I0627798

GHOSTHUNTER

THE SPECTRES OF SAINT LOUIS

EDWARD J. KNIGHT

Copyright © 2025 by Edward J. Knight

All rights reserved.

No part of this book may be reproduced in any form or by any electronic or mechanical means, including information storage and retrieval systems, without written permission from the author, except for the use of brief quotations in a book review.

This is a work of fiction. Names, characters, businesses, places, events, locales, and incidents are either the products of the author's imagination or used in a fictitious manner.

10 9 8 7 6 5 4 3 2 1

Ebook ISBN: 978-1-966819-00-4

Paperback ISBN: 978-1-966819-01-1

Date	Event
April 12, 1861	United States Civil War begins.
April 9, 1865	Robert E. Lee surrenders the Army of Northern Virginia to Ulysses S. Grant.
April 14, 1865	President Lincoln is assassinated.
April 21, 1865	The Rift to Jotunheim is opened at Andersonville Prison, Georgia. Specific details are unknown as there are no human survivors.
April 27, 1865	General Wilson and his Union Army raiders become the first humans to encounter an army of Jotun giants in Georgia and have survivors. The human army is soundly defeated but is able to dispatch reports to Washington and Richmond.
August 6, 1865	A combined Union/Confederate Army under the command of Ulysses S. Grant, with Robert E. Lee as his second, fights a large Jotun army outside of Lynchburg, Virginia. The humans are defeated, but "Grant's Last Charge" kills the Jotun commander, temporarily halting the Jotun army advance.
July 13, 1866	Richmond, Virginia, falls to a Jotun army.
Sept. 2, 1866	Washington, D.C., falls to a Jotun army.
December 25, 1866	The Christmas Miracle. General Lee defeats a Jotun army attempting to cross the Hudson River into New York City. The Jotun make no further attempts to invade New England or upstate New York.
June - July 1867	Jotun cross the Ohio River in multiple locations. Fighting rages throughout lower Illinois, Indiana, and Ohio. The area becomes known as the Contested Lands.
August 10, 1867	The First Battle of St. Louis. Believing he has superior numbers, General Custer crosses the Mississippi from St. Louis and attacks a Jotun army. General Custer and his army are annihilated.
August 31, 1867	The Second Battle of St. Louis. A Jotun army crosses the Mississippi and sacks the under-garrisoned city of St. Louis.
September 1867 - May 1868	The Long Retreat. The Army of the West under General Sanborn makes multiple raids on St. Louis. The Jotun assemble a force to crush the Army of the West. The human army begins a long retreat along the Platte River. The Jotun pursue, as they believe that the Army of the West is the last capable human resistance.
May 24, 1868	The Battle of Golden City. The Army of the West lures the Jotun army into a trap between the Table Mesas outside of Golden City, Colorado. In a Pyrrhic victory, the Jotun army is destroyed.
1873	Plague sweeps New England and Europe.
June 1875	Giant Killer Cassidy returns to Golden City. Billy McCarty's adventures with him, as described in *Sidekick*, occur.
August 1875	Billy McCarty joins the Tennessee Raid, as described in *Sharpshooter*.
March 1876	Billy McCarty sets out for the Black Hills, as described in *Scout*.
April 1881	Beth Armstrong heads to Yellowstone, as described in *Gunslinger*.
February 1882	Beth Armstrong looks for ghosts in Saint Louis, as described in *Ghosthunter*.

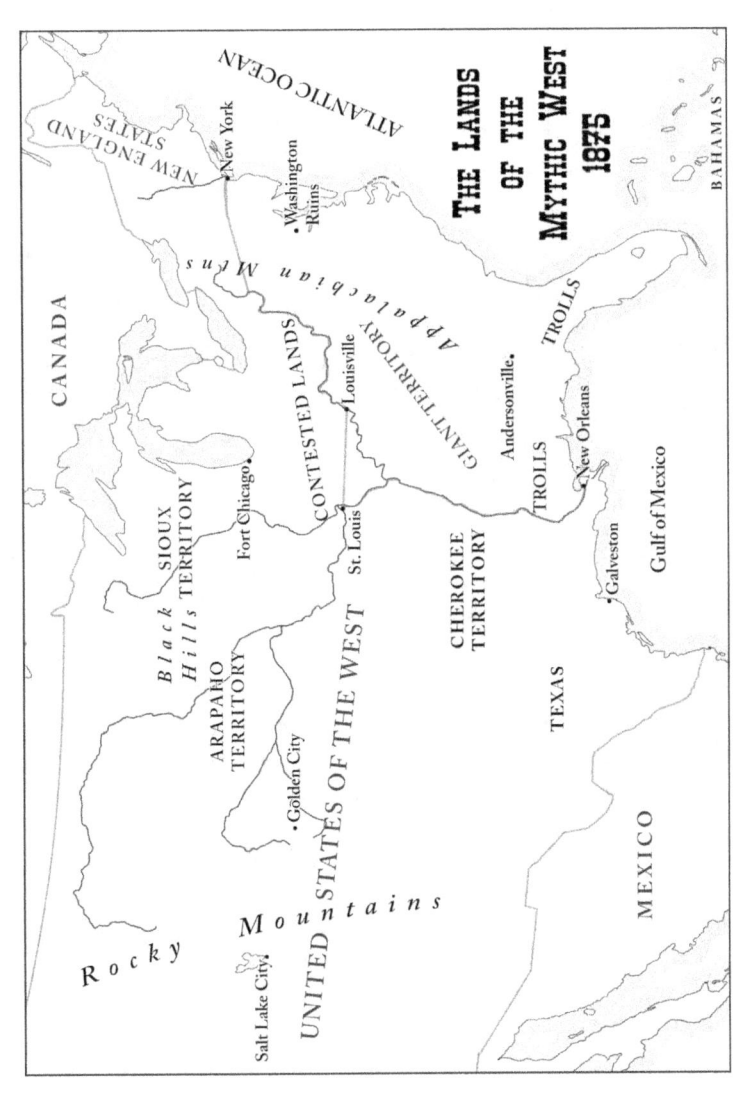

THE LANDS
OF THE
MYTHIC WEST
1875

ATLANTIC OCEAN

BAHAMAS

NEW ENGLAND
STATES

New York

Washington
Ruins

CANADA

Appalachian Mtns

GIANT TERRITORY

TROLLS

Louisville

Andersonville

TROLLS

New Orleans

Gulf of Mexico

Galveston

CONTESTED LANDS

Fort Chicago

St. Louis

CHEROKEE
TERRITORY

TEXAS

SIOUX TERRITORY

Black
Hills TERRITORY

ARAPAHO
TERRITORY

Golden City

UNITED STATES OF THE WEST

Rocky Mountains

Salt Lake City

MEXICO

ONE

BETH STARED at the falling snow in frustration. Her hand drifted to her hip where her Colt normally hung. She needed to get out. She needed to be doing something. Instead, she stood in the doorway of her ma's cabin. Trapped.

She hated feeling trapped.

Fat snowflakes drifted down. They danced a bit with the breeze. Overhead, the gray afternoon sky spread out like an unwashed wool blanket. Even the late February sun of two days ago seemed like a pale memory. The flakes just piled up into drifts and fields of dull white.

Yesterday, the snow had coated the dead corn and tomato stalks left in Ma's garden. Today, it threatened to bury the lowest fence railings. It'd already turned the walk to the barn into a slog. Tomorrow? Who knew? Her overnight visit to Ma's had already lasted a week, and now the snow threatened to extend it even more.

Beth let out a long sigh. If she wanted to do any shooting practice, it'd be either in the snow or the barn. She should've done it first thing when she woke up, like

Hickok often advised though rarely did himself. But Ma had wanted help with the goats...

She stepped back and closed the door. No point in letting in more cold than necessary. As it was, Ma was already huddled by the fire with three blankets wrapped around her. She'd said she was going to knit, but she'd fallen asleep. Like she'd done often this past week.

To Beth, the room felt stuffy. The thick log walls kept out most of the cold. She and Ma'd made sure there weren't any leaks in the mortar long before winter started. The glass windows had long iced over but still let in enough light to keep the cabin from being gloomy. It could've been downright cozy if she hadn't wanted to get out so badly.

It wasn't that living with Ma was a problem. Ma had, in fact, been especially courteous. She'd treated Beth more like a guest than anything. Which Beth supposed she was now, what with having a permanent room at the Astor.

But Ma's house was a trap. A comfortable trap, but still not the same as being on the road. Yes, there'd been days during the trip to Yellowstone last summer that had been miserable. Days where she'd loathed each step, each night, each meal.

But even in the bad days, it had never been stuffy. Or boring.

With a sigh, she quietly walked over to Ma to check on her. Ma's blankets had slid down, so Beth tucked them in again. Ma stirred and mumbled something but didn't wake.

Beth stirred the fire and fed it another small log. It crackled, and a few tendrils of acrid smoke wafted into the room instead of heading up the chimney. Ma stirred, but just turned her head. After a thoroughly undignified snort, Ma settled back into a deep sleep.

Beth smiled. Ma had worked hard running the small farm by herself. She'd earned her rest.

But Beth felt restless. She'd spent too long inside and her hand itched to hold her gun. She backed away from Ma and found her long coat and her broad-brimmed hat. She had a decent duster now, courtesy of the Army. She liked to think of it as a gift of gratitude but Hickok had laughed and said they were probably too embarrassed to say no when she'd implied she wanted one. She hadn't actually asked, though. She was just admiring them during a visit to the barracks and the next day a private had showed up at the Astor with one just her size.

Still, as she'd told Hickok, she wasn't giving it back.

She lifted her gun belt off the peg by the door and buckled it on over her denim trousers. She could at least do quickdraw practice in the barn even if she didn't pull the trigger. Shots would wake Ma. Quickdraw was better than nothing. She pulled her coat tight around herself and headed out into the snow.

Beth was almost to the barn when she noticed someone in the distance forging their way down the path toward Ma's little farm. Beth smiled when she recognized the brown wool hat and the skirts sticking out from under the long coat. She stepped away from the barn to make it easier for Rose to see her.

Somehow Rose made even a slippery walk through falling snow seem elegant. She carried a large leather bag with the straps over one shoulder, but also held it tight to her body with one hand. She didn't stutter-step to avoid icy spots, though Beth suspected she wasn't stepping in them either. Rose waved a leather-gloved hand. Even at the distance, Beth could sense her smile.

When Rose was close enough, she called out, "Beth! What are you doing out in the snow?"

"Ma's asleep," Beth said with a nod toward the house. "I thought I'd do some quickdraw practice in the barn."

"Of course," Rose said. "Left handed, I suppose?"

"Both." The injury to Beth's shooting arm had healed fine, but she still wasn't good enough with either hand. Not as good as she wanted to be.

"I've brought molasses and honey for your ma."

"Now that's worth waking her up for."

Ma stirred when they entered. Her eyelids fluttered, and then settled at cracked-open. She shifted in her chair and then jerked awake as she saw Rose.

"Oh, my," Ma said as she sat up straight. The blankets slid to her waist.

"Good afternoon, Mrs. Armstrong," Rose said. "Look what I've brought you." She smiled and proceeded to pull two glass jars out of her leather bag. She held them out toward Ma.

"Oh, Rose, you didn't have to." Ma still reached for them.

Rose waited until the older woman had a good grip on the jars before letting go and stepping back.

"What do I owe you for these?" Ma asked as she turned the jars in her hands and examined them. Her eyes lit up at their rich color.

"Nothing," Rose said. "They're a gift. From Mr. Hickok."

Ma's smile faded. "Mr. Hickok?"

"Bill's back in town?" Beth blurted.

"I should've known." Ma sighed with resignation. Then to Beth, "I suppose you're gonna go runnin'."

"Um," Rose said, "that's why I'm here." She looked at Beth. "He sent me to ask you to come to town."

"Why didn't he come himself?" Ma asked suspiciously.

4

Beth gave Rose a sideways look. Hickok didn't like to cross Ma, but sending someone else wasn't his style.

"He's asleep," Rose answered. "He rode all night without stopping." To Beth, "But he said to wake him when you arrive. He needs help with some ghosts."

Ma grumbled something under her breath. Then she shuffled to the shelves where she kept her tinned goods and added the jars.

Beth and Rose exchanged a pained look. Then Beth stepped to Ma's side.

"You know I gotta go, Ma," Beth said quietly.

"You don't *gotta* do anything," Ma snapped. Then her face softened. "You don't gotta."

Beth's chest tightened. She put her hand on Ma's upper arm. "I can't stay here."

"Why not?" Ma snapped, but she didn't push Beth's hand away. "It's warm. It's safe…"

"I'll be fine, Ma," Beth said. "Fine. I can take care of myself."

Ma turned her head away. "I… I know." She put a hand over Beth's, but didn't look at her. Instead, she took several deep, ragged breaths before turning back.

"Well," Ma said. Her eyes glistened with moisture. "At least let me make some biscuits for you to take."

Beth checked with Rose, who gave a small nod. Hickok could wait until Ma was done.

The falling snow had thickened by the time Beth and Rose set out. Beth's nose itched with the cold. The scarf Ma'd knit kept the rest of her face warm, but not her nose. At least her feet were dry. The boots she'd bought from

Boggs had been worth every penny. She kept her footing even in the slippery parts.

They reached Boggs's general store on the outskirts of town. He'd closed up, but a sign on the door said to knock. Beth couldn't help a smile. A foot of snow wasn't enough to stop Boggs from trying to sell anything a desperate customer wanted.

Then they crossed the bridge over Clear Creek into Golden City proper. One of the bars had piano music coming out of it and a couple of miners hurried across the street to another bar further down the road.

Even heavy spring snow couldn't keep some men from their booze, Beth mused sourly. She didn't understand that. The one whiskey she'd drunk had burned her throat. Hickok had been amused, and bought her beer when she turned seventeen instead. Maybe when she was older, she'd develop a taste for it.

A fresh wind blasted them in the face as they walked up Twelfth Street to the Astor. They paused under its balcony to shake off the snow and then stamp their boots. Rose's cheeks were pink from the cold but she smiled. After one last brush of snow off her hat, Beth led the way inside.

The warmth in the entryway made Beth sigh in pleasure. They followed the happy smell of smoke into the parlor. There, the roaring fire made her want to shed her coat right away.

She wasn't alone. Two burly men with grizzled beards sat at the nearest table eating steak and potatoes. The normal gingham table cloth had been removed, letting the polished oak shine. From their bearing and snatches of their conversation, she guessed they were teamsters up from Santa Fe.

Beyond them, Mr. Lake, the Astor House's owner, sat

at the table closest to the fire with his ledger open in front of him. Thin with gray hair, he was still buttoned up in his suit despite the warmth. He sipped from a steaming mug but looked up when she and Rose entered.

"Miss Armstrong!" he called as he stood. He bowed slightly. "Welcome home!"

The two teamsters broke off their conversation and stared. One's mouth dropped open at her name.

"Mr. Lake," Beth said with a nod of her head. Her gut twinged at the thought of what Ma would think of his words. But the Astor *was* home. Mr. Lake had promised her a free room in the hotel as long as she liked, though she suspected it would be as long as her fame brought in additional guests. He'd even posted flyers advertising "The Home of the Girl Gunslinger!" Though it wasn't clear how much that helped.

"Mr. Hickok left word to be awoken when you arrived," Mr. Lake said. Then his eyes fell on Rose. "And Miss Chamberlin, perhaps you could see if these gentlemen would be interested in some more of Mr. Coors's finest, or perhaps some pie?"

Rose grimaced, but then pasted on a smile for the customers. "Certainly, Mr. Lake. But I thought my shift ended after breakfast?"

His eyes tightened, but he kept smiling.

"Just so," he said, "but I'm afraid Mrs. Archer went home feeling a bit under the weather."

Rose and Beth exchanged a quick, knowing look. Mrs. Archer's spells of poor health were always exceedingly convenient.

"Well, if you will see to these men," Mr. Lake continued, "I will go alert Mr. Hickok to Miss Armstrong's return."

"I'll help," Beth said to Rose, who smiled in thanks.

The teamsters agreed to the beer but skipped the pie. They remained agog as Beth helped Rose clear their dirty dishes and tidy up some of the other tables that still bore crumbs. The younger one seemed to be trying to work up the nerve to ask her something, but broke into a string of um's and ah's when Rose asked if they needed anything else. He couldn't seem to take his eyes off Beth.

Until the door to the entryway opened and Hickok came in.

He looked ragged—he was in a stained white shirt instead of his usual impeccable three piece suit. His long brown hair hung limp around his shoulders and his mustache was unkempt. Worse, she'd never seen him look so pallid, like he was eighty instead of forty. The sharp-eyed gunslinger looked more like a drunken bum, except she knew he wasn't drunk.

"Beth," he said. "Oh, good. We have to leave for Saint Louis as soon as we can."

She furrowed her brow. "Why?"

"The ghosts—the ghosts there are killing people. We have to go."

TWO

BETH STARED AT HICKOK. She did her best to not let her mouth drop open. Other than the crackling of the parlor fire, the room had fallen still. For a few heartbeats, only the smell of smoke filled the room.

"How?" she finally asked. "Ghosts can't touch people." In fact, most people couldn't even see them.

"These can, apparently." Hickok's hand drifted toward his gun belt. It was his tell that he was worried. Beth's gut tightened in reply and her mind raced.

"You need a witch."

"They killed the witch," he said grimly.

"What?!"

"She was one of the first to die."

"Oh, that's not good," Rose interjected. "That's not good at all. The poor woman."

"Girl," Hickok corrected. "She was barely fourteen."

"Even worse," Mr. Lake echoed. Now standing, he gripped the back of his chair like a church pew.

"How many have died?" Beth asked.

"Too many."

"How do you know it's ghosts?"

Hickok nodded toward his usual table at the back of the parlor, which was also the furthest from the teamsters.

"Let me get some coffee and I'll tell you about it," he said.

"Oh, let me fetch it," Rose said. "You two go on and get settled."

"Mr. Lake," Hickok said as he turned to the Astor's proprietor, "pardon me for another indulgence. Could you please send a messenger to Mr. Boggs? We'll need fast horses in the morning."

"Of course," Mr. Lake said as he straightened up. "I'll dispatch someone immediately." He packed up his ledger and headed toward the door.

Hickok looked at Beth and then gestured toward the back table.

Rose arrived at the table a few steps ahead of Beth and Hickok. One of the gingham table cloths that normally covered the table hung over the back of a nearby chair. She quickly threw it over the table and slid it until it was centered correctly. Then she stepped back and raised an eyebrow, daring Beth to challenge her.

Beth just smiled and rolled her eyes. She sat in the chair next to Hickok's as he sagged into his. Sitting, he looked even more tired than he had coming through the door. Rose took one look and pursed her lips in thought.

"I'll be right back," she said before she headed for the kitchen.

"Are you all right?" Beth asked Hickok.

He slowly nodded. "Just tired."

"Riding hard?"

He nodded.

"So what's so urgent?"

"The ghosts and the trolls." He let out a long breath and looked toward the kitchen door.

Rose bustled through it as they watched. She bore a small serving tray with Mr. Lake's ornate silver coffee pot and three china cups on saucers. They rattled as she pushed through the door, but then settled smoothly into place as she approached.

"May I join you, Mr. Hickok?" she asked sweetly as she put a cup and saucer in front of him.

"I don't—"

"Please," Beth interrupted. "I'll just tell her everything later."

He looked at her, and then to Rose, and then back again.

"Very well," he said with a sigh. He leaned back in his chair, but then took the coffee and raised it to his lips. After a deep sip, he smiled in appreciation.

Rose poured coffee for Beth and herself and then sat on Hickok's other side. She leaned forward on her elbow and cocked her head to listen.

"Ghosts and trolls," Beth prompted.

"Yes," Hickok said. He took another sip of coffee and let out a happy sigh. "The trolls first. I went to Saint Louis because we'd heard the trolls were up to something. They've spent the winter massing across the river. We figure they have ten thousand, maybe more."

"Oh my," Rose said. "But they can't cross the river, can they?"

"They can if they have enough boats," Hickok said, "but they haven't started building them. So we don't know what they're doing. Are they going to try to cross, or are they going to march north toward Fort Chicago? Or is it something else? We don't know."

"What about our troops?" Beth asked.

"We have about a thousand in Saint Louis. We've asked the Texans to send men, but who knows what they'll do." He shrugged.

Beth nodded. The newly formed Republic of Texas wasn't outright hostile to the United States of the West, but it was pretty close. If some of the senators back in San Francisco had had their way, the War Between the States would've started up again when Texas announced its second secession. Fortunately, cooler heads had prevailed.

Hickok had been one of those heads. He'd even brought a Jotun giant axe to the Capitol to remind the senators who the real enemy was. The man knew how to persuade.

"General Sanborn doesn't want to stay in Chicago. He wants to go east," Hickok continued. "We've almost got Ohio secured and he's eager to push the Jotun out of Pennsylvania."

"Which he can't do with an army of trolls behind him," Beth said.

"Obviously," Hickok replied. He took another sip of coffee and smiled. "I do miss this."

Beth smiled too. Rose had brought out the good stuff. She wondered how Mr. Lake's dwindling supplies were holding up.

"So the ghosts," Rose prompted.

"Relentless, aren't you two?" Hickok smiled. Some of his color was back. The magic of coffee, it appeared.

"We make a good team," Rose said, and Beth nodded in agreement. Then Rose looked expectantly at Hickok.

He pursed his lips in amusement. Then he took another sip.

"So, Saint Louis had a lot of ghosts," he said, "after the Jotun sacked it in '67. The Army's gotten most of them to move on, but..." He shrugged.

Beth nodded. She'd seen a dozen ghosts on the Golden City battlefield that hadn't moved on, either because they hadn't wanted to or because they were "broken."

"It's not just that," Hickok said, having figured out what she was thinking. "We haven't even found them all."

"Why not?"

"The ruins are a pretty big place." He shrugged. "Witches are better employed elsewhere."

"But Saint Louis had one recently, didn't they?" Rose asked.

"The daughter of one of the officers assigned to the river watch, a girl named Laura," Hickok said. "She was really green, but she was the only witch between the front and the Rockies."

Beth grimaced. That was a real problem, that a girl was the only one.

"Another witch spent a week with her once her abilities started to show, but that was all her training. It wasn't much, but…" He shrugged. "Anyway, Laura'd go looking for ghosts from time to time."

He let out a heavy sigh.

"One night she didn't come back," he continued. "The next day they found her in the old ruins."

The haunted look had returned. He stared into the distance for a moment.

"It was bad?" Beth prompted.

"Really bad." He sighed again, before his jaw tightened.

"A dozen more people died," he said. "All cut up like her. The last one when I was there…"

He suppressed a shudder. Then he breathed deeply and purpose returned to his eyes.

"The witch," he continued, "the day before she died, told a friend she'd seen a new kind of ghost. It didn't make sense, but..." He shrugged. "She was clearly worried."

"Which is why you want me," Beth said.

"Yeah. With your sight..."

It was her turn to grimace. Sometimes being able to see ghosts was a curse.

"The longer we take to get back, the more people will die."

She sucked in her breath. "So we leave in the morning."

In the hotel room she now called home, Beth gave her bags another once over. It was hard to pack both light and for the cold at the same time. She'd decided to forego a dress and pack both her pairs of denim pants. If the folks in Saint Louis couldn't handle that, well, they'd have to learn. She trusted Rose could be girly enough for both of them.

The problem was how much ammunition to take. Hickok said the Saint Louis garrison was adding soldiers faster than they were getting supplies. That meant they had to be running low on bullets. But she didn't have room to take all she wanted to.

She pulled a shirt and a pair of socks out of her bags. She might get a little colder, but that was better than having her Colt click on an empty chamber.

She looked around the room to see what she might've missed. She'd placed her dresses in a trunk, along with her extra unmentionables and her second pair of shoes. She'd offered to let Mr. Lake rent out her room while she was gone if he'd store her things. She could've taken them to Ma's, she supposed. But that would just lead to another round of Ma trying to make her feel guilty for going on the road.

Beth's breath caught as she thought of Ma, alone in her cabin, waiting. Beth knew she'd be fine, but knowing it and feeling it were far, far different. Ma worried, and nothing—not sun, not good fortune, not success—could keep her from doing so. She was the master of spotting potential rain clouds.

But Beth had to go. Ma wanted her safe on the farm, but if there were people dying in Saint Louis and Beth could stop it...

She picked up her bags and headed down to the parlor.

There, she found Hickok and Rose standing near the back table and glaring at each other. Fortunately the room was otherwise empty, because their anger was palpable.

"That's final," Hickok snarled. "You're not coming."

But then they broke off when they saw Beth. Rose's face was pale and she was breathing hard, her eyes full of anger. Hickok looked more irritated than anything.

"She says she's coming with us," Hickok jabbed the air with his finger, pointing at Rose.

"Well of course she is," Beth said.

"We need to ride hard and fast," he said. "She'll slow us down."

"But she'll be able to help in Saint Louis."

"Yeah, how?"

"She's the most resourceful woman I know."

Rose crossed her arms and nodded in agreement, but Hickok would not be deterred.

"She's not coming," he said again.

Beth crossed her arms and glared at him.

"Don't make this a contest of wills," Hickok warned. He'd narrowed his eyes, but his hands remained at his side. Not drifting toward his guns. Not that he'd draw them...

"I won't slow you down," Rose interjected. "I can ride better than Beth."

"She can," Beth said. "A lot better. She won't slow us down."

Hickok looked from one woman to the other. His glare deepened, but then he shrugged.

"Fine," he said. "We leave in thirty minutes. If she's not ready, we leave without her." Then he strode out of the room.

Beth watched him go. He couldn't be angry about being slowed down. She'd spent too much time with him over the years to believe it. Too many times *he'd* been late himself.

Rose stepped to her side and also looked at the door he'd gone through.

"He said he couldn't protect us both," Rose said quietly. "Before you came in."

"He doesn't need to protect either of us," Beth retorted. "We can take care of ourselves."

"That," Rose said, "is most certainly true." She smiled and glanced at the clock on the wall. "Now I must go find Mr. Lake and arrange for Mrs. Archer to cover my shifts. Hopefully he's close, since I only have thirty minutes."

Beth grinned. She was sure that no matter how far away Mr. Lake was, Rose would be back on time.

THREE

NINETEEN MINUTES LATER, Rose and Beth stepped out
the front door of the Astor and stood under its balcony.
The speckled gray and brown rough stone of the walls
made it feel like a cave, protected from the snow still
drifting down. The fat flakes fell less frequently now and
drifted more lazily to the ground.

Rose held two small rucksacks ready to be tied to her
horse. Beth had loaded her saddlebags herself, though
she'd added two small pouches of bullets to her belt. She'd
also decided not to bring her rifle—an old Winchester her
friend Billy had given her when he'd bought himself a new
one. It didn't feel comfortable in her hands like the Colt,
and they needed to travel light. Both women had bundled
up warm with layers and coats and boots. Rose wore her
thickest wool dress over leggings, the better to ride with.
They were ready.

Except for Hickok.

And the horses, which Hickok was supposed to bring.

Rose gave Beth a knowing look followed by an exasperated sigh. Beth nodded in agreement at the irony. She turned to look down Twelfth Street toward the stables.

After what had to be several more minutes—Ten? Fifteen?—Hickok turned the corner from Washington Street leading three horses: a buckskin bay Morgan and two smaller palomino mustangs. He bent forward, his head bowed, which kept the snow out of his face. It also meant Beth couldn't read him well. Was he still angry?

From the way he yanked on the leads, he appeared to be. But after a bit, he looked up and his face was calm.

No. Masked.

She knew his tells well enough after all the time he'd spent training her. He was angry, but determined not to let it show. She steeled herself. Sometimes he couldn't hold the sarcasm back no matter how much he tried.

Still, he slogged through the snow until he and the horses were under the balcony. They exchanged greetings and then he passed the Morgan's reins to Rose.

"Boggs didn't have three palominos so you'll have to keep up on this one."

Beth frowned. Palominos were much faster than the Morgan would be, despite their smaller size.

Rose's eyes flashed but then she said, "Thank you." Before Beth could argue on her behalf, Rose shot her a look that cut her off.

"I'm sure I'll be just fine," Rose said, as much for Beth's benefit as Hickok's. "Shall we?"

Hickok muttered something under his breath, but nodded. Then he looked at both women to make sure he had their attention.

"We'll follow the Platte northeast," he said. "As fast as we can. We'll gallop whenever the horses can stand it. Once we get to Julesburg, we can change horses and keep going."

"There's an outpost at Julesburg now?" Rose asked.

"Mmm hmm," Hickok said. "The Army's trying to put the old Pony Express back together, at least until they can get telegraph wires strung."

"That'll be ages," Rose shook her head with annoyance. "Why, I think they've been talking about running wires from Salt Lake to Golden City since I was a baby."

"And they'll be talking about it after you're in your grave, too. Fool Congressmen." He spat. "Let's go. We've no time to waste."

They rode east, skirted the ruins of Denver City, and picked up the Platte River on the far side. By then, the snow had stopped and the sun had at least partially succeeded in poking through the blanket of gray clouds. True to Hickok's word, they galloped when they could and walked when the horses needed to rest. As dusk fell, he led them to an old abandoned cabin not far from the river. The roof leaked and the door was gone, but it was a decent shelter for the night.

"I know I said to practice your quick draw every day," he said as they unloaded their horses, "but we need to get there as soon as we can."

"I'll still do some," she promised.

But it was dark all too soon, so after a dozen tries she gave up and called it a night. They ate Ma's biscuits with some tack before setting watches and getting some sleep.

By the afternoon of the third day, the horses had begun to falter. Even the palominos didn't want to race. The trail had turned slushy and muddy as well. Beth shed her overcoat and tied it to her horse, at least when she was riding. But afternoon turned to a cold night, and Hickok urged them on. They slowed to a trot and then a walk, but he didn't let up.

Finally, exhausted, sore, and ready to collapse, they

spotted lights ahead. Hickok called for them to gallop, and several minutes later they arrived in Julesburg.

The little town wasn't much—maybe six buildings total. Most were constructed out of wooden planks, but one was made of sod. The biggest, with the most light leaking from its window, was still a single story not much bigger than Ma's one-room cabin. Hickok headed for it.

"Open up!" He pounded on the hardwood door. "Open up! It's Captain Hickok!"

A minute later, a soldier let them in.

"Have someone take care of the horses," he ordered, "and bring in our bags."

Warmth hit Beth immediately. A fireplace crackled, full of flames. A thick older soldier in blue stood gaping at her. With his black hair frazzled and his unshaven chin hiding his thick neck, he reminded Beth of a grumpy bear. Two younger soldiers sat at a small plain table nearby with playing cards in their hands. The other side of the one large room held simple beds.

The soldiers remained still, blinking.

"Get going," Hickok barked.

Grumpy Bear pointed his finger at one of the card players, who jumped to his feet and hustled to the door.

"Captain Hickok, sir," Grumpy Bear said, "we weren't expecting you."

"Now why would that be, Sergeant?" Hickok asked. He tilted his head. "Seeing as how I told you seven days ago I'd be back?"

"Well...., um..." The sergeant ducked his head and suddenly seemed to find his boots fascinating.

"We wasn't expecting girls!" the other card player said. He was a thin man except for his nose, which looked like it'd been smashed flat.

Hickok gave him a hard, flat stare. "Private. We need

food and water. Dry blankets if you have them. Do you understand?"

Hickok's hand had drifted to hover above his gun. Flat Nose swallowed hard and nodded.

"Uh...," Flat Nose said, "uh... sir... there's more blankets in the barn for the horses. We could use some of them but I can't carry 'em all."

"I'll get them," Sergeant Grumpy Bear said quickly. "You take care of the food." To Hickok, "You want to pick out your new horses, sir?"

"Yes," Hickok said. "Let's go."

As the men headed out, Beth let herself sink into Flat Nose's now empty chair. It wobbled when she sat down but quickly steadied at a slight tilt. She ignored Flat Nose as he bustled around the small kitchen area.

Rose hung her coat and hat on a rack near the fire and put her gloves on the hearth. Then she joined Beth at the table.

"It's so nice to be warm," Rose said with a relieved smile. Her cheeks were actually rosy as they recovered from the cold.

Beth nodded. As the heat seeped into her bones, weariness followed. She needed food and then sleep.

But even before that, she needed to take off her outer winter clothes. Slush that had splashed on her pants had begun to melt and she could feel the drips down her legs. She stood and went to the fire and wooden rack where Rose had hung her things. She had just taken off her coat when she heard Flat Nose wheeze. She turned around to see him with his mouth agape.

"Are you a girl or a boy?" he said.

She stared at him.

"You dress like a boy. You sure you're a girl?"

Rose tensed up and leaned forward in her seat, but

Beth shook her head slightly and Rose held still. Beth's own shoulders were tight, but she kept her hands loose and away from her body.

"I'm a woman," she said, sweetly but firmly, "who carries a gun and wears trousers. Is that a problem?"

"Yes! Um—"

Beth brushed her side above her Colt. Flat Nose's eyes followed her hand, and then he swallowed.

"Uh, no. No problem. I'll be gettin' your food now." He turned his back to them and got busy chopping something he'd pulled out of a basket.

Rose raised an eyebrow and looked at Beth. Beth just rolled her eyes and finished hanging her wet outer garments up to dry.

Hickok and Sergeant Grumpy Bear returned a few minutes later, and shortly thereafter Flat Nose had food on the table for them. The soldiers were finally introduced— Sergeant Meyer and Private Howard (Flat Nose), with Private Schwenker still in the barn tending the horses. They ate overly salty cured ham with mushy beans and diced onions, and some semi-competently cooked biscuits. The soldiers, having eaten earlier, mostly watched or talked about the local weather and events.

"There's just not much going on, sir," Sergeant Meyer said. "You're the only travelers in a week and we haven't seen any Indians."

"Any news from the Express riders?" Hickok asked.

Sergeant Meyer shook his head. "Sorry, sir. Haven't had any."

"That's... troubling." When Hickok saw Beth's furrowed brow, he continued, "There should be express riders every three days. If they haven't had a single one in a week..."

"They may not have sent any, sir," Sergeant Meyer said. "It's happened before. Around Christmas, actually."

"Uh huh," Private Howard added. "No riders at Christmas. None at New Year's either. Holidays, you know."

"But it's early spring," Beth said. "There's no holidays now."

"If something's wrong in Saint Louis," Hickok said, "there should've been riders. It's the first thing they'd do."

"It's probably just some lazy soldier taking his time, sir," Sergeant Meyer said. "Why hurry in the snow?"

"No excuse," Hickok said firmly.

Sergeant Meyer shrugged. He glanced at Beth, as if looking for her support, but her flat look led him to change the subject.

Private Schwenker returned a bit later and said the horses were taken care of. They'd all but finished eating, so Hickok pushed his chair back from the table. It scraped loudly across the floor, getting everyone's attention.

"You'll give the ladies your beds for the night," he said. "We'll depart at dawn."

"But where will we sleep?" Private Howard exclaimed. His eyes went wide and his lower lip trembled. Combined with his nose, he looked enough like a basset hound for Beth to smile.

"The barn's real cold, so bedrolls by the fire," Sergeant Meyer looked at Hickok. "Right, sir?"

"There's hope yet," Hickok muttered. He turned to Beth and Rose. "I'm sorry I can't do better."

"I'm sure it will be just fine," Rose said with a smile. "Now, gentlemen," she said, looking mostly at Sergeant Meyer, "where might there be a spot where we ladies can wash up?"

Beth snapped awake. She opened her eyes, but she'd fallen asleep facing the wall and couldn't see anything other than flickering shadows cast by the firelight. Her blankets had slipped below her shoulder, but her right hand remained tucked next to her pillow. She kept her breathing steady as she listened.

Mostly she heard the crackle of the fire. Then a floorboard squeaked.

She inched her hand under her pillow until she touched the handle of her Colt. Gently, carefully, she slid her fingers around it. She held off drawing it, though. Instead, she listened.

Another floorboard squeaked.

It was probably just someone headed out to the outhouse. Something simple. But that's not what her gut said. It twinged and tightened into a knot.

Then her mattress sagged as someone knelt on the edge.

The sound of a gun being cocked cut through the quiet. The person climbing onto her bed froze.

"Stop." Hickok's voice was hard and firm. "You touch her, you die."

FOUR

BETH SLID toward the far edge of the bed and rolled over. As she did, she yanked her gun from under the pillow and brought it to bear on the man kneeling on the side of the bed. Kneeling, but not moving.

Private Howard — Flat Nose.

And he looked like he was about to cry. His eyes were scrunched shut. He trembled and he held his hands up.

"Back away from the bed," Hickok commanded.

Beth glanced over. Hickok had taken the third bed and was propped up on one elbow, his Colt pointed at Private Howard. His flinty eyes only briefly glanced her way before returning their focus to the private.

"Back away," Hickok repeated.

With a whimper, Private Howard eased off the mattress. He tried to stand, but his legs went wobbly and he sank to his knees.

"What the Hell?" Sergeant Meyer called.

"He was climbing onto her bed," Hickok said, loud and clear.

"I didn't mean nothin'!" Private Howard cried. "I

didn't! It's just… it's just she dresses like a boy! I wanted to look!"

"That doesn't mean you get to touch me," Beth said coldly. She kept her gun leveled right between his eyes.

"But I didn't!" he sobbed. "I didn't touch her!"

Hickok glanced at Beth for confirmation, and she nodded. Then he turned to Sergeant Meyer. "Get him out of here. And get him a change of pants."

Sure enough, Private Howard had wet himself.

The room exploded into motion. Sergeant Meyer and Private Schwenker scooped Private Howard off the floor and hustled him out the door while Hickok climbed to his feet and Rose found her way to Beth's side.

"Are you all right?" Rose asked.

"I'm fine." Beth let out a long breath and felt the tension leave her muscles.

Hickok loomed in front of her.

"Are you okay?" he asked.

"I just said I was," she snapped. "What'd he think he was doing?"

"He wasn't," Rose said. "Some men… don't think."

"I'm not even sure he's all there." Hickok looked at the door. "I'm surprised he's in uniform."

Beth nodded. She knew the Army was desperate for men, but Private Howard didn't even sniff the standards she'd come to expect from soldiers.

"I'll make 'em sleep in the barn," Hickok said. "All of them. I don't care how cold it gets." He walked back to his bed, sat on the edge, and started to put his boots on.

Beth glanced at the fire, where the soldiers' boots sat. Sergeant Meyer had hustled everyone out in their stockinged feet. She snorted softly. He'd chosen speed over comfort.

"No." Rose shook her head. "That's not fair to Meyer and Schwenker."

"Fine. Just Howard." He gave Beth a stern look. "But I meant it. If he'd touched you, he'd be dead."

"Isn't that a little much?" Rose asked quietly.

Beth grimaced, and then nodded in agreement. That was going a little too far.

Hickok snorted and shook his head. Then he grabbed his coat and went out the door.

Beth pulled a chair over to the fire and sat. She wrapped one of the blankets from the bed around her and made sure to tuck her stockinged feet inside it. The flames had mostly faded into deep black coals, with dull red glowing from inside the larger logs. A few feet away, Private Schwenker snored like he was cutting wood. He'd rolled onto his side, which had cut the giant sawmill down to a quiet hand saw. Beth wasn't sure it was enough for her to get back to sleep.

At least Hickok didn't snore. Or Rose.

She looked glumly at where Hickok slept. He'd spread a bedroll out in front of the door, so that no one—and by no one he meant Private Howard—could get in without waking him. She didn't know whether she appreciated it or not.

On one hand, she liked having someone watch her back. On the other hand, she could take care of herself just fine! She'd already proven that at Yellowstone, rather spectacularly, hadn't she? She could certainly handle a no-account soldier. She'd woken up before he'd done anything, hadn't she? She'd had her gun ready, hadn't she?

But Hickok.... She sighed. He sometimes called her the "daughter he'd never had." Occasionally when he was sober, but often when he'd been drinking and thinking about Calamity Jane. All these years, he still grieved for her and the family they'd never had.

At first it had been endearing. Especially through all their long training sessions like when she'd first learned to shoot. But it'd gotten old.

She didn't know how to tell him that. Or how he'd react if she did.

Private Schwenker snorted and shifted in his blankets. His snores cut off.

Beth let out a relieved sigh. Maybe she could get some sleep.

They were up at dawn. A half-frozen and very contrite Private Howard mumbled an apology that he'd clearly been forced to memorize by Sergeant Meyer. The words weren't much, but the misery in his face was sincere.

"I shouldn't'a done it," he said at the end as his voice cracked. "I just wanted to know…"

"I'm a woman," she said firmly.

"I know." He looked completely miserable. "Even if you wear trousers."

He looked away before she rolled her eyes.

After a quick meal of eggs, biscuits, and some very watered-down coffee, they mounted their new steeds and rode off.

To Beth's surprise, they didn't ride quite as hard as they had the previous days. Hickok kept them at a canter for most of the morning. The road followed the river, and every few minutes he'd spur his horse ahead, ride to the bank, and look around.

The fifth time he did it, Beth followed. The river was

icy but not completely frozen. The banks were muddy with strands of dead grass peeking up here and there through the snow.

"What are we looking for?" she asked.

"The missing express riders."

"Okay..."

"I can't believe they weren't sent, or got lazy. Most soldiers aren't like those yokels in Julesburg."

"You think they were killed along the way?"

"I hope not, but..." He grimaced and scanned the river once more.

"How far to the next station?" Rose asked. She'd ridden up behind while they'd talked. All morning, she'd been cheerier than Beth, intermixed with looks of concern when she thought Beth wouldn't notice.

"About a day's hard ride," Hickok said. "We'll be spending our nights in the stations until we get to Saint Louis."

"Well, maybe instead of checking the river, we should see if the next station has seen the riders," Rose said. "That would certainly narrow down the places one has to look."

Hickok snorted in agreement.

"Besides," Rose added, "those men are better suited to search. They know this part of the country."

"Good point," he said. "We're needed in Saint Louis more anyway." He turned his horse back toward the road. "Let's ride!"

They reached the next station just after dusk. A solitary cabin and barn by the road, it housed three soldiers who were much more courteous and professional than the men at Julesburg. They, too, reported that they hadn't seen a single Pony Express rider, and that in fact Hickok himself had been the last man to ride through.

They ate a quiet meal that night. Hickok was lost in his

thoughts. Beth was just happy that none of these men snored.

The next few nights were much the same. Each station reported no new riders since Hickok had gone through. Each set of men had their own speculation, but no facts. The sergeant at one station had been enterprising enough to send one of his men to the earlier station in the line, but that station had turned out to be undermanned and he chose not to keep investigating.

"I'm sure the commander in Saint Louis has need of every man he can get," the sergeant of the undermanned station said. "If they haven't sent anyone, it just means that there's no news since you came through."

"The riders are supposed to be regular," Hickok retorted.

The sergeant shrugged. "That's Saint Louis's problem, sir."

Hickok's eyes flared. Beth put a hand on his upper arm. He turned his glare on her, but his face quickly softened. Then she gently shook her head. This was not the time, she tried to silently say.

He frowned, but then nodded.

"Your problem," he said to the sergeant, "is getting us dinner. Now."

The sergeant didn't move fast, but he did move. Before long, they had a serviceable stew.

The days mostly blended together. The ones that stuck out were the ones on the edges of the ruins of Fort Kearney and St. Joseph. When the giants had come through, they'd smashed them, and the settlers had been slow to return. Farming in California was much more profitable these days. And safer.

Leaving St. Joseph, they followed a road that paralleled the Missouri River. Most of the time their view was blocked by trees, but Beth remained impressed with how much wider it was than the rivers in Colorado Territory. She could probably shoot a troll on the other side, but it'd be a difficult shot.

Beth's team rode hard, to the point where her thighs and rear were constantly sore. Beth and even Rose lost track of the names of the small crews at each of the stations. Only the small details like beards and whether they had biscuits or bacon varied, and even those became easy to confuse.

The one thing that was not confusing was the ignorance about the missing riders. No one had seen a single rider since Hickok had ridden through. To Beth's mild surprise, he didn't become more agitated with the news. Instead, he became more and more polite to the soldiers at the stations.

"It's not their fault," he said as they rode away from what he said was their next-to-last stop. "No point it making it harder for them out here than it is."

"Why is it hard?" Rose asked. "They're not at the front where the fighting is."

"Exactly that," he said.

"I don't understand."

"They wouldn't be here if the Army thought they'd be good in battle."

"Oh." Rose tilted her head, as if in thought.

"Now for some men," Hickok continued, "that's a relief. For most, it's an insult."

"They *want* to fight?" Rose looked incredulous.

"Not all of them," Hickok said. "Remember Sergeant Meyer, in Julesburg?"

Beth couldn't help but remember the man. He and Private Howard were the only distinct faces of the trip.

"What about him?" Rose asked.

"He fought in the War Between the States," Hickok said. "He said after that, he was happy to be away from the fighting." Hickok fell silent for a moment. When he spoke again, he was somber.

"He was at Shiloh."

Beth bowed her head. Her old childhood neighbor Mr. Jenkins had fought at Shiloh. He'd said it was the bloodiest battle ever, after Golden City. Pa had disagreed. He said the giants had done worse at Lynchburg and the Second Battle of Saint Louis. In the end, they'd agreed that Shiloh had been the worst human versus human battle.

She snorted. It seemed strange to think of humans acting as evil to other humans as trolls and giants did. But maybe that's because she'd never known a world without the monsters who'd come through the rift.

Beth remained lost in her thoughts for much of the afternoon. She apparently wasn't the only one. Neither Hickok nor Rose spoke during their short stops for water, or when they gave the horses a breather by dropping to a walk.

Finally, just after dusk had truly begun and the scarlet colors of the sunset had faded into grays, they spotted the station that would be their last stop before Saint Louis. The squat dark building sat on a rise, silhouetted against the gathering evening sky.

Hickok, in the lead, pulled up on his reins and stopped. Beth and Rose slowed and came beside him.

"There's no lights," he said.

"It's not really dark yet," Rose pointed out. "Maybe they haven't lit any yet."

"Let's go slow," Beth said.

Hickok nodded, and they proceeded to slowly walk their horses forward.

Beth concentrated hard on the station. In the night, all

she could hear was the clomp of the horses' hooves and the occasional call of a distant bird. The air was almost still, with just a light cold breeze nipping at her ears. Meanwhile, her eyes slowly adjusted to the growing darkness.

But even as the last of the sunlight disappeared, a gray shape appeared to form just outside the closed cabin door. It was the height and width of a man—

"Stop," Beth said. "There's a ghost."

FIVE

BETH STARED at the distant ghost. She almost shivered, but that could've just been the cold. The air was still except for the sounds of their own horses snuffling and shuffling.

"What do you see?" Hickok asked quietly.

"We're too far to make out details," she said, "but there's a ghost standing just outside the door."

"I don't see anything," he said.

"It's there."

"Oh, I trust you. Let's go slowly, though."

They started their horses forward at a walk. Beth's eyes darted from the ghost to the silent cabin and back. Behind the cabin sat a small barn, with a little corral between them. The corral was empty and the barn dark.

As they closed, the ghost became more distinct. A soldier in his uniform, including a broad brimmed hat. She couldn't make out his face, but he stood still and stiff, as if at attention. His hands were by his side.

Still nothing stirred in the cabin or the barn.

When they were about twenty yards away, the ghost

turned its head to face them. Beth pulled up on the reins, and Hickok and Rose did quickly as well.

"What?" Hickok asked.

"The ghost's a soldier," Beth said. "He looks like he's on guard duty."

"Why?" Rose asked. "That's just an express station."

"Agreed," Hickok said. "I don't like it."

"The ghost's seen us but he's not doing anything," Beth said.

"Hmm." Hickok studied the cabin.

"I think we should check out the barn before we approach the cabin," Beth said. "In case—"

"Yeah," Hickok interrupted. "Let's make sure there isn't something hiding in there."

Beth kept her eyes on the ghost as they circled around. It stared back, but didn't otherwise move.

The squat wooden barn didn't look like the ones that dotted the farms near Golden City. The walls weren't quite straight and the planks that made them up were uneven. Its roof peaked no higher than the cabin's, and if it hadn't been for the broad open door, it could have been the cabin's twin.

Except it reeked of rotted flesh.

The closer they moved, the stronger the smell. Their horses started to snort and toss their heads and Rose's even balked when she nudged it forward.

"Let's walk from here," Hickok said when they reached the corral fence. He dismounted and loosely tied the reins around the top rail.

"I'd like to stay here," Rose said, "if you don't mind."

"You got a gun?" Hickok asked.

Rose nodded slowly. She reached into one of her saddlebags and pulled out a Colt .45.

Beth had to suppress a smile. Rose didn't like guns but

she knew carrying one was a good idea. The saddlebag, instead of a holster at her waist, was her compromise.

Hickok and Beth drew their guns and stole quietly toward the barn.

Beth couldn't hear a thing. Despite the door being wide open, she couldn't see anything inside, either. The darkness was too thick.

They crept up to within a few feet of the threshold. Nothing moved inside. Nothing changed. Hickok swore softly and looked back toward the cabin.

"Gonna have to risk some light," he said quietly. "Keep an eye on the cabin."

Beth nodded. She turned away before he struck a match.

Nothing moved at the cabin. The small window that looked back at the corral remained dark even as the shadowy light from Hickok's match played across it.

Hickok cursed under his breath again.

"What?" Beth resisted the urge to turn her head and look herself. Instead she focused on the cabin. Nothing moved.

"The horses. They're... well, it's ugly."

All dead, obviously. Beth sucked in her breath. "How many?"

"The barn's full. I figure six."

Then the match went out.

Beth heard Hickok slowly backing away from the barn. They quietly made their way back to Rose. At Hickok's signal, the remounted and rode back up the road several hundred yards. With the cabin now in the distance again, he turned to them.

"Something vicious killed all the horses," he said. "They looked like they'd been savagely chopped up."

Beth blanched. Rose stiffened.

"And there's too many of them." Hickok stared at the barn.

"Too many?" Rose asked.

"These stations are supposed to have four horses. They've got six. Or did."

Rose grimaced.

"What about the Express rider?" Beth asked. "He'd have a horse."

"Yeah. I figure this is as far as he got."

"Or they got," Rose said. "If they sent two."

"Would they do that?" Beth asked.

"I don't know." Hickok let out a long breath.

"The question is, are they still here?" Beth added.

"I'd rather know about the thing that killed those horses," Hickok said. "Whatever it was, didn't stop when they were dead. It doesn't look like it ate the bodies either."

"Didn't eat them?" Rose's voice quivered.

"Predators would've taken part of the flesh. This was... just butchery."

Beth looked back at the cabin. "We have to know what's in there."

"Yeah." Hickok looked grim. "Can you talk to the ghost?"

"I can talk to it," Beth answered, "but... I can't hear it."

"Maybe he can, I don't know, pantomime?" Rose suggested.

Beth shrugged agreement. "We have to try, though. That's the only door into the cabin, and he's blocking the entrance. We could walk *through* him, I suppose."

"Lord, no." Rose fanned her face with one hand. "That'd be so unpleasant. Let's see if he'll move first."

"Agreed." Beth turned her horse toward the cabin. "Let's go."

To her surprise, Hickok didn't argue. Instead, he fell in behind her as they rode back toward the cabin.

About twenty yards from the door, Beth halted and dismounted. She passed the reins to Rose. Beth took three steps toward the ghost. Then she paused and studied it.

Like she'd noticed before, the ghost wore the regulation coat and pants of a soldier, but with a broad-brimmed hat instead of the regulation cap. Other than the hat, the uniform was crisp and in good shape, without wrinkles. His beard was thin and wispy, that of a young man just come of age. With a start, Beth realized that it *was* a young man, not much older than she. Well, had been a young man. Now...

Her stomach tightened. Her own brushes with death fluttered through her mind. She steeled herself and looked the ghost in the eyes. It looked back, its face gaunt.

"Hello," she said. "Can you hear me?"

Its mouth moved, and she grimaced. She couldn't read its lips at all.

"I can't hear you," she said. "Nod your head if you understand."

It slowly nodded. Desperation seeped into its eyes.

"Are you guarding something?"

It nodded again.

"Can we go in?"

It shook its head.

Beth grimaced in frustration. She needed better questions. The problem was, the questions she really wanted to ask weren't ones that could be phrased as a yes or no. She didn't see a way to get longer answers, either. She spent some time in thought.

"Are you protecting what's inside?" she asked.

It shook its head and Beth's eyes widened.

"Are you trying to keep us away from what's inside?"

The ghost's nod was emphatic.

"Did what's inside kill the horses?" she asked.

Another emphatic nod.

"Did what's inside kill people, too?"

The pained looked on the ghost's face was answer enough. He'd probably been one of the victims.

She took a deep breath. Then she turned to Hickok, who still stared in the general direction of the ghost he couldn't see.

"He said yes?" Hickok asked. "What's inside killed the soldiers?"

"Yeah. What do we do?"

"We have to kill it," he said.

"You sure?"

"How many more would die if we just went around it?"

She nodded. "But how? What is it?"

Beth stared at the cabin. Her breath formed a little cloud in front of her, crystalized in the cold night air. The cabin was pitch dark, which meant whatever was inside didn't need a fire for warmth.

"Don't know," Hickok said. "But it's got a body, or it couldn't have killed those horses. That means we can kill it."

Beth slowly nodded. But something still nagged her— something she couldn't put her finger on.

"I'm a bit hesitant about walking into its lair," Hickok said. "Especially at night."

"We could wait until morning," Beth suggested. She didn't like the idea, but it felt necessary to suggest it.

Hickok shook his head. "Better to deal with it now."

Beth nodded. "So let's lure it out, then. If we can."

"Yeah," Hickok said. "Fight it on our terms. But how? If that ghost is in the way…?"

"I'll ask it to help." She turned back to the ghost. "We want to kill it. Will you help?"

The ghost hesitated. It tilted its head to the side as if considering her.

"We need to lure it out," she continued, "where we can shoot it. I'll bang on the door and run back fast. I just don't want to... reach through you."

"I'll bang on the door," Hickok said quietly. "I can run faster."

She looked at him in confusion. "But you're a better shot."

He gave an ambivalent shrug, which caused her eyes to go wide in surprise. She'd never considered he might think she was as good as him.

The ghost stepped to the side. At the same time, it raised its hands like it was ready for a wrestling match.

"He's clear," Beth said to Hickok. "Go."

He nodded, drew his Colt and raised it, and then slowly walked forward. Beth took a deep breath and scampered sideways so she'd have a different angle when she aimed at the door. It wouldn't do to shoot Hickok accidentally. Once she'd gotten far enough around, she drew her gun and dropped to one knee. The cold started seeping in through her denims where the snow was melting, but it gave her a steadier aim.

Hickok stopped at the door. He lit an oil lamp and set it down along the wall. He was making it easier for her to see the target, she realized. Then he looked back at her and waited.

"Go," Beth said again.

Hickok pounded the door with his fist. The bangs echoed through the still night air and he yelled, "Come out! Come out, you coward!"

Then he turned and ran.

At first nothing happened. Hickok made it about twenty yards back, before he turned and dropped to one knee as well. Beth only spared him a quick glance as she kept her focus on the door.

And waited.

And waited some more.

And then finally the door opened. It swung in, revealing nothing but darkness inside. Beth strained her eyes.

Then something strode out. A ragged man, in a torn blue uniform. His face was all torn up and rotted, as was his flesh where she could see it. He also glowed a bit, gray and dull.

No, Beth realized. Not a man. A corpse. A walking corpse.

Beth fired. Hickok's shot rang out immediately as well.

The corpse staggered as both bullets slammed into its chest. Pieces of bone and flesh flew. But then it straightened and turned toward Beth. She couldn't make out its face—too much was torn away. But its eyes glowed white.

It lifted an axe.

Beth fired again. Twice. Both bullets struck home. Then Hickok added two more. The corpse jerked and twisted as the lead slammed into it.

Then it hefted the axe and threw it at Beth.

SIX

TIME SLOWED as the axe flew. It tumbled end over end and filled Beth's vision. Her heart almost stopped. She still managed to throw herself to the side.

The axe went past her into the dark.

She rolled across the rough ground. A sharp rock stabbed her ribs but she was back to her knees in an instant. She leveled her gun at the cabin. The echoes of Hickok's shots still rang.

The ghost grappled with the walking corpse, if that was possible. To Beth's eyes, the pale gray soldier held the corpse by the shoulders while the walking corpse pummeled the ghost's chest. The blows seemed to be landing.

No. The soldier's ghost wasn't touching the corpse's body. Its arm passed through the flesh. It was grappling with the soul still trapped in the corpse. As it did, the soldier's ghost brightened from gray to bright white. The more the soldier struggled, the brighter it got.

She glanced at Hickok. He was reloading while he kept nervously glancing at the walking corpse.

Beth took careful aim and fired. The bullet passed through the ghost and smashed into the corpse's head. Dead flesh exploded, but the corpse kept fighting.

How would they kill this thing?

She checked her Colt. Two bullets left. She fumbled open the pouch at her waist as she started to reload. She couldn't tear her eyes off the monster.

It kept attacking the ghost, to no avail. From its reactions, the ghost felt the pain of each punch, of each kick, but it didn't let go. The monster couldn't pull away and it couldn't break the ghost soldier's grip.

How is it even touching it? Ghosts moved through matter, but the ghost had a firm grip on the monster, as if they were both fully physical.

Or both ghosts. She'd seen ghosts touch other ghosts. The monster was part ghost! Which gave her an idea. She scrambled to her feet.

"Pull it down!" she yelled at the soldier ghost. "Pull it down to the ground!"

It caught her meaning and immediately flopped backwards, yanking the monster on top of it. Except when they hit the ground, the ghost sunk through the surface and into the dirt. It wrapped its arms around the corpse. Those arms were all of the ghost that was above the earth.

Beth ran forward, and then realized Hickok had as well. The corpse was trapped—pinned to the ground by the ghost. It tried to snap its teeth and hands at the arms. She stopped three feet away and allowed herself time to catch her breath and reload.

Then she fired into the monster's skull.

The decayed flesh and bone shattered. She blasted it again. Then Hickok was beside her and shooting its knees, elbows, and shoulders. The rotting sinews parted and bone broke. As they did, those parts of the corpse fell limp. More of the ghostly glow shone through.

They emptied their guns into it. When they were done, it still twitched and fought the ghost holding it down, but now it was more ghost itself than flesh.

"Looks like we'll have to destroy it completely," Hickok growled. "I'll get my saber."

Beth nodded. She reloaded yet again and briefly gave thanks she'd brought the extra ammunition. Once the gun was full, she kept it pointed at the corpse.

It didn't look right, she realized. Enough of the body had faded away that she could see the ghost underneath the decayed flesh. That ghost looked like a man—another soldier in a military cap in fact—except for the rabid, crazed expression on its face. Like a wild man in blinding white instead of a soldier. It was also streaked with a spiderweb of red. Every ghost she'd seen before had been some combination of grays and whites. But not red.

Hickok hustled up. "Step back."

She watched as he hacked the corpse to pieces. At one point the mad monster almost pulled out of the ghost's grip, but then its fleshy arm came completely off, severed just below the shoulder.

She'd been still enough that the smell of rotted meat finally reached her nose. She'd seen butchering before, but that was fresh meat, not this... grotesqueness. Nor had the animals she'd seen slaughtered before been remotely human.

She forced herself to watch. Just in case something went wrong. Just in case Hickok needed help.

He didn't. He methodically sliced the corpse into pieces. As he did so, the web of red in the ghost faded to black. Finally, only a single strand remained, tied to the pelvic bone.

Hickok stepped back and caught his breath. Despite the cold, he wiped his brow.

The monster still struggled against the ghost, but much more feebly now. It reminded Beth of a child beating her hands on her daddy's chest.

"Break the hips," she said.

"What?" Hickok's stare was more exhausted than confused.

"Break the hips. It's still here as a ghost. There's... something tying the soul and body together."

Hickok gave her a confused look, but instead of asking he started hacking at the last whole piece of the corpse. Slowly, the red faded.

And then a small dark gray circle appeared above the corpse. The ghost within the monster floated toward it and then both it and the circle vanished.

The soldier ghost rose out of the dirt. Its arm brushed through Hickok's as it did and Hickok shuddered. He looked wildly at Beth.

"You touched the ghost," she said.

He shivered and stepped back.

"It's dead," Beth said. She indicated the hacked-up corpse. "Its spirit has... moved on."

"Moved on?" He looked down at the body.

"There was this... ghost inside the body. That's... the best way to describe it. But it's gone now."

"What about the other ghost?" he asked.

"Still here." She nodded to where the ghost soldier now stood. He didn't bear any wounds, and he looked relieved.

"Are there more?" Hickok asked.

Beth blinked. She should've asked.

The ghost heard Hickok anyway. It was shaking its head.

"No," she said.

"Then let's see what's inside." Hickok stepped over to the open door, but then pulled back.

"Smells like dead bodies," he said. He picked up the lamp and shone it inside. Then he grimaced. "Yeah. Several dead bodies. No one's alive."

He turned to the Beth. "It's ugly in there. I'd rather investigate in daylight."

She grimaced and nodded. If nothing was alive inside, then there wasn't a rush.

Rose walked up leading all their horses. "So where do we sleep?"

Beth nodded and turned to the ghost. "Is there somewhere nearby we can sleep?" she asked. "A nearby abandoned farmhouse? Or something like it?"

The ghost hesitated. Then it pointed south, away from the road.

"How far?" Beth asked. She raised her hand. "In hours? One?" She held up a single finger. "Two?" She extended a second.

The ghost slowly nodded. Then it raised a single finger.

"Thank you," she said. She looked down at the dismembered corpse that had been the monster and then back at the ghost. "You protected us. And then you helped us kill it. Good work, soldier."

"Yes," Hickok added. "You've done your duty."

The ghost slowly nodded. Its face fell, as if exhaustion had overtaken it completely. But then the air behind it shimmered into a dark circle. A moment later, it faded into the dark circle and both disappeared.

"He's gone," Beth said quietly. "He saved us, and now he's moved on."

The dilapidated farmhouse turned out to be in really poor shape. The roof was filled with holes, but at least it was there. Even better, the house had a hearth. Unfortunately, that hearth had a raccoon who'd decided it was the perfect place to winter.

Hickok did his best to dislodge the animal by yelling and throwing rocks in its general direction. It hissed and refused to move on until one rock hit it square on the snout. Then it charged at Hickok, who scrambled away, much to Rose's amusement. Fortunately it wasn't so much chasing him as trying to get to the door, while Hickok had been in the way. That didn't prevent Beth from stifling at laugh at Hickok's expression.

Once the raccoon was gone, they were able to use some of the broken timbers from a collapsed wall to start a fire. It smoked heavily, but blessedly the smell was only burnt wood. The warmth was a welcome relief.

They talked about the ghost, the corpse, and what they'd seen.

"I think that was a barrow wight," Hickok said.

"What's that?" Rose asked.

"A Norse monster that's basically a walking corpse." Hickok looked grim. "At least that's how Cassidy described them."

"Cassidy the Giant Killer?" Rose asked.

"Yeah. Him. He fought something like that down in Mississippi."

"Oh, my."

"Said it was one of the toughest fights he'd had."

"Did he say how he beat it?" Beth asked.

"He said his witch did it, in the end. She exorcised the

wight's spirit. It put up a heckuva fight, though. Killed one of his team."

"It didn't feel pain," Beth said. "It looked strong, too.

Hickok nodded. "Even though it was decayed."

"Mmm hmm."

"And the way it threw that axe?" Hickok snorted and shook his head. "I can't do that."

Beth nodded, and suppressed a shudder.

"You okay, dearie?" Rose asked.

"Just memories," Beth couldn't help but reach up and touch the old scar on her shoulder.

"Oh, my dear, it's not the same," Rose said. "It's not the same at all. You couldn't dodge that first one."

"What?" Hickok asked.

"When I was hurt in Yellowstone," Beth explained, "I got hit from behind. I hadn't expected…" She shrugged and rubbed her shoulder.

"Yeah…," Hickok said. He unconsciously rubbed his own side, where he'd told Beth he'd once been shot himself. "The near misses get to you."

Beth nodded in agreement.

"So…," Hickok said. "We'll go back in the morning and see what we can learn in the cabin."

"Then we bury the bodies?" Rose asked.

Beth shook her head. "No. The ground's too frozen. We burn them, along with the dead horses."

"Fair enough," Hickok said. "Now let's get some rest."

Hickok woke her in the middle of the night to take her turn on watch. By the low light of the fire's coals, she could just make out his expression—worn and somber. He waited until she'd rubbed her eyes and sat up. Then he spoke and kept his voice low.

"I've been thinking," he said. "We should've switched places. I should be the one the wight targets."

"He could've thrown that axe at you just as easily."

Hickok shrugged. "Still."

She grimaced but climbed out of her bedroll.

"Keep a good watch," he said. "Wake me at the slightest sign of trouble."

"I will." She moved to the building's doorway. The night was clear and still. They wouldn't have any trouble.

She glanced back at Hickok. Despite his worries, he was already nestling into his own bedroll.

Beth sighed. She didn't quite know what to make of his concern. She turned away and settled in for her watch.

By day, the station wasn't much better than the night before. Clouds had drifted in, which meant a gray pall filled the air. The wind had picked up as well, and the open cabin door swung and banged against the wall. They tied their horses to the corral fence between the barn and cabin. Rose looked nervously from one to the other.

"We need food," she said, "especially for the horses."

"The horses were killed in their stalls," Hickok said. "The hay should be fine."

Rose nodded. "I can get that."

"That leaves the cabin to us," Beth said to Hickok.

He clenched his jaw, and for a moment it looked like he might say something, but then he just nodded. He gestured for Beth to follow him around to the front.

Enough light shone into the open door to reveal the horror within. The cabin reeked of rotted flesh and she had to look carefully to identify three bodies inside. The soldiers had been savagely killed and blood covered nearly everything. Furniture had been smashed. Food from the kitchen lay scattered everywhere. It reminded her of the rat's nest she'd found in Ma's barn once, but with dried blood and a far worse smell.

Hickok looked grim. "Get the window." He moved to the closest body.

Beth picked her way through the room's debris to the window that faced the corral. She swept the curtains aside, and to her relief, saw that it could be opened. The slight breeze blowing in helped the smell, at least when it first brushed her face.

Hickok had moved to the first body. He closed the unfortunate soldier's eyes and then motioned to Beth.

"You get his feet," he said.

They carried the body outside and then set it down on the ground. Hickok turned out the soldier's pockets and poked around for anything under his shirt. He found a small square locket with the picture of a young woman, a few coins, and not much else.

"Poor woman," he said as he looked at the picture.

"Poor soldier," Beth said. "He's the one that's dead."

"True," Hickok said, "but he signed up for this. She just fell in love with an unlucky man." He passed her the locket.

She looked closer at it. The light-haired woman was smiling, but it looked forced. She probably knew what she, too, had signed up for.

Then Beth looked a little closer at the dead soldier and her eyes widened. The face was the same as the ghost's who'd helped them.

"It's him," she said. When Hickok gave her a curious

look, she repeated, "It's him. He was the ghost that helped us."

"Well, then," Hickok said, "we better learn his name, so we can make sure he gets the honor he's due."

They brought the other bodies out and searched them for anything that might identify them. Other than some money and a few personal effects like handkerchiefs and a comb, they found nothing. They started searching the cabin itself and Hickok found the station's ledger, mostly intact, thrown under a bed. The book's spine was broken, but most of the pages were still there.

Beth looked for some salvageable food but found nothing. The handful of cans had all been smashed and the cold box completely broken apart. Even a barrel of flour had been split open, to the delight of some bugs that had found it. The whole time she searched, she had to keep a bandanna over her nose and try not to breathe too deeply. When she did, her stomach lurched at the smell.

Hickok had started searching the beds. Beth was relieved and happy to let him do it. That's where two of the mangled bodies had been, apparently killed in their sleep. The contents of their bags and trunks were strewn everywhere, most coated with dried blood. Hickok picked up each piece of clothing gingerly between two fingers, looked at it, and then discarded it.

Beth put her hands on her hips and looked around. Something wasn't right. She furrowed her brow while she thought. There'd clearly been a fight in the cabin, and the barrow wight had killed the three men. Their bodies hadn't been hacked as savagely as the horses but it wasn't pretty. Something was missing...

"Wait a minute," she said.

Hickok looked up. "What?

"You said there were two extra horses in the barn, right?"

He nodded. "That's right. The station's usual four and two more."

"And these stations usually have three men staffing them, right?"

"Well, except for the one that was short-handed back near Julesburg."

"So there should've been five men here. The three manning the station and the two that brought the extra horses."

Hickok's eyebrows rose. "But there's only three bodies."

"Four, counting the barrow wight. I think he was one of our soldiers once, too.

"Really?"

"I think he was turned into the wight somehow."

"Fine," Hickok said. "Four. But that begs the question..."

Beth nodded. "Where's the fifth man?"

SEVEN

THEY SEARCHED the cabin and the barn once again. They didn't find a fifth corpse. Then Rose walked a wide circle around the outpost looking for footprints or some trail that the missing soldier could've left. While she did so, Beth and Hickok moved the bodies to the barn. It was difficult work, given how torn up and gory the bodies were. Beth's gut felt like she'd swallowed a lead cannon ball. At least she wasn't going to vomit.

Rose returned just as they finished laying out the last body for their fiery funeral. She looked grim, though she walked quickly.

"Found him." Her eyes were cold but she was breathing hard, upset.

"Where?" Beth asked.

"He was headed toward Saint Louis on foot."

"And didn't make it." Hickok grimaced.

Rose shook her head.

"Might as well bring his body back." Beth gestured toward the barn.

"Yeah." Hickok turned to Rose. "How far is he?"

"Far enough we should take the horses."

Beth nodded. She was already weary and quite cold. Somehow the day felt more frigid than the night before. Her nose and cheeks tingled now that she wasn't working so hard. She knew it had to be mid-morning, though with the clouds it felt like dusk would arrive soon.

Rose led them down the road toward Saint Louis about five hundred yards. As she did, she pointed to the blood drops she'd spotted in the snow. They were hard to see in the well trampled old snow—a mixture of hoof prints and human tracks made the icy ground uneven. The drops grew closer together as they approached the body. The soldier, in his blue uniform, sprawled face down with one arm pinned underneath.

"See anything?" Hickok asked Beth. "Any ghosts?"

"I can't see ghosts in the daylight." Still, she looked closely. Nothing.

He sighed in mild frustration and dismounted his horse. Beth did the same and then passed her reins to Rose. She took the opportunity to rub her frozen face with her hand. The glove was rough, but her cheeks felt better when she'd finished.

Hickok approached the body. He knelt by it and frowned.

"This is a bullet wound," he said. "He was shot."

Hickok touched the back lightly and then rolled the body over. The dead soldier flopped over and stared at the sky. A leather pouch that had been clutched to his front fell to the side.

He was another youth, barely more than a boy. He was lanky, with wisps of brown hair on his chin that weren't thick enough to be a true beard. His mouth hung open until Hickok closed both it and his eyes.

Dried blood covered the corpse's stomach and the

back of the leather pouch. He'd clearly been clutching it to him as he ran. Hickok gently picked it up and opened it.

"Letters," he said as he peeked inside.

"He must've been the final rider." Beth knelt by Hickok's side.

"Mmm hmm."

"What are the letters?"

Hickok pulled out four envelopes and scanned them. His eyes went wide. He set three back in the pouch and cracked the seal on the fourth.

"This one's addressed to me," he explained before she could ask. He unfolded the paper and quickly read.

"Oh, no," he murmured.

"What?" Beth couldn't quite read over his shoulder.

"The trolls have started building boats."

"To cross the river?"

"Right." He flipped over the page, checked the back, and then returned to the front. "The commander's sent messengers to both Fort Chicago and New Orleans asking them for help. He wants the ironclads to sail up from New Orleans."

"Will that help?" Beth vaguely remembered that most of the the West's ironclads had been sunk in a battle a few years ago. She was sure they'd built more, but most of the shipbuilding these days was on the Pacific coast.

"It should. If they get the dispatch."

"Why wouldn't they?"

"I didn't get this one." He tapped the paper. "It orders me to bring the Colorado militia." He looked at the letter again and frowned. Then he picked up the other letters again.

"The commander says he sent a letter to the President, too," Hickok said, "but it's not in the pouch."

"You think it was stolen?" She frowned. "But that doesn't make sense."

"Not by the wight," Hickok said.

"Could it have been sent earlier?" Rose asked. She'd crept closer while Hickok had been reading.

"We would've met the messenger along the way." Hickok folder his letter and put it in his pocket. "It makes more sense to have sent them all at once."

Beth couldn't help the chill she felt run up her spine at the thought of an army of trolls. She'd heard that trolls weren't much harder to kill than humans. They didn't have the thick skins giants did, but they seemed to breed like rabbits. Troll armies were... huge.

"So what do we do?" Rose asked.

"We take this body back to the barn and give the men the funeral they deserve." Hickok grimaced. "Then we continue on to Saint Louis."

The barn blazed far hotter than Beth had expected. The three of them stood together a decent ways away, but still the heat washed over them. Beth's gut twinged a little with guilt. She should be feeling reverence or grief for the departed soldiers instead of grateful for the heat.

But as she watched the flames consume the old, dry wood, she had second thoughts. Maybe they could've just left the bodies frozen somewhere until someone could come back and give the soldiers a proper burial. It was cold enough, and maybe she and Hickok would've been able to find a place that the local scavengers couldn't get at them.

But she wasn't sure when anyone would come back. She suspected it might not be for a long, long time.

Because the wight's presence didn't make sense this far from Saint Louis. Actually, she realized, it didn't make sense for a couple of reasons. She turned to Hickok.

"How are wights created?" she asked. "Did Cassidy ever say?"

"No." Hickok grimaced. "But that barrow wight had to have been created here."

"Why is that?"

"The others wouldn't have let it into the cabin if they knew what it was."

She nodded. "He changed... from a soldier into... that."

"That's what I reckon."

"But that raises another question," Beth continued. "How'd the messenger die?"

Hickok furrowed his brow in confusion.

"The ghost trapped the wight inside the cabin," Beth explained, "but the messenger died outside. So the wight couldn't've killed him."

"Well... if it was earlier..."

Beth shook her head. "The others would've heard the gunshot."

Hickok blinked. "That's... a very good point."

"Besides," she said. "The wight didn't use a gun to kill anyone. It tore them apart."

"Oh, God." Hickok's face turned grim. "There were two of them."

"Has to be," Beth agreed.

"Two wights?" Rose asked. "Or a wight and something else?"

"Someone else," Hickok said. "The gun, remember?"

"So...," Beth said. "How does this work?"

"The outpost soldiers had to be dead by the time the messenger arrives, or they'd've come outside."

"Or the messenger would've gone inside," Rose said. "Remember, the Julesburg men didn't come out."

"But either way, his corpse would've been with theirs," Hickok said. "And it wasn't."

Beth nodded. "So the messenger arrives. He dismounts. He goes to the cabin door. Something happens."

"And after that 'something,' he runs on foot," Hickok continued. "Which means he couldn't get back on his horse fast enough."

"Right," Beth said, "so the horse was tied up."

"There wasn't a hitching post out front," Rose added.

"Good observation, Miss Chamberlin," Hickok said. "That means—"

Beth interrupted. "The other person was a soldier. The messenger arrives to see a soldier standing outside. He hands him the reins to his horse and goes to the cabin—"

"No!" Hickok's excitement was palatable. "He gives this soldier the letter for the President for some reason. Not the entire mail bag. Only then... something happens."

"He must've seen the wight," Rose said. "Or he'd have gone into the cabin instead of down the road."

"Right." Hickok nodded. "So he runs."

"And the other soldier," Beth said excitedly, "the evil one, he shoots the messenger. Then he rides off on the messenger's horse!"

"Mmm hmm."

The exhilaration of having figured it out surged through Beth's blood, but faded when she saw Rose's worried expression.

"Umm," Rose said. "So... we have a soldier working with a wight?"

Beth and Hickok both nodded.

"That sounds awful."

"Yeah," Hickok agreed. "But it's clear the wight didn't kill the messenger." He paused, and then swore quietly. "We have a traitor in the Army."

Beth felt the certainty in her gut. It made too much sense. The dread settled deep as she watched the flames.

"So what do we do?" Rose asked.

"It's too late to make Saint Louis before dark," Hickok said. "Normally, I'd ride anyway, but now... we'd better not."

Rose looked at Beth questioningly.

"We could be walking into a trap." Beth explained. Then she thought for a moment. "Bill, did you look at that ledger yet?"

"No. But perhaps now's the time."

The waited by the barn as it burned. The blaze faded to coals by mid-afternoon. Most of the barn had just collapsed inwards. Beth and Rose scooped snow onto anywhere near the edge that still smoldered. Beth was pretty confident it'd go out soon, given the cold and all the surrounding snow. Still, they didn't want to set the surrounding area ablaze.

Hickok studied the ledger and other papers from the cabin. Most of the time he had his head down with his brow furrowed. After a bit, he headed back into the cabin to find a lost page. It took him a while, but he came back out with a paper held high and a look of triumph on his face. He gestured for Beth and Rose to join him.

"Got something," he said with a snap of the page. "Three days ago, a Private Simmons arrived. The log says he was taking messages to San Francisco, but there's a note: 'got sick.'" Hickok jabbed the page with a finger.

"And then another note: 'Slept in barn.'" He smiled. "There's no entry about Simmons leaving, which there should be. So he didn't. Simmons is either our traitor or our wight."

"But that's only one name," Beth said. "Is there another entry?"

Hickok shook his head.

"So the traitor might still be out there." Rose bit her lip nervously.

"I think Simmons is the wight." Beth paused to order her thoughts. "The wight had to have killed the horses before he got trapped in the cabin."

"Good thinking," Hickok said.

Beth nodded. "He turned into a wight, somehow. He killed the horses and then went after the men."

"Mmm, yes," Hickok said. "But where's the traitor in all this?"

Beth thought a moment. "I think he arrived either later that night or early the next day—"

"Right," Hickok interrupted, "because the outpost soldiers didn't enter him into the log."

"Mmm hmm." Beth glared at Hickok for his interruption, but he didn't seem to notice. "And then the traitor waited for the messenger."

Hickok expression grew grim. "Betrayed by one of his own."

"But why?" Rose asked. "Why would he do it?" She waved at the barn. "We've got wights and ghosts and trolls. Why would a soldier, a *human* soldier, betray one of his own?"

"Men do evil for many reasons." Hickok's face tightened as he stared at a memory Beth couldn't see.

"And the poor boy just handed over the President's letter without seeing a hint of that evil," Rose said.

Beth started and pursed her lip in thought.

"Bill," she asked, "why would the messenger pass another soldier a single letter instead of the entire mail pouch?"

"Good question." Hickok stroked his beard as he thought. "He should've passed the entire pouch. That's how the old Pony Express worked."

"Oh." Beth's eyes widened as the realization hit her. "Oh. He handed over the letter because he was ordered to."

Hickok cursed under his breath. "Our traitor is an officer."

"So," Rose asked, "how do we find him?"

EIGHT

THEIR CONVERSATION WAS INTERRUPTED by the fire. One of the last logs shifted and dropped, sending up a shower of sparks. They swirled in the breeze and Beth kept a wary eye on the ones that drifted highest. Fortunately, none drifted far.

"We'll have to figure out the traitor when we get to Saint Louis," Hickok finally said. "Let's hole up in that farmhouse."

Rose nodded. "We need to leave this place." She gave the smoldering funeral pyre a sour look.

Beth couldn't help but agree. It wasn't the gruesome nature of the deaths. She'd seen death before. It was the wight. She kept expecting to see it lurch out of the ashes and throw an axe at her. She knew it couldn't—she'd seen its soul move on—but that didn't stop the nagging sense that it would.

She'd taken comfort in the knowledge that ghosts couldn't hurt her. But now...

She wished she could talk to her friend Maria. She'd know about wights. Heck, if the story about Cassidy and the barrow wight in Mississippi was true, she'd banished one. Beth just didn't know enough about them beyond the name.

And if there were more in Saint Louis...?

"We should get some rest," Hickok said. "We'll need to leave early so we can arrive in the afternoon."

Beth nodded. "So if something's really wrong, we'll have time to find shelter before night."

"Really wrong?" Rose's brow was furrowed. "How wrong can it get?"

"I don't know," he admitted. "If these are roaming around..." He gestured at the fire.

"I'm sure it's okay," Beth tried to project more confidence than she felt. "Wights can't be that common, or we'd have run into them before."

"Yeah." Hickok stared east at the horizon. "I just hope nothing's changed."

"Well... if it has," Rose said with a small smile, "we will manage. Wights, trolls, dragons, whatever. We can handle it."

Hickok nodded. "Yes, we can."

They watched the fire a bit longer but eventually the horses started to snort and shuffle. They'd been tied up long enough, Beth realized, so maybe it was time to move on. The three of them headed south to the abandoned farmhouse where they'd spent the night before.

Hickok insisted on second watch and said they wouldn't have a third. When it was time, he'd just wake them both up and they'd get on the road. He quickly settled down next to the small fire while Beth sat near the open door.

Nothing moved anywhere she could see. She sat quietly with the blankets pulled tight for warmth. Her stomach grumbled. It'd been hard to eat after all their work with the bodies. She couldn't even touch the hardtack but at least had managed some of the dried apples. Ma would've turned them into muffins or flapjacks, but on the road, they didn't have the time.

Ma. The pang in Beth's gut struck deep. Ma was right to be afraid she'd never see her again. If that axe had been a foot or two lower...

Beth suppressed a shudder.

Ma wanted her to be safe. Hickok, too. But... she couldn't stay back where it was safe.

If they hadn't destroyed the wight, how many more would've died? What would've happened when the next messenger arrived?

Her mind raced through the possible scenarios, but none of them were good. They'd done what they had to do. And at least they hadn't had to kill another human. Private Simmons had probably been dead before he'd turned into a wight.

At least she hoped so. The thought of being alive... trapped in a dead body... she had to take a deep calming breath.

No one knew for sure whether soul would go to Heaven or Hell, but being trapped like that had to be worse than being a ghost. Most of the ghosts she'd encountered had been able to move on, eventually. Except the Broken Ones. Those...

She sighed. She wished, once more, that Maria was around. There was so much she didn't know about ghosts, and no one to ask. But she could do this. She'd spent almost four years training with one of the best gunfighters ever. Yes, Hickok could get on her nerves, but he knew what to do.

She snorted softly. Except that wasn't always true. He didn't know how to cope with ghosts any better than she did. In some ways, she was the teacher here. She'd spent several months living with an Indian shaman's ghost. Hickok couldn't even see them.

Hickok taught her to never give into fear. Make friends with it. Own it. Let it serve you, and not the other way. She didn't have to be afraid. If they ran into more wights, they ran into more wights. She could deal with them. She could beat them.

Them or her. If she was fast enough, and smart enough, she'd win. She only knew two men who were better gunfighters than she was. Both were friends. One was sleeping only a few feet away. As was her best friend, too.

Beth couldn't help a smile at that. Rose had carefully brushed and braided her hair before going to sleep. She'd washed her face in some melted snow and cleaned out under her fingernails. They might've spent the day moving corpses, but Rose would be a lady at the end.

If Rose could manage a day like they had, then Beth could, too.

She settled back for her watch.

Beth awoke cold and stiff and not at all as quickly as she usually did. In the dark, she could sense more than see Hickok moving around. The fire was barely more than coals, and the farmhouse chilled. She rubbed her arms to get some warmth. A moment later, Rose stirred.

"We'd best be on our way," Hickok said. "We'll eat on the trail."

Beth grumbled, but Hickok ignored her. A short time later, they were on horseback.

The morning broke bright, with the sun beating down all too soon. They didn't ride as hard as they'd done on days past. Hickok seemed more interested in slowing from time to time to check the horizon. About mid-morning, he stopped and stared into the distance. When he'd gotten Beth and Rose's attention, he pointed.

"That smoke?"

Beth shaded her eyes and stared. A faint black curl drifted up ahead of them.

"Looks like a campfire or chimney."

"Good, that's good." He nodded, and when he saw Beth's confusion, he explained. "The farms that feed Saint Louis are out here. That's probably one of them."

"Oh thank you, dear Lord," Rose muttered. When she caught Beth's amused look, she added, "It'll be nice to talk to someone who isn't a soldier."

"Just not used to you praying."

"I pray a lot these days." She gave Beth a sheepish look before shifting to face down the road.

Beth blinked in surprise. Maybe she hadn't paid as much attention to her friend as she should've.

Hickok urged his horse forward. "Well, let's go say hello."

The farmer stood outside feeding some goats. About a half dozen of the animals bleated and jumped in their little pen while he tossed handfuls of hay over the four foot fence. The goats were so loud that the farmer didn't notice Beth and her companions until they were only a half dozen yards away. Then he turned, startled.

He was younger than Beth had expected from his worn clothes. Maybe thirty, his muscles were tight and his skin and face smooth. His deep brown eyes quickly looked them over and shifted from wary to relaxed.

"Good day," Hickok said. "I am Captain Bill Hickok and these are my companions Miss Armstrong and Miss Chamberlin. I wonder if we might trouble you for a bit? We have questions about Saint Louis."

The farmer's eyes drifted to Hickok's army jacket. He'd worn it only loosely buttoned and without much of the rest of the uniform, but it was apparently enough. When his eyes took in Beth's trousers, he raised an eyebrow, but that was the extent of it.

"I'm Mr. Sawyer," the farmer replied. "You can go on to the house and tell Mrs. Sawyer I said to look after you." He nodded at the goats. "I'll be along after a bit."

Mrs. Sawyer turned out to be a tiny dark-haired woman with the energy and bustle of a woman three times her stature. She invited them in and introduced them to her children—two boys about four and six—before sending the children outside to help their father. Then, in a whirlwind of activity, Beth found herself seated at a simple but sturdy wooden table with milk and biscuits in front of her. Hickok, sitting next to her, looked equally bemused, but Rose's face was alight.

"How beautiful," Rose said as she took note of the embroidered napkins that accompanied the biscuits. "Are these Chinese?"

"Oh, just a Chinese design," Mrs. Sawyer said. "My cousin had some like those from San Francisco and they inspired the pattern."

"You made these yourself?" Beth said. She held one up and looked more closely at the stitching.

"Oh my, no. I just did the decoration." Mrs. Sawyer pulled a pan out of a cupboard and some bacon out of the cold box. "Mr. Sawyer purchased the fabric a number of years ago." She smiled. "That was a better time."

"The stitching is quite lovely." Rose examined her

napkin with a critical eye. "Such fine thread. Has it been hard to get?"

"No, not particularly."

"We've had some difficulty in Golden City."

"One of the gleaners found it in the ruins," Mrs. Sawyer explained. "She was happy to sell it for a modest price."

"Gleaners?" Beth asked. "What's that?"

"One of the people who explores the ruins of Saint Louis," Mrs. Sawyer said. "They sell what they can find."

"They still find things to sell?" Beth couldn't help raising her eyebrows. "I would've expected it to be completely scavenged by now. It's been, what, fifteen years?"

"Nearly." Hickok's face grew tight. His shoulders tensed. "The Jotun destroyed it fifteen years ago this coming summer."

Beth let out a long breath. He'd been there. Often when he was drunk, Hickok had muttered about the mistakes they'd made. He'd never been specific, though. But after Saint Louis, it had been his idea to lead the Jotun army down the long, long road back to Golden City and into the trap in the mountains.

She'd once asked him why the Army had listened to him. It seemed like an awfully long way to go. It also seemed like a plan that depended on luck and Jotun carelessness more than anything. He'd never explained why they'd listened. He'd just said that the plan had worked, and that was all that mattered.

But now his face was filled with old pain.

"Oh, my," Rose said. "Fifteen years? People stopped exploring the Denver City ruins after a year."

Hickok snorted and shook his head. Then he looked at Rose. "Denver City had a population of ten thousand, just before it was destroyed, and everyone had a week's warning to evacuate. They took all the possessions they could move with them."

He leaned back and let out a heavy breath.

"Saint Louis had a quarter of a million people," he said quietly. "They only had hours to flee."

Mrs. Sawyer grew somber and nodded in agreement.

Roses eyes were wide. "I can't even imagine a quarter of a million people. The city must be huge."

"Was," Hickok said. "Was."

"So how big are these ruins?" Beth asked. *How many places could hide barrow wights?*

"Big enough that we haven't explored it all," Hickok said.

"Big enough," Mrs. Sawyer added, "that they haven't found all the ghosts."

NINE

THE SAWYERS' cabin suddenly felt small. It wasn't particularly. In a lot of ways, it was light and airy and homey. When the door opened and the boisterous boys entered, it even felt loud and crowded. But small.

Beth still tried to grasp what Mrs. Sawyer had said. A city where they hadn't found all the ghosts was too large to imagine.

A minute later, Mr. Sawyer came in. He greeted them and kissed his wife on the cheek before washing his hands in a basin by one of the windows. His boys crowded around him and he admonished them to wash as well before finally turning his attention to his guests.

"Welcome," he said as he sank into the last available chair. "It's good to have visitors. Especially womenfolk." He nodded at both Beth and Rose, and still didn't seem at all put off by Beth's clothes. Then he turned to Hickok.

"Now, Captain," he asked, "how might we assist you?"

"I was hoping for news from Saint Louis."

"We don't get much." Mr. Sawyer looked at his wife

for confirmation. When she nodded, he continued, "We see the riders pass by from time to time, but none stop."

"Did you see any in the last week?" Beth asked.

"I don't believe so," Mr. Sawyer said.

Hickok furrowed his brow.

"We spend most days inside on account of the cold," Mr. Sawyer explained. "When we don't need to feed the animals, of course."

"A soldier did ride by two days ago." Mrs. Sawyer moved behind her husband's chair and put her hands on its back. He gave her an affectionate smile. "He seemed in a bit of a hurry."

"They usually are," Mr. Sawyer said. Her reached back and gently touched his wife's hand.

"What did he look like?" Beth asked before Hickok could.

"I didn't get a good look," Mrs. Sawyer said. "He was in uniform on a brown horse, if that helps."

"Any particular reason for the interest?" Mr. Sawyer's smile was friendly, but his shoulders tightened as he asked.

Beth exchanged a look with Hickok and Rose. Hickok grimaced and cleared his throat.

"The express station west of here was attacked two or three days ago." His eyes flicked to the young boys before returning to the elder Sawyers. "All the soldiers were killed."

"Oh, my." Mrs. Sawyer turned to her children. "Boys... could you please go see if there's some eggs? Hattie should've laid one by now."

"We looked this morning," the older boy whined. His lower lip stuck out like a fat worm.

"Well, look again."

"Perhaps I can help," Rose said. To the boys, "Would

you like to show me your chickens? I'm sure they're lovely."

"The little one's got black and brown feathers!" The smaller boy beamed at Rose. "Both!"

"Well, you'll have to show me." Rose stood and extended a hand to the boy. He glanced at his mother. When she nodded, he took it. After some effort to get bundled back up in coats, they were out the door.

"So what happened?" Mr. Sawyer asked once the boys were just distant voices.

"It was horrible," Hickok said. He described what they'd found and how they'd fought the barrow wight.

Both the Sawyers flinched. Mr. Sawyer squeezed his wife's hand tight. They asked a few questions for clarification, which both Beth and Hickok answered, before Hickok continued to describe the funeral pyre.

"We could've given them a good Christian burial," Mrs. Sawyer said.

"Well, pardon, ma'am," Hickok said, "but we didn't know you'd be here, alive at least. And from what I understand, a wight can make more wights from the dead."

"What?" Beth interjected.

"It was something Cassidy said. If a wight kills someone, they can rise from the grave a few days later as a new wight."

"You could've mentioned this when we were at the station," she muttered. Her tone would've been louder and harsher if they hadn't been in front of others.

"I didn't want to worry you," he said. "Or Rose."

She shot him a glare, but he just shrugged, not at all repentant.

"So how did the wight get there?" Mr. Sawyer asked.

"We don't know," Cassidy answered. He proceeded to describe what they had found.

72

"Show them the locket," Beth urged. "Maybe they know the girl."

Hickok fished it out of his pocket and passed it over. The Sawyers looked carefully at it, but shook their heads.

"We don't know many people in Saint Louis." Mr. Sawyer handed the locket back. He sounded apologetic. "Mostly the merchants who buy our grain."

"Down at the waterfront market?" Hickok asked.

"And the stores by Jefferson Barracks." Mr. Sawyer smiled. "We also sell to the Army, but you know those men."

"Perhaps," Hickok said. "When was the last time you were at the Barracks?"

Mr. Sawyer shrugged. "A few weeks. Sorry."

"The Benton girl might know the young lady." Mrs. Sawyer nodded toward the locket. "She knows many of the girls in town."

"Ah, yes," Mr. Sawyer said. "At the boarding house." To Hickok and Beth, "Her father owns the Soulard Inn, though it's not really an inn."

"Just a fancy boarding house in the old Soulard neighborhood," Mrs. Sawyer said. "They don't serve food unless you're staying there, but they do take good care of some of the lost souls."

"They're near the church," Mr. Sawyer added.

"Which church?" Hickok asked.

"The one Father O'Neill runs."

"In Soulard?" Hickok asked. "That'd be... the tall church? Um... Saints Peter and Paul's?"

Beth furrowed her brow. She couldn't imagine a tall church.

"Mmm hmm," Mrs. Sawyer said. When she saw Beth's confusion, she added, "The giants didn't destroy Saints Peter and Paul's Church when they invaded."

"Some consider it a miracle," Mr. Sawyer added.

"More like dumb luck," Hickok said.

Mr. Sawyer just shrugged, deigning not to argue.

"So what do you know about the ghosts?" Beth asked.

"Not much, I'm afraid." Mrs. Sawyer glanced down at her husband, who furrowed his brow in thought.

"Well...," he said to her, "what about Father O'Neill's map?"

"Oh, I'd forgotten about that!"

"Map?" Hickok prompted.

Mr. Sawyer nodded. "I've heard that Father O'Neill keeps a big map of the city that he uses to keep track of the ghosts."

"How have I never heard of this?" Hickok quickly amended his outburst. "My apologies. I realize that's not something you'd know."

"It's all right," Mrs. Sawyer said. "The folks in Soulard don't mix much with the barracks men. I doubt many soldiers know of the map."

Hickok grumbled under his breath, but just nodded to Mrs. Sawyer.

"So how does Father O'Neill make this map?" Beth asked. "Most people can't even see ghosts. Can he?"

"Why, I don't rightly know," Mrs. Sawyer said. "You'll have to ask him, I suppose." She looked at her husband, who nodded.

"Well, we know who we'll visit first then." Beth looked at Hickok. "After we visit the Barracks?"

He nodded. "Assuming everything's fine." He turned to Mr. Sawyer. "Thank you for your hospitality."

"Yes," Beth said, "we should be going." They'd need to tell Rose, which made Beth think of what Rose would say. "But first, Mr. Sawyer, is there any chore we could help you with?"

"Oh," he demurred, "our hospitality was just the Christian thing to do." He actually looked abashed at her offer.

"We really should be going," Hickok said.

"We can spare the time for me to help Mrs. Sawyer in the kitchen and you, perhaps, to help Mr. Sawyer bring in more water from the well."

Hickok's eyes flared, but he forced a smile. Then he turned to the Sawyers. "I do believe we can stay a bit longer. Mr. Sawyer, if you could show me the way...?"

Hickok didn't speak to her as they left the Sawyer farm. He rode stiff and angry. Not the fury Beth had seen from time to time, but more like over-the-top irritation. Still, it was unsettling. She knew him well enough to know why — he hadn't wanted to "waste time" helping the Sawyers — but that didn't make it less annoying. She exchanged a few looks with Rose, who just shook her head in sympathy. Whatever blowup was coming, Rose wasn't going to intervene.

So when Hickok slowed his horse, Beth steeled herself. But instead of yelling, he waited until their horses were side by side.

"I don't like being contradicted by my apprentice." He glared at her for emphasis.

"I haven't been your apprentice since I killed the dragon," she shot back. "Before then, actually."

"I taught you. I trained you."

"And you did a very good job. But I'm my own woman now." She met his glare with her own. Her gut churned, though, and she tried to keep the tremor out of her shoulders. He would notice that.

And apparently he did. His eyes widened just a mite.

He'd taught her that if a gunman's shoulders were calm, they were serious, and someone to be reckoned with. Maybe he'd realize she was.

"You need to follow my lead," he said. "I can't protect you otherwise."

"From the Sawyers?" She snorted. "They weren't a threat."

"We want to be at the Barracks before dark."

"Oh, I don't think one more night camping would be a bother." Rose had come up on Beth's other side.

Hickok glared at her.

"Being polite to the Sawyers was the right thing to do and, besides, it didn't take that long."

"And I don't need your protection," Beth added.

Hickok snorted and spurred his horse forward. Beth mimicked his snort with one of her own. They didn't talk for another hour.

Beth gawked when the ruins of Saint Louis came in sight. She'd poked around in the Denver City ruins once or twice —every kid growing up in Golden City did, sooner or later. But that was a village compared to this. Destroyed and decaying buildings stretched across the entire horizon. Even in the bright sun, they looked depressing. How many lives had been lost when the Jotun had surged across the river?

At first, Beth thought Hickok was going to lead them into the heart of the ruins, but he mostly skirted along their northern edge and headed east. They didn't avoid them entirely. More than once they rode down what had been streets between scattered buildings, but they kept completely to the edge of the former city. The grass and weeds had already reclaimed the roads they chose, growing up between the stones. She supposed that was true further in as well.

Hickok's mood softened as they rode. His eyes kept drifting over the desolation. His shoulders sagged. The one time Beth caught his eye, he actually gave her a forced smile. He held his reins loose, as if the urgency had faded now that they were all but there.

It was unsettling. Beth felt both relieved that his anger had passed and disconcerted that he seemed distracted. Back in Golden City, the only time she'd seen him this unaware of his surroundings was when he'd been drunk. Here, he stopped more than once and stared around, as if he'd forgotten which direction they should ride.

They continued east until the buildings faded more and more to the south and the view ahead opened up. A scattering a trees blocked the view but beyond them...

"Oh, my," Rose said. "I do believe it's the Mississippi."

"You wanna see it up close?" Hickok asked. When Rose nodded, he actually nudged his horse into a trot through the trees. The women quickly followed.

Beth gaped when the water came into view. The wide blue expanse seemed more like a small sea than a burbling river. It was huge! The river was several times wider than the Missouri. She guessed it was as wide as Grand Lake, back in Colorado. Maybe wider! There was no way she'd be able to shoot across it, even with a rifle. She'd had no idea...

Rose's face was also filled with wonder. "I can see why the Jotun and trolls can't cross this."

Hickok's chuckle was most unsavory. "Well, they did, but we're making sure they can't do it again."

"How?" she asked.

He pointed upstream at a tower perched on the edge of a bluff on their side of the river. "There's a lookout there, or should be. We also send boats to scout the far shore. If we see 'em building their own boats, we destroy them."

"Couldn't they just build them somewhere else and bring them to the river?"

"They could... but boats big enough for the Jotun are hard to build without our spies spotting them, and the trolls aren't that smart."

Beth suppressed an exasperated sigh. She couldn't believe what he'd just said. Hadn't Hickok himself told her to never rely on the stupidity of your enemy? But as she watched him, she saw a small twitch in his cheek. He must be distracted, she realized. He normally controlled his tells better than that.

The trolls weren't stupid, and that's what scared him. He didn't believe what he'd said. He was lying for Rose's benefit.

Except Rose seemed to pick up on it too. She sat stiff on her horse and stared across the water. She squinted, and then shaded her eyes with one hand. Then she pointed.

"Mr. Hickok," she said, "what's that?"

TEN

ACROSS THE WIDE RIVER, something flashed brightly, and then did it again. It was like sunlight off metal, which was strange.

Hickok squinted. "I don't know what that is." He gestured toward the tower. "But the lookouts have spyglasses."

"Ooh!" Rose would've jumped in excitement if she hadn't been on horseback. "Can we see? I've always wanted to use a spyglass!"

"Well, I don't see why not."

"I thought we were in a hurry," Beth said.

"True, but the lookouts may know what's happening with the wights."

Beth thought that unlikely, but they'd still have some news. Besides, she herself was curious to see what a troll looked like.

They rode the short distance to the watch tower. The building stood on thick pine log posts and rose easily fifty feet into the air. The raised platform had short walls more like the balcony walls at the Astor, except logs instead of stone, and was probably only eight feet long by eight feet wide or so. A rickety ladder ran up along the cross beams and posts on one side. They couldn't see anyone up top, but that may have been the angle and the short walls as much as anything. Still, she felt her gut tighten as her imagination raced.

But to Beth's relief, another horse was already tied beneath the tower, happily munching on a bale of hay. A nearby small slat shed contained more feed, and a long tin trough with dirty water stretched out beside it. The horse looked up as they approached but then snuffled and returned to its meal.

"Who's there?" someone called.

Beth craned her neck. A young clean-shaven soldier with brown hair sticking out every which way from under his blue cap looked back down at them from the top of the ladder. The cap started to slide and he immediately slapped his hand to his head to hold it in place.

"Captain Hickok, with companions. May we come up?"

"Uh... sir, yes sir."

"I should go last." Rose pointedly looked at her skirts, which would clearly flare as she climbed.

"I'll go first." Beth didn't even have to glance at her own trousers. She dismounted, tied her horse to the post next to the other animal, and started to climb. The ladder shook a little as she did, but didn't sway enough to do more than unsettle her. Still, Hickok chose to wait at the bottom until she was all the way up.

The soldier looked goggly-eyed at her and his mouth opened and closed like a fish.

"You're a girl!" He'd finally gotten control of his chin but his eyes still bugged out.

"Yeah, I believe so." She didn't bother to keep the

annoyance out of her voice. Instead, she moved off the ladder onto the little observatory platform.

The cold breeze stung her cheeks. It smelled fresh, of pine with a hint of rain. The sky seemed brighter, too, though the same scattered clouds they'd had all morning persisted. The soldier shuffled where he stood and cleared his throat, which broke up the moment of peaceful silence.

She looked at him more closely and furrowed her brow. He was younger than she'd first thought. He stood no taller than her and his boyish face implied he might even be younger than her. His oversized uniform hung loosely from his shoulders and he'd rolled up his sleeves to keep his hands free.

He's a boy, pressed into service, she realized. And he was alone, which made the hair on her neck prickle. It was a lot of responsibility for one so young.

A moment later, Hickok's head poked up at the top of the ladder. He quickly bounded up and turned to the soldier.

"Status report, Private." Hickok shifted into parade rest as he spoke.

The private saluted. "Yes, sir! Watch tower secure, sir! No sign of trolls massing on the river, sir!" He trembled slightly as he stood, his eyes wide.

"At ease. Any sign of them at all?"

"Some, sir. They appear to be foraging."

"How do you know?"

"We're getting sun glints off their swords."

"Let me look." Hickok turned toward the river where a spyglass rested on the broad wooden railing.

"Yes, sir!" The private hurried over to the spyglass.

"Beth, give me a hand?" Rose had reached the top of the ladder. Beth helped her step off.

"Oh, my," Rose said as she looked about. "I don't think I've ever been this high."

"Not even in the mountains?" Beth thought of some of the passes she'd crossed. The views had been spectacular, but mostly of other mountains. She'd never seen so far in every direction.

Rose shook her head.

"Miss Chamberlin," Hickok held up the spyglass. "Would you like to see a troll?"

"Oh, most assuredly." She smiled at him and then her gaze settled on the private. "Are you going to introduce us, Mr. Hickok?"

He frowned, but turned to the private, who responded before Hickok could ask.

"Private Matthew Johnson, sir. Second Platoon of Saint Louis."

"Ah. Under Lieutenant Busch?"

"No, sir, Lieutenant Grieves."

Hickok nodded and the corners of his mouth turned up just a bit. He didn't directly look at Beth, but she got the message. The private had passed some sort of test.

"Well, Private Johnson," Hickok said, "please let me introduce Miss Chamberlin and Miss Armstrong."

"Delighted," Rose said. She didn't quite curtsy, but it was close enough. The private stuttered and then bowed so deeply he almost fell over.

"The ladies would like to see a troll." Hickok held up the spyglass. "Would you mind?"

"Um, no sir!" The private reached for the glass, and then yanked his hands back. "Sorry, Captain! I'll... I'll stand over here." He backed up until he banged into the side railing.

"Miss Chamberlin." Hickok extended the spyglass to

her. "If you'll lean your elbow on the railing, you should be able to hold the glass steady. Here, let me show you."

While Rose and Hickok worked the spyglass, Beth casually walked to the rail next to Private Johnson. She leaned back and watched Rose and Hickok until she sensed that Johnson was paying more attention to her instead of them.

"Any problems besides trolls?" she asked as casually as she could.

"Uh... um... aren't the trolls enough?" Private Johnson looked at her like she was crazy.

"But they're on the other side of the river."

"They'll be on this side soon enough," he scoffed.

"What makes you think so?" Beth looked toward the river, but Rose and Hickok blocked the view. Rose was bent over with her eye to the spyglass while Hickok explained how to focus it.

"Everyone says it. We know what's gonna happen," he said firmly. "When they get enough boats built, they're gonna try to cross. But we're gonna stop 'em."

"Mmm." She hoped her tone would encourage him to go on, and apparently it did. His face brightened and he actually straightened up.

"I'm a key part of that, you know." He burnished his knuckles on his shirt. "Me, keeping watch up here. If they try to cross here, I'll signal the Army and then start shooting."

She spotted the signal flags and an unlit signal lantern propped against one wall, but no rifle.

"I'm a good shot. A real good shot! I'll get 'em before they even get their boats launched!"

She bit her lip to keep from responding. Did he really think this bragging was going to impress her? No way was he shooting all the way across the river—no rifle had that range with any accuracy. And she hadn't even seen a—

An old Enfield from the War Between the States lay on the floor along the little wall in front of Rose and Hickok. If either of them had shuffled their feet, they would've kicked it. She wasn't sure the Enfield would have the range to get *to* the river, much less hit a target on it. The far side —was laughable.

He raised his arms and mimicked firing a gun. "I'd be going bang! Bang! Bang!"

Her forced smile apparently encouraged him.

"They can't shoot back, you see," he went on. "They don't have guns, and if they didn't, their fingers are too fat to use 'em." He smiled smugly.

"Do you have enough ammunition?"

"Enough to hold 'em off until the rest of the Army got here! We'd drive 'em back."

"Mmm," she said, which was about as encouraging as she wanted to be.

Hickok cleared his throat. "Miss Armstrong, perhaps you would like a turn with the spyglass?"

"Thank you," she said, and then, "Excuse me," to Private Johnson. She strode over to the wall facing the river and Rose passed her the spyglass.

"Now, Private Johnson," Rose said, "did I hear you say you were here all alone?" She drifted back toward the private, which gave Beth the room to look out across the river.

She propped her elbows on the watchtower railing and set her eye to the glass. It didn't take long to focus it on the far shoreline. She slowly began scanning from left to right until she found the troll.

It was an ugly thing. It had large, floppy ears and gray-green skin that reminded her of rotten unripe tomatoes.

Worse, it seemed to be dressed in hides that still had fur on them. At least she didn't think that was its own skin.

It carried a small sword and wandered by the shore. She watched it peer into the river a couple of times before it quickly jabbed the sword into the water. When it pulled the fish out, it threw it into a pack on its back. Then it continued walking along the river.

"Doesn't seem like much." She handed the spyglass back to Hickok. "Though in large numbers…"

"Even one on one," he said. "They're fast, strong, and not always stupid."

She laughed. "Not always?"

"No, and that makes them dangerous. Remember who the best gunslinger fears most?"

She nodded. He'd made that point often her during their lessons. The best gunslinger didn't fear the second best gunslinger. The best gunslinger knew what the second best gunslinger would do and how to beat him. No, the best gunslinger feared the man with a gun who didn't know what he was doing. He could do something dumb but lucky.

"Nine out of ten are stupid," Hickok continued, "but that last one is really smart."

"But you don't know which one he is."

"Exactly."

"Complacency?"

He nodded. They'd had that lesson a ton of times, too. The worst thing a gunslinger could do was get complacent and think they knew what came next. Complacent gunslingers filled the cemeteries.

"Don't get me wrong," he said, "I'd much rather fight trolls than Jotun, but you can't underestimate 'em. Now let's talk to Private Johnson."

They turned to see Rose in an animated conversation

with the young private. She broke it off and smiled at Beth and Hickok.

"Why," she said, "Private Johnson has been a fount of knowledge." She patted him on the shoulder and he actually blushed. "He says that all is well in the Barracks and the city, as best he knows. He didn't know Private Beaumont well, or if there was a young lady he might've been with, but he says that a Miss Benton might, if we could speak to her." Rose grinned at Private Johnson. "He's a bit sweet on her, Miss Benton. I promised to put in a good word for him."

If his face could've turned more red, he'd have become a tomato, Beth thought.

"The trolls are still gathering?" Hickok asked.

"Yes, sir," Private Johnson replied.

"And the garrison?" Hickok continued. "In good shape?" Private Johnson nodded and Hickok continued. "What about reinforcements?"

"I heard they were sent for, sir, but we ain't seen none."

Hickok grimaced.

"Tell them the other news, Private." Rose nudged him gently with her elbow.

"They saw a monster in the ruins, sir," he said. "A couple of people saw it, so we figure it's true. They said it was a walking dead man but they didn't want to get too close."

"A walking dead man!" Rose said.

Beth's chest tightened. "So. Another barrow wight."

ELEVEN

PRIVATE JOHNSON STARED at her like she was from the moon. His mouth did that fish thing again where it opened and closed and opened and closed. Beth kind of wondered what would happen if a fly wandered by. There weren't any bugs up on the watch tower, though. Not in the cold.

"A... a what?" he finally asked.

"Barrow wight," she replied. "A ghost still in a dead person's body. We've already fought one."

The fish mouth reappeared, but this time Private Johnson seemed to know it. He clamped his jaw shut on the second cycle.

"So... uh... there's really a monster there?"

"Well," Rose said, "I'm afraid we don't know where 'there' is, so we can't be sure. Might you know where those sightings were?"

"South of Soulard." His eyes went wide. "You don't think... I mean, it wouldn't...!"

"We'll make sure it doesn't hurt anyone," Beth reassured.

He turned to Rose. "You gotta protect Miss Benton!"

"We'll do that," Hickok said. He stepped forward, close to the private. "Your job is to keep watch on the trolls, at least until your relief arrives. When is that?"

"Dusk, sir."

"From how far away?"

"We have a small house on the edge of town."

Beth couldn't help wondering if they'd ridden right by it without realizing it was occupied.

"Carry on, then," Hickok said. "Be sure to note our visit in your report."

"Sir, yes sir!" Private Johnson snapped a salute which Hickok returned.

"Miss Chamberlin." Hickok gestured toward the ladder. "I believe you're first?"

"Thank you, Private Johnson," she said. "You have been a delightful host. I shall be sure to convey that to Miss Benton."

Private Johnson's smile could've lit the sky.

Hickok led them south along the shore of the Mississippi. They passed a few more watchtowers but didn't stop. Hickok seemed in more of a hurry the further they went. Most of the ruins close to the river had been torn down and cleared, leaving a wide road between the banks and the remnants of the city. Occasionally, Beth glanced across the river but she never saw anything there.

The ruins seemed less desolate as well. Besides the areas that had been completely cleared, they passed the occasional house that had been reclaimed, with the land around it turned into extensive gardens.

But the ruins kept going. As the afternoon sun faded,

they still hadn't come to the end of them. They stretched down the shore as far as Beth could see. As evening began, Hickok finally pulled up on the reins.

"We spent too long at the Sawyers," he said. "We're not going to make the Jefferson Barracks tonight. We'll stop in Soulard."

"How far is that?" Rose asked.

"About ten minutes south, then into the city a bit." Hickok gestured in the general direction. "Jefferson Barracks are another ten miles or so beyond that. I don't want to arrive after dark."

"Not with wights around," Beth agreed.

"We could stay at the Soulard Inn," Rose suggested.

Hickok nodded. "That's the plan."

"Good." Beth said. That's where she wanted to go first, anyway.

They turned into the ruins when they spotted the spires of a church rising above the rubble. The area here had been more tended, Beth noted. While the neighboring buildings were still husks of stone, the roads between had been cleared of debris. A well-worn path even led between the buildings from the river. They followed it to the church.

The church itself was smaller than Beth had expected. It had two large spires, but other than them, was only about forty or fifty feet tall. It took up less land than Mr. Coors's new brewery back in Golden City. While the church was bigger than the ones she'd visited before, it wasn't by much. What made it appear large was the smallness of the buildings around it. Several had been rebuilt, but none stood more than two stories. By comparison, the church steeples were giants.

She glanced around and spotted a sign for the Soulard Inn on a brick building across the dirt street from the church. Hickok saw it about the same time. He nudged his horse forward and led the way.

The inn itself was half old brick and half new wood. The front facing them had a half dozen stone steps leading up to wide oak double doors. The side held a few glass windows of varied sizes at irregular intervals. It looked as much like a patchwork quilt as a building.

There wasn't a hitching post out front, which was a bit confounding. They stopped their horses just in front of the steps. As they dismounted, the door burst open and a teen boy in long pants and a white button-down shirt hustled out. He was a gangly kid with a mop of dark, unkempt hair, but his face shone with eagerness.

"Evening, folks!" he called out. "Are you coming to stay at the inn? We've got rooms!"

"We might be," Hickok said, "and who might you be, young man?"

"Jack Benton. My dad owns the inn."

"I see. And where might we stable our horses?"

"I'll be happy to take them around back."

"Well, by all means." Hickok held out the reins and gestured for Beth and Rose to do the same. Then he gestured toward the stairs to the door. "Ladies?"

Beth went first. Inside, she found a small sitting room not much bigger than her bedroom back at the Astor. A large paneled desk filled most of it and the man behind it was rising to his feet.

He was a surprisingly skinny man in a black wool suit with a thin tie. His neatly trimmed black beard and dark hair made him look younger than he probably was. His eyes darted everywhere at once and opened wide as he sized her up. Then he let out a notable sigh of relief when Hickok and Rose appeared behind her.

"Mr. Benton, I presume?" Hickok said.

"Why, yes, sir." Mr. Benton gave Hickok a business smile that Beth was all too familiar with from the greedy merchants back home. "Owner and proprietor of the Soulard Inn. How might I help you this evening?"

"We'd like rooms," Hickok said. "And some dinner, if that can be arranged."

"Indeed, sir. We can arrange simple but hearty fare. At a reasonable price, I might add. Now…" His eyes flicked from Hickok to Rose and then to Beth, where they lingered. "…how many rooms?"

"Two. And when might we be able to eat?" Hickok reached into his money pouch and pulled out a silver dollar. Mr. Benton's eyes went wide.

"I'll get to it right away, sir!"

He hurried back to his desk and shuffled through some papers. Then he pulled a key from a pocket at his waist-coat, used it to unlock a drawer in the desk, and extracted two large iron keys. He passed them over to Hickok and then extended his hand for the dollar. The coin disappeared into Mr. Benton's pocket a moment later. He straightened up with a smile.

"Your rooms are at the end, numbers nine and ten," he said. "The parlor's the first door on the right. You dinner will be served there as soon as it's ready."

"We'll be down as soon as we're settled," Hickok said. "Have your son bring our bags around."

"Yes, sir! I'll have my daughter get cooking right away!"

Rose and Beth exchanged a knowing look, but Hickok was already headed for the hall.

———

Beth and Rose's room was clean and surprisingly well decorated. Paintings hung on almost every inch of the wall above both beds. Most were of pastoral scenes but a few were images from the Bible. The one small window let in enough light for Rose to find the oil lamp and the matches. She lit the lamp as Beth checked for mouse droppings and bugs and let out a relieved sigh when she didn't find any. She hadn't been sure what to expect of Mr. Benton, but he seemed to keep a good room.

They found the parlor in equally good shape. Like the bedroom, its walls were covered with paintings, though a large fireplace filled the south wall. Beth watched in amusement as Rose surreptitiously checked for dust on the picture frames and on the mantel. Whoever worked here had done a good job.

She and Rose had only been in the parlor a minute or so when Hickok strode in. After greeting them, he took the seat at the biggest table with his back to the wall.

She frowned. She would've liked that seat so she could watch the room better. But this was probably not an argument to have. She took the chair that let her face the door to what had to be the kitchen. They didn't wait long before a young woman bustled in.

Miss Benton, for it had to be her, was about the same age as Beth, or maybe a little older. She had Rose's curves, though her brown wool dress was modest. Her dark brown curly hair spilled out the back of her hair ribbon. Her cheeks dimpled when she smiled, and Beth could easily see why Private Johnson was sweet on her.

The young woman carried three glasses and a ceramic pitcher much like the one Beth was all too familiar with from the Astor. Unlike when Beth had been serving water, this girl managed to walk quickly and not spill a drop. Beth glanced at Rose, who gave her an amused grin in return. Rose had apparently had the same thought.

"Good evening," the young woman said. She had a flat midwestern twang in her voice. "I'm Miss Benton and I'll be serving you dinner."

"Good evening, Miss Benton," Hickok said.

She smiled. "Tonight, If you'd like, we have pork cutlets with potatoes and dumplings."

"You have pork?" Beth blurted. "At this time of year?"

"Oh, yes," Miss Benton said. "We smoke it in the fall and keep it on ice in the cellar. It's quite fresh."

Beth bit back a retort. That wasn't *fresh*. But it wouldn't make them sick.

"Any whiskey?" Hickok asked.

"I'm afraid not, sir. But we have plenty of beer."

"That'll do." Hickok looked at Beth and Rose. "Ladies? I know it's not your normal drink, but if you're interested…"

Rose quickly shook her head. "Oh, thank you for the offer, but I must decline." She gave Miss Benton a knowing smile.

Beth paused. She'd only had beer twice, and still hadn't decided if she liked it, though whiskey was foul. She thought for a moment longer.

"I'll have some too, Miss," Beth said.

Miss Benton smiled. "Coming right up. And… three pork cutlet dinners?" After a round of nods, she said, "Thank you. They'll be out shortly." Then she left the room.

"My," Rose said, "a proper service. I'm surprised this place is not more popular."

Beth looked around the empty room and nodded. "It should be."

"It's the location," Hickok said. "They're too far from

the Jefferson Barracks. If there's trouble, they're on their own."

"But it looked like a nice area," Rose said. "They're certainly trying to bring the city back."

Hickok harrumphed. "I'm not sure it's salvageable."

"Oh?"

"Saint Louis was the gateway to the West. Now it's the gateway to nowhere."

"At least they're trying." Rose gave him a sour frown. "What would you have them do, give up?"

He snorted, but before he could say anything, the door swung open again and Miss Benton emerged with two beer steins.

"Here you go," she said cheerily. "Those pork cutlets will be right out in a few minutes. They're already in the pan."

"Do you think you could join us?" Beth nodded toward the fourth seat at the table.

Miss Benton balked, but then Rose jumped in. "It'd be mighty nice to talk to someone who knows the area. We've come a long ways and we've heard some very nice things about this inn and its owners."

"Besides," Beth said. She took the locket out of her pocket and popped the clasp. "We're hoping you might know someone."

Miss Benton paled as she looked at the picture. "Oh, my."

TWELVE

THE ROOM suddenly seemed deathly silent. Beth could actually hear the tick of a distant clock and Hickok's breathing. She found it hard to look away from Miss Benton's shocked face.

Rose recovered first. "Why, I take it you know the young lady?"

Miss Benton nodded vigorously. "She... she died six months ago. Her name was Ellen Lemp."

"I'm so sorry for your loss," Rose said.

Miss Benton picked the locket up and looked wildly at them. "Where did you get this?"

"From a dead soldier." Hickok's voice was calm and reassuring. "We were hoping she might be alive so we could bring her the news."

"Oh, my." Miss Benton pulled out the empty chair and sank into it. Tears formed, but before they could fall, Rose extended a clean handkerchief. "Poor Michael." Miss Benton took it and wiped the corners of her eyes.

"Michael?" Beth prompted.

Miss Benton nodded. "Michael Beaumont. He was so in love with her."

"He was at an express station about a day's ride from here." Hickok's tone was soft, comforting. Beth's eyebrow started to go up, but she suppressed it. As angry as he'd been the last few days, it was a nice change.

"He didn't want to stay here after she died." Miss Benton sniffled, and then took a calming breath.

"I see," Hickok said.

Miss Benton took another breath. "He asked to be reassigned."

"He died a hero." Beth did her best to give Miss Benton a comforting smile, but her mind was already racing. Ellen Lemp died six months ago?

Miss Benton fought back a sob and rested her elbows on the table. She twisted the handkerchief between her fingers. Rose reached over and put her hand on top of the young woman's.

"Join us for supper, Miss Benton," Rose said. "I can help you cook. I work in a hotel much like this one back in Golden City."

Miss Benton nodded. Then she gave Rose a winsome smile. "Call me Margaret." She stood and Rose joined her.

After they'd left the dining room, Beth turned to Hickok.

"Coincidence?" she asked.

"Maybe." He frowned. "I hope so."

"Why?"

"I'd hate to think the wight, or the traitor, was chasing him."

Beth nodded.

"What do you think of Miss Benton?"

"I don't know yet." Beth leaned back in her seat. "Are you actually asking my opinion?"

"Well, yes." Hickok furrowed his brow. "I ask your opinion all the time."

"You haven't lately."

"This is different." He shrugged dismissively.

She wasn't going to let it go this time. "Why?"

He paused and thought for a moment. After he'd chosen his words, he said, "It's dangerous and I don't want you getting hurt."

"Then why'd you bring me?" she snapped.

"I need you. That doesn't mean I can't try to keep you safe."

She bit back her retort. Nothing she could say would make a difference. Instead of arguing, she just took a sip of her own beer.

That caused her to blink. The ale was darker and thicker than the beer Mr. Coors brewed back in Golden City. More bitter, too. She took another slow sip.

Hickok broke the silence. "I hope you realize, you're still green. I know you fought that dragon and you're one of the best gunslingers around, but you still don't know enough."

"What don't I know?"

"A lot of things. But you'll learn."

"I shoot better than you."

He grinned. "Let's not put that to the test."

They talked a while longer before the kitchen door opened and Rose and Miss Benton emerged with dinner. Both were actually smiling. They each balanced plates brimming with food on their arms while Miss Benton also held water glasses and Rose carried a ceramic pitcher.

"I've decided to join you," Miss Benton said as she set a fourth plate down. "Rose was very persuasive."

Rose smiled. "Margaret has a remarkably good head on her shoulders."

"Thank you." She set each plate down and distributed the glasses. When Hickok stood, she waved a hand at him. "We don't need all the formalities, Mr. Hickok. I can pull out my own chair."

He shot Beth an amused smirk—they'd had the same conversation years ago—and sat back down.

Once Margaret was settled, she shooed them to start eating. She asked if they'd gotten settled and if they needed anything in their rooms.

"Not for the room." Hickok held his beer stein up. "But perhaps more of this. It's quite good."

"They brew it cold and keep it cold year round." Margaret's eyes sparkled. "I'll pass your compliments on. Now, are you just passing through?"

"I'm afraid not," Hickok said. "We're here to look into the deaths."

"And how will you do that?"

Beth," he nodded to her, "can see ghosts."

"Ooh!" Margaret's eyes danced. "You need to talk to Father O'Neill."

"Oh?" Beth said.

"He's such a wonderful man," Margaret gushed. "He's so kind and strong."

"I'm sure he is," Hickok said.

She gave him a small smile before turning back to Beth. "He's trying to help all those ghosts—excuse me, he calls them 'lost souls,'—find peace so they can rejoin God."

"Ah," Beth said.

"If you can see them, you really need to talk to him."

Beth nodded, as much at Margaret's enthusiasm as her words.

"He holds mass every morning," Margaret continued. "You'll hear the bells. Oh! And if you want to break your fast before, just let me know. In fact, that's probably best. After mass, I help Father O'Neill feed the poor."

"You have enough to do that?" Hickok asked.

"It's only soup." Margaret's face darkened. "But it is our Christian duty."

"I'll go with you," Beth said, "though I may just watch the mass."

"Well, all are welcome," Margaret said. "You don't have to be Catholic to pray." She smiled at Hickok again.

"I believe I'll head down to the Barracks," he said. To Beth and Rose, "Think you'll be safe here without me?"

"We'll be fine," Beth said with only a touch of exasperation in her voice. Of course they'd be safe!

"Besides," Rose grinned, "Margaret has some canned berries set aside, so I'm going to teach her my tart recipe."

The two women shared a smile while Hickok just rolled his eyes.

Beth hesitated on the steps of the church. She shivered in the morning cold. As she looked at the stone building in the early light, she couldn't help but crane her neck. It made her realize how tall the spires were. Especially standing so close, the stone seemed to touch the sky.

Faint music wafted from the church. As she stood there, a thin woman with two small children bundled in heavy coats bustled toward the door. The woman nodded her head in greeting but tugged on the children's hands. Someone must've been watching, because the door creaked open as they approached. Organ music spilled out —a hymn Beth didn't recognize. A raggedy looking man with a long unkempt black beard held the door as the small family hurried in.

Beth took a deep breath and followed. She idly wished for Rose's company. Rose knew what to do in church, but her friend had opted to join Margaret in preparing the soup for after the service. Beth hadn't gone regularly and never to a Catholic church. The only guidance she'd been given was to stay seated when it was time for communion.

She wasn't prepared for the size of the sanctuary or how ornate it was. The ceiling soared and the stone columns and walls contained carvings the likes of which she'd never seen. No, that wasn't quite true. She'd poked her head into one of the destroyed churches in Denver City and seen some carvings as fancy, but those had been in wood.

"Please take a seat, sir." The black-bearded man's voice was gruff but not insulting. She started to retort, but caught herself. As bundled up as she was, he'd only made an honest mistake.

She shuffled down the aisle and, when she could no longer feel the cold from the door, stepped into an empty pew. That still put her in the back of the meager congregation.

The dozen congregants filled part of the first six pews. Given that it was a weekday, Beth didn't know if that was good attendance or not. She studied them closely—most wore torn or mismatched clothes. Some coats hung loosely, like they'd been cut for a bigger person. The one common element is that all the clothes were thick and warm.

The music slowed and then stopped. A boy coughed and a couple of people shuffled their feet. Then the priest strode to the lectern.

Beth blinked in surprise. She'd always imagined priests to be her mother's age. He was a "Father," wasn't he? But Father O'Neill, for it could be no one else, was at most in his early thirties. His trimmed brown beard didn't have a hint of gray nor his face any wrinkles. He stood tall and held his shoulders back, like he'd once been a soldier. His muscles were relaxed, though his stance made her think of a mountain lion—ready to spring at a moment. He scanned the crowd and paused only for a second when he saw her, but then moved on as if she'd been expected.

The priest began with a prayer. Beth stood when the others stood. She sat when they sat. She bowed her head when they bowed their heads. She tried to follow the words when they prayed out loud but mostly ended up mumbling along.

Finally, the priest paused. He stared down at the lectern for a moment as if collecting his thoughts. When he looked up, his expression was grim.

"Dearly beloved," he said, "I am grieved to report the untimely death of our brother in Christ, Thomas Melville."

Beth furrowed her brow. This was a new name.

"He was known to many of us for his constant cheerfulness after morning services," the priest continued. "He led a hard life, but was one of God's children, as are we all. So while we mourn our loss, we can rejoice that he is now at peace, in Heaven with our Father. May God bless his soul." He crossed himself.

"May God bless his soul," the congregation responded. They, too, crossed themselves.

"His service will be held here at one o'clock this afternoon," Father O'Neill continued, "with refreshments after for those who attend."

Beth let out a deep breath. She hoped Thomas Melville's death had been innocent, but she wasn't confident it had been.

She was eager to ask, but first there were hymns to

sing. She hated singing. She grimaced and endured it and hoped it'd be over soon.

Father O'Neill stood by the door as the parishioners left the sanctuary. He greeted each person by name and clasped their hands. When the children approached he crouched down to their height. They shared a smile and a few words. He honestly beamed with pleasure when he stood back up.

Beth hung back several feet until after all the others had made their way out. Father O'Neill patted the last man on the back and then turned to her. He warmly smiled.

"Miss Armstrong, I presume?" His eyes twinkled and his shoulders remained relaxed.

"How did you know?"

"Margaret told me to expect you."

"Ah."

"Can you really see ghosts?"

"I can."

He nodded, though his expression turned grim.

"How did Mr. Melville die?" Beth asked.

Father O'Neill's shoulders sagged. He let out a deep sigh and bowed his head. After a silent moment, he crossed himself and looked up.

"The poor man was a gleaner. You know what that is?"

Beth nodded, remembering Mrs. Sawyer's description of those who scavenged the ruins.

"Yes, well… the day before yesterday, he stayed too late in the ruins."

Beth's mind raced ahead, with her heartbeat not far behind. "And…?"

And something killed him."

THIRTEEN

BETH STARED AT THE PRIEST. Despite his words, every muscle in his body remained loose. Instead of tense over the implications, he seemed... resigned. Saddened, but unsurprised.

"He told his friend Luke where he was going," Father O'Neill said, "which is why we were able to find his body last night. He'd clearly been trying to get back to safety..."

"Where's safe?"

"With other people." He gestured toward the church. "We let those who wish sleep here, in the sanctuary."

"And that helps?"

"Whatever's out there seems to stay away."

"Seems?" That word carried a lot of weight.

"We know so little." He sighed. "Come. Let me show you my map." He closed the front door and motioned for her to follow him back down the aisle.

They went through a discreet door off to the side of the altar and then into a small room that reminded Beth of Mr. Lake's office back at the Astor, except with more books. A wooden chair sat in front of a small but solid oak desk.

Across from it, a filled bookshelf ran from floor to ceiling. A small window let in light, but was too frosted over to see out.

And then there was the map that filled the wall above the desk.

Beth marveled. This was a map of the city? It was huge! It took her nearly a minute to find the church and the Soulard Inn, and that was only because someone had added small dots of green paint at their locations.

"I started this years ago." Father O'Neill smiled sadly as he studied the map with her. "I wanted to find all the ghosts from the battle of fifteen years ago and release them."

She nodded.

"I did not realize that they wouldn't all go."

"The Broken Ones." Beth nodded. The ones that couldn't accept their deaths and so would not pass to the next world. Even Maria found it difficult to get them to move on.

"You know of them?"

"There are a few on the battlefield near Golden City."

"Ah. Well, I keep track of them." He pointed to the map. "The brown dots."

"There's not very many," Beth observed.

"No, but we've only explored a small part of the city. Everything inside this pencil line." The gray line surrounded less than an eighth of the city, in an amorphous blob spreading out from the church with tentacles down what looked like the major roads.

"It's difficult," he continued, "more now with Laura's passing."

"She was the witch?"

"Yes, God rest her soul." He crossed himself.

"Ah." Beth paused as she considered how delicately to

104

phrase her next question. "Could anyone besides Laura see them?"

He shook his head. "None of the people who live here."

She grimaced. This was going to be difficult if she was the only one who could see ghosts. But then, everyone could see wights, and they were the problem.

"Where are the new deaths happening?" she asked.

"The black dots." He pointed at a cluster frighteningly close to the church, a mere dozen blocks to the south. Then he swept his finger down to another scattering of dots that stretched to the Jefferson Barracks further to the south. There weren't as many, and they were more random, but it still sent a chill up her spine.

"There are twenty or so dots," she said. Many more than when Hickok had left to get her.

"Twenty-six. That one," he pointed at a black pip about six blocks north of the nearby cluster, "is Thomas Melville's."

"Anyone survive an attack?"

He let out a deep breath and shook his head.

She studied the map some more. The city was so big! It'd been over a decade and they still hadn't explored all the ruins. Now she understood why.

"I can help." She put her finger on the map where the black dot cluster was the densest. "But I can't see ghosts during the day. Only at night."

"We would love your help. However, it's very dangerous after dark."

"Then I'll just have to be very careful."

"Perhaps we could visit the area during the day?" He nodded toward the map.

"Might as well. We might find something else."

They served the soup in the church reception hall not much bigger than the parlor at the Astor. Paintings and other art covered the walls, though it varied wildly in style and quality. The only consistency was the religious themes. Small tables filled the rest of the space, some already occupied with people eating.

Rose and Margaret stood behind a low table with a large porcelain tureen. Rose smiled and gave Beth a little wave before turning to chat with a woman holding up a soup bowl. She ladled in a dark broth without spilling a drop.

"It's only potato soup with a little beef stock," Father O'Neill murmured. "But for some, it's the best they'll have today."

"Is food that short?" Beth surveyed the parishioners again. Their coats and clothes weren't as ragged as she would expect for the poor.

"During the winter, yes. The Army takes what food they can."

Beth frowned. "Takes? Not buys?"

"Does it matter if there isn't any left?"

She gritted her teeth. With the trolls amassing, the Army *needed* the food. But this was the price?

"Excuse me," Father O'Neill said, "I must see how Mrs. Becker is doing." He eased from Beth's side and waved at the woman with the small children Beth had seen earlier. As he approached them, Beth decided to join her friend.

"Good morning," Rose said. "Would you like some soup?"

"Umm." While she was a bit hungry, they'd eaten

bread and eggs that morning. It didn't seem right to have soup when so many needed it more.

"There's plenty," Rose said. "Margaret was worried about the potatoes."

"They were starting to sprout," Margaret said.

Beth nodded. Ma'd had trouble in the past keeping the root cellar cool enough. Though the current cold made her wonder just a bit.

Margaret must've read her expression correctly.

"They were in the outer room of the cellar," Margaret explained. "The inner room is much cooler."

"Your cellar has two rooms?" Beth goggled at the idea. That was huge!

"Why, yes." Margaret furrowed her brow. "Doesn't yours back in Colorado?"

Beth shook her head, but then Rose cleared her throat.

"This afternoon, Margaret's going to take us to meet the Lemps," Rose said. "Ellen Lemp was the girl in the locket."

"I remember," Beth said. "I also want to look at the area where all the recent deaths have been happening."

Margaret tensed, but her smile quickly returned as she served another bowl of soup.

"What about the funeral?" Rose asked.

"That, too." Beth glanced over at Father O'Neill. She should've asked more questions about Thomas Melville, but she'd been too distracted by the map.

Most of the people had their soup by then, so Beth accepted a bowl and found her own table in the corner. She drew a few looks, particularly from the children, as the adults were more discreet. After a bit, Father O'Neill finished circulating and came over.

"Thank you for your indulgence." He nodded toward

the congregation. "If you'll let me change out of my robes, we could go explore the city."

"Yes. Let's."

Father O'Neill wore heavy trousers, a long coat, and a knit wool hat as they headed off into the city. Beth looked at the hat in envy—hers was more for sun than warmth and her ears already stung from the cold. Fortunately, Father O'Neill set a quick pace and Beth had to hustle to keep up. The exercise kept her warm.

They went south down a broad street much like the one Beth's party had come in the night before. The lane was wide and clear of debris. Weeds poked up here and there, and only a few buildings had intact roofs or walls.

She marveled at the buildings. Many were clumped together, side by side, so that the stone houses went on for a block. They didn't have space between them like in Golden City, where only the saloons and stores clustered so close. They were all brick, too, another huge difference from what she was used to. Their doorways gaped open, and it took her a minute to realize there weren't any doors. In fact, there wasn't much wood at all. Whatever could be scavenged had been taken.

As they walked, Beth noted that a couple of the houses had old gardens in front, though nothing grew in them. These houses also had some patching done, mostly on the roofs, but their doors were still missing. Those houses looked just as cold and empty and lifeless as the others.

Finally, after several blocks, Father O'Neill paused at a crossroads and put his hands on his hips. He looked left and right and up and down the street.

"This is it?" Beth asked.

He nodded. "Most of the deaths were within two or three blocks of here."

"People who lived here?" Most of the nearby houses had been destroyed beyond the point of being livable.

"Gleaners. Some soldiers passing through. And Laura." He let out a heavy sigh.

"Where'd she die?"

"This way." He gestured for her to follow him down the western street.

They walked two long blocks and the stone houses changed to businesses. These had the same scavenged look as the houses they'd passed, with damaged walls and missing wood. Debris lay scattered here and there in the street as well. It ranged from small broken branches and dead leaves up to several large stones and even some roof tiles.

Father O'Neill stopped in front of what looked like a large warehouse on the south side of the street. This building had a high second story and far more windows than Beth was used to. All the glass in the windows was broken. She spotted a name carved into the stone above the main door: "Anthony and Kuhn."

"What was this place?" she asked.

"A brewery." He gestured down the street. "This neighborhood was filled with them."

"But not since the Jotun came."

"No." His face grew grim and he gestured toward the triplet of steps leading up to the brewery doorway. "We found her body there."

Beth tensed, but strode over with Father O'Neill a step behind. Dark brown stains covered the stone steps. Some areas, on the edge away from the door, seemed lighter, as if the stain had been partially washed away. Beth knelt and examined it more closely. Then she looked up and saw that only the top step was still covered by the broken porch roof. The darker stains were more protected from the elements.

"A true tragedy." Father O'Neill knelt beside her. He closed his eyes and muttered a few words of prayer that Beth didn't quite catch. Then he nodded toward the brewery.

"Several men searched inside," he said. "They didn't find anything. We also searched the surrounding buildings. Nothing."

She grimaced. She hadn't really expected them to find anything, but she'd had a glimmer of hope they'd find some clue or another.

"I can show you some of the other sites."

Beth nodded. She didn't think it would help, but she didn't know what else to do.

None of the other half dozen sites that were nearby gave any better clues. When they found bloodstains, they varied in size. Some were near buildings. A couple were inside. Some were in the middle of the street. There didn't seem to be any meaningful pattern. Finally, Beth and Father O'Neill made their way back to the original brewery so Beth could look again, but she didn't find anything new that could be a clue as to what had happened.

"I just don't understand," she said. "If it's a predator of some kind, there should be tracks or other marks."

"We haven't found anything that wasn't human," he said.

"What did you find?"

"Human footprints." He gestured toward the city. "But they don't mean much here. There are so many."

She sucked in her breath.

Father O'Neill tilted his head and looked at her questioningly.

"It could be human," she said. She suppressed a shudder. "Or a former human. I should've told you earlier. We encountered a barrow wight on our way to town."

His eyes went wide. As she told him an abbreviated version of the story, his face went paler and paler. Finally, he lowered his head and uttered a small prayer and crossed himself.

"Your description of those soldiers," he said when he looked up, "the murdered ones you found in the cabin. Those descriptions match the poor souls here. They were all savagely treated."

"I think it was a barrow wight." She quickly amended her words. "Another barrow wight. Thomas Melville couldn't have been killed last night by the one we fought."

"No," he agreed. "But... then how many of them are there?"

FOURTEEN

STANDING NEXT to the abandoned brewery in the late morning chill, a shiver ran down Beth's spine. She almost jumped when a shadow shifted, but as she looked closer, there was nothing there.

She couldn't help looking around the deserted street at all the ruined buildings. There were plenty of places for a wight to hide, even if Father O'Neill's men had checked them once. Heck, maybe it had left and come back. Ghosts were bound to their bodies or their place of death, but what if you could take your body with you?

She thought about Father O'Neill's question about the number of wights. Ghosts were, unfortunately, not rare. But ghosts that could walk?

"There can't be many wights," she said.

"Oh?"

"I've only heard of one sighting other than ours. If wights were common, there would've been many over the years."

"That's wise." Father O'Neill still frowned.

"Well, there's at least one here," she said, "and Hickok

and I think we know how to kill it. We just need to find it. Maybe we should check your map again."

"This is the only cluster." Father O'Neill put his hand to his chin as he thought. "Most are along the road between Soulard and the Barracks, and I had assumed that was because that's where the people were. If some poor soul met their end out in the greater ruins, we would be unlikely to find them."

"But they'd be missed."

"We would hope." He let out a ragged sigh. "There are so many lost souls here. So many."

"We should head back," Beth said. "I really want to look at your map again."

"And I should begin preparations for the funeral."

She nodded and wondered if Hickok would be back from the Barracks by then. He'd want to hear what they found.

Beth found Rose in the Soulard Inn kitchen washing dishes with Margaret. They had two large wash bins on a wide wooden table. Margaret scrubbed bowls in the soapy one and then passed them to Rose for rinsing and drying. The two women happily chatted and laughed before they spotted her.

Beth let out a deep breath. Hearing their laughter made the grimness of the trip more bearable.

"You two sound like you're having fun." Beth leaned tiredly against the wall.

"Margaret was telling me stories about some of the silly things the men here have done, trying to impress her."

"So was Rose!" Margaret mock-protested. "Except not here. In Golden City."

"Men are all the same." Rose rolled her eyes.

"I don't know about that," Beth said. "They don't do silly things to impress me."

Rose stopped. She bit back whatever she was first going to say before giving Beth a soft smile.

"There are some that want to impress you," Rose said. "They just don't know how to do so."

Margaret turned and leaned against the table. "Matthew Johnson, the private you met at the watchtower, brought me wildflowers once. But he just stammered and blushed when I told them they were pretty. If he'd talked...?" She shrugged.

"And he's a nice one." Rose rolled her eyes and looked at Beth. "Remember that miner I accidentally-on-purpose spilled the coffee on?"

Beth snorted. How could she forget? He'd been furious, but Mr. Lake had heard his curses and ordered him to leave.

"What'd he do?" Margaret's eyes danced with amusement.

"Well, let's just say his suggestion of what I might enjoy was not at all fit for polite company."

Beth grinned. Rose had later told her the miner's exact words and they weren't fit for impolite company either.

"Men are going to treat you differently because they're scared of you," Margaret said. She nodded toward the gun on Beth's hip.

"With reason," Rose added.

"Not all men!" Beth objected. Two or three immediately came to mind. But they were hard men, scared of very little.

"That's true." Rose looked at Margaret. "It's one of the things that makes traveling with Captain Hickok bearable."

Beth harrumphed.

Rose gave her an apologetic look. "Oh, Beth. He can be gruff and surly and sometimes mean, but he listens to you."

"I don't know about that," Beth groused. Their argument the day before came to mind.

Rose chuckled and turned back to the dishes. Then to Margaret, "You'll see when he gets back."

Beth frowned, but realized Rose had answered the question she'd come in with. Hickok was still down at the Barracks.

"I'm going to look at Father O'Neill's map some more," she said. "Meet at the funeral?"

Rose nodded agreement before Beth slipped from the room.

The map was maddeningly unhelpful. It was just too big. She'd walked the area near the breweries and she knew how far apart the dots really were, even though they were right next to each other on the map. Other than "many here," they didn't tell her anything she'd hoped for. Still, she studied it. With Father O'Neill preparing for the funeral, Beth had his little office to herself. Finally, she gave up and sagged into the only chair.

There had to be a way to figure out where the wights were, other than wandering the streets at night. She could do that, but daytime would be far less dangerous.

Maybe the men had missed something in the buildings, but as she herself didn't know what to look for, she didn't see the point in just randomly searching them. There had to be a better way.

She stared at the map again. She needed to search where they hadn't already done so. Unfortunately, that covered a lot of the city. She started looking more closely at the pencil lines Father O'Neill had drawn to indicate the areas they'd looked for ghosts.

He'd drawn several lines, she realized. He'd erased old ones as the explored area had expanded, but she could still see the erasure marks in most places. She traced her finger along one line and then stopped at some small pencilled-in numbers. Twelve and twelve, separated by a slash.

She furrowed her brow. They were "inside" an area to the north of the church. She scanned further north and spotted another set of numbers. Twelve and fifteen, also separated by a slash.

Dates! They were dates! December twelfth and December fifteenth. Father O'Neill had recorded the dates they'd searched each area for ghosts.

She skipped down to the big cluster of black dots. The last date was January twenty-fifth. She did some quick mental calculations. That would've been two days before Hickok left to get her, assuming it took him as long to ride out to Golden City as it had taken them to ride back.

Hickok definitely would've searched that area. Or at least made sure it was searched, even if he hadn't done it himself.

She looked for dates in the areas nearby. She found a marking for January eighteenth on a street slightly to the north of the breweries and west of the road between Soulard and the Barracks.

That had to be it, she thought with smug satisfaction. The witch Laura had seen the wight before it killed her. So she'd seen it on the Eighteenth and it'd killed her a week later. That meant lair had in that general area.

But how could she find it in all those destroyed buildings?

Beth didn't have a clue.

Most of the people from the earlier service turned up for Thomas Melville's funeral, along with several people Beth hadn't seen that morning. Margaret and Rose hurried in at the last moment, with Margaret pausing to bow her head and cross herself. Rose nodded when she spotted Beth and they joined her in the pew.

"I thought you'd be preparing food," Beth murmured to Margaret. Father O'Neill stood at the podium with an open Bible in front of him.

"Margaret knew Mr. Melville," Rose whispered back. Before she could add more, Father O'Neill raised his arms. The rustling in the rest of the congregation stilled.

"Let us pray," he said.

All three women bowed their heads and the service began.

Beth fought back her frustration. She hadn't learned anything useful at the funeral or the following reception. She'd even followed along to the burial while Rose returned to the kitchen of the Soulard Inn to clean. The one saving grace was that Margaret gave Beth the names and histories of everyone that had been at the funeral. It turned out she really did know everyone.

The graveyard sat on the grounds of a deserted old church a couple of blocks north of Saints Peter and Paul. That church had been completely smashed. Not a single wall stood higher than four feet. Margaret quietly shared that since it was already consecrated ground, it just made sense to use their gardens and lawn for burials.

The grave had already been dug by the time they

arrived. Father O'Neill said a few words and two burly men lowered Thomas Melville's body into the ground. After a short prayer, the men started shoveling dirt down onto the coffin. Most of the people drifted off. Father O'Neill retrieved his own shovel from a small wooden shed and pitched in.

Beth found a low broken wall she could sit on. She brushed the frozen mud off some of the stones and was glad that there wasn't snow. Then she hopped up onto the wall and enjoyed the chance to be off her feet. Not that she'd done any real work, like the grave diggers who were digging in nearly frozen ground.

Margaret joined her. She gave the dirty wall a wary look and remained standing. She turned to watch the men filling the grave.

"Why do you do it?" she asked out of the blue.

"Do what?" Beth blinked in confusion.

"Wear a gun and trousers." Margaret caught herself. "I apologize. It's rather forward of me to ask, I know. But I can't help but wonder, and Miss Chamberlin was not forthcoming."

Beth's indignation was overwhelmed by the mental image of Rose refusing to answer Margaret's questions. She could imagine the smile and roll of her eyes as she avoided giving a direct answer. She looked over at Margaret and saw that the young woman was earnest. There wasn't a touch of derision in her face.

"I wear the trousers because they make it easier to wear the gun," Beth said. "Gun belts don't work well over most dresses."

"So why the gun?"

Beth shrugged. She wasn't sure she could explain.

"My father would throw a fit if I wore a gun." Margaret's tone was flat, almost resigned.

"Do you want to?"

"No." With a sour frown, Margaret turned her attention back to the gravediggers.

Beth's eyes followed Margaret's, but the men didn't seem to be doing anything special. She thought more about Margaret's question. She really wasn't sure she could explain why she wore a gun in words. It was like the world wasn't right unless she did.

"We should go," Margaret said after a while. "We're supposed to meet the Lemps soon so you can return that locket."

Beth nodded. She climbed off the wall and they headed back to the inn.

They found Rose in the Soulard Inn kitchen washing towels in the sink. The kitchen itself smelled of baking bread and apples, though there wasn't a trace of flour on the counter or small work table. She smiled and hung a washcloth on a makeshift clothesline next to the stove. The warmth of the room led Beth to unbutton her coat.

"I hope you don't mind," Rose said to Margaret. "I made a pie as well as the bread. There's also some warm tea on the stove. Help yourself."

"Yes, please," Beth said, suddenly aware of her dry mouth.

"Mugs are in the cabinet." Margaret pointed at the exact one.

Beth pushed past Rose and reached for a mug.

"Oh, Dearie," Rose said, "what did you do to your trousers?"

"She sat on a muddy wall at the graveyard," Margaret said.

"It's just dirt." Beth protested. "What's wrong with a little dirt?"

Rose and Margaret exchanged an eye roll.

"What?" Beth protested.

"Well, brush it off as best you can," Rose said. "We must be on our way."

The Lemps lived in a small house with a large garden only a few blocks northeast of the church. Nothing grew in the cold, but Beth spotted rows and rows of what had to be vegetables during the summer, as well as two bare apple trees not far from the house's side.

A small gray-haired woman wearing several shawls wrapped around her shoulders met them at the door. She had a weary smile with tired eyes.

"Mrs. Lemp," Margaret said, "I'd like you to meet Miss Armstrong and Miss Chamberlin. May we come in?"

"Why of course. Please do."

A crackling fire kept the main room quite warm. Beth spotted a stack of broken lumber next to it. A heavy oak table sat in the middle of the room with a small plate of what looked like cookies on it, as well as a white ceramic pitcher. Mrs. Lemp led them to the table and waited until they were all settled.

"Shortbread?" she said with a gesture toward the cookies.

"Thank you, Mrs. Lemp," Margaret said.

"Yes, thank you," Beth added.

"We appreciate this," Rose added. "Especially in such a difficult time."

"Civility is next to Godliness," Mrs. Lemp said. "Especially in difficult times."

"Very much," Rose said, "and you keep such a lovely home."

They talked about the decor for a minute or so while Beth fought to suppress her growing impatience. When would they get to the point?

She still forced a smile as she listened and nibbled on her cookie.

"Well," Rose eventually said, "about our visit. Miss Benton told you about Private Beaumont and his unfortunate passing."

"Yes." Mrs. Lemp sighed. "He was such a sweet boy."

"He died a hero, if that matters," Beth interjected.

Mrs. Temp just snorted softly and shook her head.

"We brought you the locket he carried, with the picture of your daughter." Rose pulled it out from a purse at her waist and passed it to the older woman. "We thought you might like to have it."

Mrs. Lemp accepted the locket and opened it. She stared down at it and then took a deep breath. She took another, and then another. Beth blinked when she realized the woman was quietly sobbing.

"It must've been a horrible loss," Rose consoled. She held out a lacy handkerchief.

"She was so... so beautiful." Mrs. Lemp took the handkerchief and dabbed her eyes.

"Yes," Margaret said. "She was. Very lovely."

"Yes." Mrs. Lemp shook her head ruefully.

"And helpful, too." Margaret said.

"Too helpful at times."

"She was helping Laura Masterson when she died," Margaret explained to Beth and Rose.

"Wait, what?" Beth bolted to attention. "Laura, the witch?"

"Why, yes," Mrs. Lemp said.

"Helping how?"

"My Ellen helped her gather healing plants. Ellen wanted to be a nurse."

"Where was she gathering them the day she died?" Beth asked.

"Why, in that little garden next to the graveyard."

Beth's eyes went wide.

FIFTEEN

THE FIRE CRACKLED LOUDLY in the three heartbeats it
took Beth to recover her wits. Mrs. Lemp stared at her
with a furrowed brow, her cookie held halfway to her
mouth.

"There's an herb garden in the cemetery?" Beth said.

"Yes, there is," Margaret replied.

"Really?" Beth said. She hadn't expected herbs in a
cemetery. But then, nothing but weeds grew in the cemetery in Golden City.

"The Lutheran pastor grew all sorts of plants there
until the church was destroyed," Margaret said. "Most of
them have gone to seed since."

"Nobody dug it up for graves?" Beth asked. It was
hallowed ground, after all.

"It's around the side of the church," Margaret said.
"Well, the ruins now. The mint's largely taken over."

"Oh my," Rose said. "There must be more than mint."

"Quite a bit, but," Margaret smiled sympathetically at
Mrs. Lemp, "we can have this conversation another time."

"True." Rose looked around. "Mrs. Lemp? Do you live here alone?"

"Mr. Lemp stays at the Barracks most nights." She sighed wistfully. "He didn't want to join up, but..."

"But he's a good man," Margaret said with a solemn nod.

"Yes," Mrs. Lemp agreed.

"He'll do his duty well." Margaret said.

Mrs. Lemp nodded fretfully.

"Hopefully this will be all over by planting time," Rose said. "I couldn't help but notice your garden, Mrs. Lemp. What all do you grow?"

Mrs. Lemp blinked at the subject change, but Margaret smiled.

"She brings the most amazing tomatoes to market in the fall," Margaret gushed. "She won't tell us how she does it."

"You just have to take good care of them," Mrs. Lemp said. "Water and the right amount of sunshine..."

They talked gardening until they'd finished the cookies. Then Margaret thanked Mrs. Lemp for her time and Mrs. Lemp thanked them once again for the locket. She escorted them to the door and closed it shortly after they'd left.

Beth waited until they were back at the street before she turned to Margaret. "You have to show me that herb garden! We need to see where she died."

"Think she's a ghost?" Rose asked.

"I dunno." Beth looked at Margaret. "Was she... torn up... like the others?"

"Not at all. The ones that were..." Margaret shuddered. She didn't say anything as they strolled until the church came back in sight.

"So how did she die?" Rose prompted.

"We don't know." Margaret shook her head.

"Oh?"

"She wasn't... well, like the others. She was unconscious when we found her and died the next day."

"No wounds?" Beth asked.

"She just had a scratch on her arm. We thought poison, but none of what grows near the graveyard is poisonous."

Beth sucked in her breath. Now she *had* to see that garden.

The shadow from Saints Peter and Paul's steeple stretched all the way across the road and shaded some of the nearby buildings, though not the Soulard Inn. The afternoon seemed later than Beth was sure it was. However, she was colder than she'd been earlier that day.

Hickok stood in front of the church door along with another army officer talking to Father O'Neill. The priest was the first to notice the approaching women. He gave a big wave, which Margaret returned. All the men turned when the women were close.

"Miss Armstrong, Miss Chamberlin, Miss Benton," Hickok said, "I'd like you to meet Sergeant Chalmers. He's the quartermaster for Jefferson Barracks."

"We're acquainted," Margaret said with a slight nod toward the army officer.

"Charmed to meet you," Sergeant Chalmers said to Rose. He bowed low and smiled, but his eyes barely left her. He only gave Beth a quick glance.

"What did you learn?" Beth asked Hickok.

"Let's have that discussion inside," he said smoothly. His eyes flicked to the Sergeant and back to Beth. She gave a short nod.

"Sergeant," Hickok said, "I know you have some work to do. I'll leave you to it."

The sergeant gave Hickok a quick salute. Then he turned to the women. "Ladies, if you'll excuse me." He gave Father O'Neill a quick nod and then strode up the street.

"What's his work?" Beth asked as she watched the sergeant go.

"He's going to talk to the gleaners he knows," Hickok said. "The Army will pay triple for any weapons, tools, ammunition, or blankets they find."

"Blankets?" Rose asked.

"The barracks are pretty drafty."

"Triple?" Beth scratched her head. "That's a lot."

"They need the supplies. Don't worry. There's still plenty to find."

"Maybe," Beth said, "but that'll send the gleaners out where the wight is."

"Wight? What did you learn? No. Later." He turned to Margaret. "How long until dinner?"

"Excuse me," Father O'Neill said. He nodded at Beth. "Miss Armstrong, please let me know when I may next assist you."

"Yes, Father."

Margaret waited a moment until the priest had stepped inside before answering Hickok. "Dinner's in an hour."

"Perhaps Miss Chamberlin could assist you?" Hickok suggested.

"Rose should join us," Beth said. "It'll save me having to tell her everything later."

Hickok scowled, but conceded with a nod.

They crowded into Hickok's room to talk. He had a window, which gave them more light. There wasn't much space to sit, so Hickok ended up standing. The worry lines in his face had deepened.

"So what'd you learn about the wight?" he asked.

"Quite a bit." Beth told him Father O'Neill's descriptions of the bodies, which slid into her discussing his map and their exploration of the brewery blocks. That turned into her telling him about the funeral and the graveyard and Ellen's death there.

"I want to go back tonight," she concluded, "after dark."

Hickok looked wary. "Looking for ghosts?"

"Of course." She powered through before he could object for her safety. "But what did you learn?"

He grimaced and stared off into the distance for a moment, in his familiar "collecting his thoughts" tell. Then his eyes widened and he nodded, just like he did when all the thoughts were herded into line.

"They haven't gotten any word back from Chicago or New Orleans," he said, "and they should've by now. The commander's sending teams to check the routes. He has no idea who the traitor is. He has no reason to suspect anyone and, besides, they've had bed checks."

"Bed checks?" Rose asked.

"Mmm hmm. Right after I left, they started checking all the beds at night to make sure all the men were accounted for. Any man outside the barracks after that got confined to barracks or the stockade."

"I'm sure some still snuck out," Rose said.

"Not after the first one got killed." When Hickok saw Rose's eyebrows shoot up, he chuckled. "No, not by the Army. By whatever's killing the city folk."

"The wight." Beth was emphatic. "We know what it is. We just don't know where it is."

"True," Hickok said. "But it could be something besides a wight."

"*I'm* convinced." Beth furrowed her brow. Why wasn't Hickok?

He noticed her frown and tensed, but before he could speak, Rose jumped in.

"What else did you learn, Mr. Hickok?"

"The trolls continue to build boats," he said. "They haven't launched any scout boats yet, which is good. It means they're not ready to invade in force yet."

"Why would they launch scout boats?" Rose asked.

"Beth?" Hickok looked at her with the same look he'd given her numerous times during her training. His "this is a test" look.

She grimaced. She didn't need more tests! Still, she forced herself to calm down. Rose had asked a fair question and deserved a fair answer.

"They'll want to figure out where to land," she said. "If we don't respond to their scout boats, they'll know we don't have many defenders along that part of the river."

"And if we do respond," Hickok added, "they'll have an idea whether we have cannons or not."

"Do we?" Beth hadn't considered the possibility.

"Only a dozen, and all by the Barracks." He gestured toward the surrounding area. "If the trolls cross the river, these people will be in trouble."

"They're already in trouble," Beth said.

Hickok looked at her with a raised eyebrow.

"None of them can stop the wight. But that's why you brought me, right?"

"I'm not sure we can either," he said. "We got lucky last time. We need to be really careful."

"Yeah." She gave him a curious look. Did he really think she needed to be told that? "But there aren't many places to hide in the cemetery. We should be fine."

"Okay." Hickok rolled his eyes. "We'll go to the grave-yard after dark. It won't be long anyway."

Beth nodded and kept her satisfied grin to herself.

Hickok and Beth set out shortly after dusk. Rose chose to remain with Margaret to help clean up after dinner. She said she'd also talk to Margaret's father about reducing the price of the room and board since she was helping so much. Beth wasn't sure he would, but Hickok liked the idea of her asking. He promised they'd be back within two hours.

They briskly walked the handful of blocks to the graveyard. Beth kept her coat pulled tight against the cold. Saint Louis was more chilling than the nights in Golden City. More like a cold wet blanket. She missed the crisp-ness of the Colorado air.

Hickok walked hard. His lantern swung freely from his arm, illuminating and shading the road and the adjacent ruins. He kept looking all around, which slowed his longer stride to match hers. The night remained quiet. They heard only the occasional clack of their boots on the stones.

Beth thought about Ellen, gathering herbs. And then Laura—so young to be struck down. Beth's chest tight-ened. She'd been the same age herself the first time someone had tried to kill her. What if they'd succeeded? Would someone be mourning her still today? Besides Ma, of course.

But Laura hadn't sought danger, Beth mused. When she herself had decided to become a gunslinger, she'd known the risks. Laura had just wanted to help souls move on. At least that's what Beth had understood. And the gleaners were just trying to survive. They hadn't expected a monster in the ruins.

She and Hickok would have to destroy that monster. To keep everyone completely safe. The question was how.

When they came in sight of the graveyard, Beth strained to see a ghost, but none were obvious. Not even when they entered the cemetery itself. Not a gray figure anywhere.

Hickok pulled up and looked expectantly at Beth.

"None," she said.

"Huh."

"Mmm hmm. Not a one. Yet."

"Maybe we should get a little closer."

They slowly entered the cemetery. Beth would've said they crept in, if they hadn't been standing straight. The silent tombstones, some granite, some wood, stuck up here and there to break up the shadows. At one point, Beth started at something moving, but it was only the flicker from Hickok's lamp.

They made their way to the wall Beth had sat on previously. She peered over it and saw nothing. Following Margaret's directions, they worked their way around to the herb garden. A handful of green shoots poked through the ground in the warm shadow of the low wall. One of the bushes looked like it might be rosemary, except it looked dead. But all was still and silent.

"No ghosts," she told Hickok.

"Well, that's unfortunate. Though I'm not surprised." He looked around the graveyard and sighed. "Too many fresh graves here."

"Yeah. Let's go visit Laura's." She ought to at least pay

her respects to the young witch. Beth frowned. "Though I'm not sure which one it is."

"Let's find out." Hickok held his lamp up and headed toward the nearest tombstone. He played the lamp over it. Then he shook his head and moved onto the next. As he did, he slowed down so Beth could walk by his side. They passed a dozen graves before they found one with a familiar name. Ellen Lemp's.

It was largely unremarkable. The simple wooden tombstone was painted with her name and dates. She'd been close to Beth's age, which made reading the dates almost painful. Other than that, the lumpy ground, where the dirt had been turned, remained dark over the grave itself.

Wait a minute...

Hickok started to move on, but Beth gently tugged on his sleeve. Then she knelt down, letting her trousered knee touch the cold, hard dirt on the side of the grave.

"What are you looking at?" Hickok asked.

"She died six months ago, right?"

"Yeah, why?"

Beth ran one hand through the loose dirt. Her eyes widened. It was barely packed.

"So...?" Hickok knelt beside her.

"If she was buried six months ago, this should be packed harder. Like the dirt does in Ma's garden." She chuckled and then turned to him. "She wants my help spading it every spring because it's almost clay."

"This isn't the same dirt."

"True... but it's still wrong. Look." She ran her fingers in the dirt off the grave and didn't raise more than fine dust. Then inspiration hit.

"Oh! I know! Mr. Melville!" She stood and looked toward his grave.

"What about him?" Hickok asked.

"They buried him today." She hurried over to his grave, careful to watch her step, with Hickok at her heels this time. She knelt down and ran her fingers through it.

"It's loose." She sank her index finger to the first knuckle.

"It should be," Hickok said. "Let's check one that's not as fresh."

"Preferably someone who died after Ellen."

"I know just the person." He gestured for her to follow.

He led her through two rows of wooden markers to a small one tucked close to the old broken wall. This one was stone, though the name was painted on it in a crude hand. It simply said "John" with a date. Hickok stopped at the foot of the grave and noticeably stiffened.

"He was a gleaner." Hickok gestured toward the head-stone. "I... I was the one that found him."

Beth knelt down. The dirt was hard packed and even had some stray weeds growing in it.

"Look." She ran her fingers through it. "This hasn't been turned."

"So someone dug up Ellen's grave recently." Hickok knelt next to her and ran his own fingers through the dirt.

"I think so," Beth said. "The question is, why?"

SIXTEEN

BETH STOOD and slowly looked around the graveyard. Hickok's lamp flickered across the nearest tombstones, but most of the area remained deep in shadow. Only the dark ruins stood out against the lighter sky.

"We need to find out if it's the only grave that's been disturbed." She tried to peer at the dirt on the other graves, but it was too dark. "We especially need to check Laura's."

"We should also dig up Miss Lemp's grave in the morning," Hickok said.

"See what we can learn?"

"Mmm hmm."

Beth nodded, but then froze. The clack-clack of running footsteps on the stone road echoed from the way they'd come. She turned to see a light bouncing along it.

Hickok had seen it, too. He ran toward the light. Beth followed only a few steps behind.

"Hold up!" Hickok yelled as they exited the graveyard.

A running man, his own lamp swinging wildly, turned and slowed at Hickok's shout. He wore dark colors which made him almost invisible in the night. But when he paused, he held the lamp up close enough to his face for Beth to recognize him.

"Captain Hickok?" Sergeant Chalmers called. The quartermaster panted hard and his arm shook.

"Yes, Sergeant?" Hickok called. He and Beth slowed to a trot as they closed the distance.

"Oh, thank God!" Sergeant Chalmers said.

"What is it?" Hickok slowed, but showed none of the tenseness Chalmers did.

"The gleaners' camp. It's on fire!" Sergeant Chalmers pointed north, the direction he'd come from.

"Lead on!"

Sergeant Chalmers took off at a run. Hickok followed, almost stride for stride. Neither looked back as Beth slowly fell behind.

She panted hard as she ran. Her stride just wasn't long enough! At first she grew surly at them leaving her, but then she caught herself. If the gleaners were in trouble, a few seconds could make a difference. She allowed herself to slow further into a jog instead of a sprint. The men didn't get so far ahead that she couldn't use their lamps to track the way.

After passing a couple of destroyed buildings, they wound through the neighborhood and made several quick turns. Beth almost lost the men until she spotted them silhouetted against distant flames.

A chill ran down her spine.

As she drew closer, she made out other figures running back and forth. The flames weren't particularly high. Whatever had caught fire wasn't bigger than a single story. Hickok's and Sergeant Chalmers's shadows grew and she realized they'd stopped. They drew close, as if talking, and then split up. Hickok ran forward to the left side of the blaze while Sergeant Chalmers headed right.

Beth got close enough to make out more of the fire. Someone had added wooden walls and a roof to a large older stone building and those now burned. The flames leapt high, but they were spotty—here and there instead of a conflagration. A few figures fought the fire by throwing dirt on the flames.

She jogged left, the way Hickok had gone. After a moment, she saw him up ahead. He'd slowed to a quick walk and seemed to be looking closely at the nearby fire. Then he stopped and stared, his hands on his hips.

Something moved in the shadows several feet behind him.

"Look out!" Beth skittered to a stop and yanked her Colt out.

Hickok spun at her words and then again as the figure from the shadows lurched toward him.

Beth fired. The gunshot echoed off the nearby ruined buildings.

The figure flinched but didn't go down. Hickok threw himself backwards just in time to avoid its grasp. They were too close together to risk a second shot, so Beth raced forward.

The figure kicked at Hickok on the ground. When he rolled away, it chased him, kicking and leaning down. Then it fell backwards when Hickok swept its legs out from under it. Hickok scrabbled away and scrambled to his feet.

Which moved him clear of the figure! It rose to its feet. Only ten feet away now, Beth couldn't miss! She stopped running, snapped the Colt up, and braced it with her other hand. She fired twice.

The bullets tore into the figure's chest. It staggered and stumbled but didn't drop. Then it turned to face her, and she got her first look at the rotting flesh of its face.

Oh, God, she thought. *Another wight!*

She fired again.

The wight charged her.

Beth fired once more and then turned and ran.

The wight gave chase. It wasn't far behind. It was almost as fast as her! She raced down the street, not daring to look back. Its footsteps sounded too close. When she finally snuck a peek, it was almost on her!

She veered toward the fire. Maybe that would shake it! But it didn't let up as the flames grew in front of her. She had to duck her head to keep the heat off her face. She swerved just before she reached a burning wall.

The wight moved to cut her off.

Beth skidded to a stop. She only had a little room to back up. The wight took three steps and lunged forward.

She dropped and rolled to the side.

Gunshots rang out.

The wight jerked and stumbled.

Beth scrambled further away from it. Twenty yards back, Hickok stood with his pistol leveled at the wight. He waited as the monster turned to face him.

Then he put a bullet through its eye.

The wight waved its arms. Beth thought it would've yelled if it could.

Hickok shot its other eye.

The wight started swinging big meaty fists wildly about. None of them came even close to Beth.

She gasped for breath. Then she climbed to one knee and readied her Colt. The wight took a stumbling step her way, throwing punches through the air as it did.

She squinted. Yes, she could see the gray ghost inside the decayed flesh. She couldn't make out its features, other than a short beard and a high brow. She couldn't see the

136

angry red lines the last one had. Not in all the flickering shadows and light from the fire.

She aimed just above its groin, where the red line had connected to the last wight's pelvic bone. She fired her last bullet.

It slammed home.

The wight tumbled on its face. It continued to claw forward, but now its legs were dead weight. Beth scrambled back a few feet and climbed to her feet.

She heard shouts and people running. She heard them but didn't tear her eyes away from the wight. She took a step closer and stared at its face. The trapped white ghost had a long nose with a broken bridge and fat bushy eyebrows. Rage filled its crazed eyes.

With one hand, it reached out toward her. It'd stopped moving forward, so she crouched down for a better view. She could make out a ghost collar—a soldier's shirt.

A burning log smashed down on it. She jumped up and back. Hickok had swung the log. A moment later, a soldier standing next to him dropped another flaming board onto it. She blinked and realized it was Sergeant Chalmers.

The wight's tattered, ragged clothes caught fire. All three backed up as the wight flared up like an oil-soaked torch.

Hickok gave her a look and a familiar nod. *Well done.*

Beth wiped her cottony mouth and tried to ignore her thirst. She sagged against a ruined wall across the street from the burned gleaner camp. By now the flames were down to coals that popped and smoldered. Men shoveled dirt on those they could reach. The fire hadn't spread, thank goodness. The lack of wind kept the acrid stench of the smoke hanging in the air, but also kept the sparks close.

Beth breathed deep. She ached, but wasn't injured beyond a few scrapes on her hands and a tear in the knee of her trousers. Rose would dramatically sigh and roll her eyes at that. At least the underlying shallow cut had already stopped bleeding.

After a bit, Hickok came over. His lamp had long been smashed and with the fire behind him, she couldn't read his shadowed face.

"All the gleaners are headed for the church," he said gruffly. "We should, too. Sergeant Chalmers can handle it from here."

Beth nodded and stood up. From the way Hickok slouched, he was as tired as she. He waited until she fell in beside him and then let her set the pace.

"How'd the fire start?" she asked.

"We don't know. It started in several spots all at once, so someone must've set it."

"I don't think the wight was a coincidence."

"No," he agreed.

She waited for him to continue. Instead, they walked in silence. Beth's mind whirled the entire time. She waited for him to start talking again, like he'd do so often during her training, but the silence stretched until the church spires loomed ahead.

"The wight was a soldier," she finally said.

"Oh?"

"Well, had been. I saw enough of the ghost to make out the uniform and face."

"Hmm. I'd've thought it was a gleaner."

Beth nodded. The attack on the gleaner camp would make more sense if it was.

"Can you describe him?"

Beth did her best, and after a moment, Hickok nodded.

"I'll ask around the next time I'm at the Barracks," Hickok continued after a bit. "Maybe someone can match your description to one of the missing soldiers."

Beth nodded. She could ask Margaret and Father O'Neill, which she suspected would be just as fruitful. It'd be easier than the long walk south. Which caused a thought.

"What about asking Sergeant Chalmers? He's here."

"Good idea. Yes... very good idea. He was quite helpful tonight."

She nodded agreement.

"As were you."

"Thank you." They were a good team. Good partners.

"Good shooting, too," Hickok added. "Could've been better, though. Maybe you should practice more before bed."

Beth blinked in surprise. She was weary, cold, and sore, and he wanted her to *practice*?

"Yes... yes, I think you should. A little bit slower and that wight might've gotten you. So fifty quickdraws, each hand, before bed."

They'd reached the Soulard Inn and warm light spilled from the parlor windows. Rose and Margaret were undoubtedly waiting. She stared at the windows and the warmth they promised.

"Fifty," she repeated, her voice stony. "Each hand."

"That's right."

"You want me to practice right now." She gave him a glare which he ignored.

"Yes."

"Are you going to practice with me?"

"Mmm... I need to talk to Sergeant Chalmers. I'll practice in the morning."

Beth gave him a hard stare. He didn't return it, but he didn't flinch. Instead, he waited.

Finally she gave up and stomped off. Inside the inn, she kept going to her room. She found the lamp and lit it, and then took stock of things.

Her heart still raced in anger. Her breathing was still ragged. This was not ideal shooting conditions.

Which meant it was indeed the perfect time for practice.

Still, she emptied all the chambers, just in case.

There was a small mirror mounted on the wall over the dresser. Beth faced it. She let her hand hover over her holster.

Then she drew.

That's one, she thought. *When I get to fifty with each hand, I'm gonna find Hickok and Sergeant Chalmers and see what's really going on.*

SEVENTEEN

BETH DISCOVERED Hickok and Sergeant Chalmers sipping whiskey in the Soulard Inn dining room. Sergeant Chalmers had his back to the door. He hunched over the table with his elbows planted firmly on the wood. His filthy coat hung over the back of the chair and his dark hair had flecks of ash and soot. The glass near his arm had barely been touched.

Hickok faced the door. His eyes darted to Beth, but just for a moment, before returning to Chalmers. Hickok had his feet up on a spare chair as he tilted back the one he was in. He'd shed his jacket, and his dingy white shirt was surprisingly clean other than the cuffs and collar. She could only see the tips of his muddy boots. Small flakes of ash remained caught in his hair, where he'd failed to brush them out.

"But you saw things I didn't," Sergeant Chalmers said.

"Still, he doesn't need reports from both of us," Hickok replied.

"Who's 'he'?" Beth asked.

Sergeant Chalmers started and turned. His eyes

widened. Before he could speak, Hickok gestured toward the fourth chair. It was blessedly not covered in mud.

"Colonel Philips, the commander of the Jefferson Barracks," Hickok answered. "Sergeant Chalmers wants us to ride down tonight and report on the wight's attack."

"Now?" Beth asked. "At night?"

"Exactly." Hickok said.

"When there's probably another wight between here and the Barracks?"

Sergeant Chalmers scowled. He leaned back and took a swig of whiskey while he regarded Beth.

"We killed the wight," he said.

"There's more than one." Beth eased herself into the empty chair. The whiskey bottle between the men was mostly full, which was good.

"Why do you think that?" Chalmers asked.

"This one was north of Soulard. Most of the deaths have been south. A wight wouldn't leave its hunting ground and go all that way to attack a gleaners' camp."

"And do it without being seen by the folks in Soulard," Hickok added. The corners of his mouth turned up in the beginning of a grin.

"Fine," Chalmers said. "Maybe there's more than one. But that supports my argument that we both go. If there is a wight, it's far more likely to attack a lone man than two."

"You can ride down in the morning," Hickok said. "There are spare rooms here."

"You should still come with me. Colonel Philips is going to want your report anyway."

"Then he'll get it when I'm ready." Hickok slammed the rest of his whiskey. "No need to be impatient about it." He looked at Beth. "Is it time for us to go practice?"

"Uh, yes." She gave Chalmers a sheepish, apologetic smile. She hoped he bought it.

"Fine." The sergeant stood. "I'll ride down in the morning. But don't be surprised if Colonel Philips sends orders for you to report tomorrow."

"I look forward to them." Hickok's boots banged on the floor as he moved to stand.

"If you'll excuse me, miss," Sergeant Chalmers nodded at Beth, "I must be going." As he stood, Sergeant Chalmers gave Hickok a sloppy salute. "See you in the morning, sir."

Hickok just scowled.

Beth shivered as she and Hickok stepped out into the cold night. He marched forward, hard and angry. The lamp in his hand swung wildly and cast beams of light across the street and the church. He only glanced back once to make sure Beth followed. She quickened her step to keep up.

She caught him at the church door. Hickok had stopped as if he was about to knock, but instead stared at the flickering lights that danced behind the stained glass windows.

"There's people in there." He shifted to look through a lighter colored pane.

"Father O'Neill said that those afraid of the wights were welcome to stay in the sanctuary."

"I want to talk to the Father." He put his hand on the door handle and tugged. The locked door didn't open.

"I thought we were going to practice."

"That was just to get rid of that coward."

"Coward? Because he's afraid of walking back to the Barracks alone?"

"Nah. It's not just that. You didn't spend time talking to him. He's a lily-livered coward—scared of the wights. He's scared of the trolls. Heck, he's scared of Colonel

Philips." He spat. "Men like him shouldn't be in the Army."

"Ah."

Hickok tilted his head and regarded her. "You... you have never run away from a fight. It's a damned shame we can't make you an officer."

She blinked in surprise.

"You'd be better than a dozen Chalmers."

She flushed, but only briefly looked away. She didn't know about being in the Army, but she never had run from a fight. It just didn't seem right.

"We need to talk to Father O'Neill." Hickok knocked hard on the door.

"What about?"

"You said the wight was a soldier. We need to find out if any soldiers died near the gleaners' camp."

"Ah." She'd been wondering that herself.

Hickok knocked on the door again. This time, a skinny boy of about ten answered it. He looked up, his eyes wide, and then called back into the sanctuary. A moment later, Father O'Neill appeared.

"Father," Hickok said, "you've heard about the fire and the wight attack?"

"Most of the survivors are here." The priest stepped back and gestured for them to come in.

Beth swallowed hard as she looked around the sanctuary. About thirty people, all told, huddled or stretched out under blankets here and there. Most were men and several were so dirty she couldn't tell what color their clothes had originally been. But she spotted two small groups of women with young children. A ragamuffin girl stared at Beth with wide eyes as she trailed behind Hickok and the priest.

"They've told me what they could," Father O'Neill

said as he led them through the sanctuary toward his little office. "It sounds horrible."

"It was," Hickok said.

"Yes," Father O'Neill acknowledged and then gestured for Hickok to go on.

"The fire itself was bad," Hickok said, "but the wight was serious trouble."

"I understand it attacked you."

"It did. And it might've killed me if Beth hadn't been along." Hickok actually smiled at her as he spoke.

"Well, Miss Armstrong certainly deserves praise for that." They'd reached the office door and Father O'Neill opened it and gestured for them to enter.

Hickok took four steps in and came to a sudden halt. His mouth dropped open as he stared at the map. He did move aside to make room for Beth and then turned back to Father O'Neill once the priest had shut the door behind him.

"This is quite impressive."

"It was originally to help with the lost souls," Father O'Neill said. "The ghosts, so to speak. When the killings started, I just added them."

"May I?"

"Of course." Father O'Neill stepped back and gestured for Hickok to approach the map.

"Do you know the names of everyone who died?"

"Of course. Well, not all of the older ghosts, I'm afraid."

"That's all right. We're looking for a soldier who would've have died more recently. The wight that attacked the camp wore an army uniform."

"Mmm." Father O'Neill pulled a thin ledger off a shelf and flipped it open. "Then I think you want one of the missing, not one of the dead." He ran one finger down the page.

"He'd have gone missing north of here," Hickok said without looking back.

"We don't always know where they went missing," Father O'Neill said. "Just that they are. And the Army doesn't always inform us about their missing soldiers."

Hickok scowled.

"But in this case," Father O'Neill tapped an entry in his book, "we're in luck. Private Pierce went missing a month ago. The Army suspected desertion, but his brother believed otherwise."

"Can we talk to the brother?" Beth asked.

"I'm afraid he was killed two weeks ago while searching the ruins southwest of here."

"He was a gleaner?" Beth knew the answer before Father O'Neill nodded.

"Think they're related?" Hickok asked. "Maybe Private Pierce wanted revenge on the gleaners?"

"Then why wait two weeks to attack?" Beth shook her head. "Even if Private Pierce is the wight, that doesn't make any sense."

"Right." Hickok nodded. "Something else triggered the attack."

"And what about the fires?" Father O'Neill asked. "Could the wight have set them?"

Hickok turned to Beth. "You're the ghost expert."

"I... I don't know," she admitted. "I suppose it could've. But it doesn't feel right."

"No," Hickok agreed. "It was too calculated. Both wights fought... savagely."

Like wild animals, Beth thought. *Not humans.*

"They must be in great pain," Father O'Neill mused.

"To be sundered from both life and the Holy Spirit. It must drive them mad."

Beth's mouth dropped open as realization hit. She stared at the priest. Hickok looked at her with a mixture of curiosity and amusement.

"What is it, my child?" Father O'Neill asked.

"It's the choice," she said. "Ghosts choose to be here. Even the Broken Ones have chosen not to move on. But the wights are souls that didn't get a choice."

"Mmm," Hickok said nodding. "I've heard that witches get ghosts to move on by just talking to them."

"Right. They persuade them." Beth couldn't tamp down her excitement. "That's why the witch Laura had to die. Whoever's been making the wights had to kill her before she could figure out how to help those souls move on."

"Do you think there's anything I could do?" Father O'Neill asked. "I can't see ghosts, but I do have the Lord and the Church behind me."

"I don't know," Beth admitted. "What have you tried?"

"Laura would sometimes ask me to bless a ghost. I couldn't see them, but she said it helped."

"It's better than nothing," Hickok muttered, "but I don't think we want you close to a wight."

"No," Father O'Neill agreed. "That's not my place in the world these days."

"So, tell me more about Private Pierce and his brother," Hickok asked the priest.

As Father O'Neill began a detailed and frequently interrupted description, Beth wandered over to the map. She slowly scanned it until she found the gleaners' camp. There wasn't a mark around it. The pencil marks also showed that the area had been "cleared" of ghosts for several blocks in all directions.

She put her finger on the map and traced the path from the gleaners' camp to the graveyard and then the church. At only one point did she come close to touching the uncleared area. It consisted of a few houses just north of the graveyard that weren't too far from the camp.

"Did you say the brother was killed southwest of here?" Beth asked without taking her eyes from the map.

"Um, why, yes I did." Father O'Neill appeared at her shoulder. He pointed at a black dot not far from where the witch Laura had been killed. "I think this is where."

"There's nothing around the gleaner's camp." Beth swept the area with her index finger. "This should've been safe territory."

"I suspect that's why the gleaners chose that spot for their camp." Hickok leaned in over her shoulder to take a closer look.

"I believe so," Father O'Neill added. "Though it's also close to territory that hadn't been picked over yet." He tapped the map to the northwest.

"They were deliberately attacked," Beth said. "I don't know how the wight figures into it, but the fires were set by a human."

"Must've been," Hickok murmured.

"And I think I know why," she said. "One of them was getting too close to discovering something out here."

She jabbed her finger at the houses on the map she'd noted before.

EIGHTEEN

THE TWO MEN stared at the spot on the map that Beth had pointed to. Hickok pursed his lips in thought while Father O'Neill looked on wide-eyed. As they did, the room fell quiet enough for the sounds of distant voices to seep in from the sanctuary. Hickok tilted his head and accidentally blocked the light from the lamp. He stepped back immediately, and then Father O'Neill did the same.

"We have much to do in the morning," Hickok said to Beth.

"Yes." She turned to Father O'Neill. "The dirt on Ellen Lemp's grave has been disturbed. We need to investigate that tomorrow, too."

The priest's expression turned grim. "That is hallowed ground."

"Well, whoever dug it up was probably human," Hickok said. "I don't think these wights could do it."

"No," Beth agreed.

"Is this really necessary?" Father O'Neill asked.

Hickok nodded.

"Then I wish to be present," Father O'Neill said.

"Especially if you decide to exhume Miss Lemp's remains."

"We probably will," Hickok said. "Do you think you can have two strong men with shovels join us?"

"Yes. After morning services. I will also need to discuss it with the Lemp family and receive their permission."

Hickok nodded and then turned to Beth. "We should get some sleep."

Hickok walked back to the Soulard Inn at a more leisurely pace. Beth had no trouble keeping up. The cold nipped her ears. It felt too frigid to snow, for which she was grateful. If Hickok was bothered, he didn't show it.

Instead, they walked in silence for a bit before Beth cleared her throat.

"Yes?" Hickok asked.

"You sent me away to practice. It was an excuse."

He shrugged. "I'll do it in the morning. Besides, I'm sore." He nodded toward his shoulder.

She grimaced at his dodge.

"You didn't want me around when you talked to Sergeant Chalmers." She kept her tone flat so it wasn't an accusation.

"You noticed."

"Yeah."

They'd almost reached the inn. "Let's talk inside."

They found the parlor empty. The fire remained lit, but had damped down to warm coals. Hickok's whiskey bottle still sat on the table where he'd left it, so Margaret had obviously not cleaned up. Beth's gut tightened. She'd promised Rose they'd be back long before now. She'd have to seek her out soon.

Hickok didn't sit, though. He glanced at the door to the kitchen and then turned to Beth.

"I wanted to speak to Sergeant Chalmers alone," he said quietly, "because I believed he would be more candid."

"Candid about what?"

"Why he ran from the fire."

She thought for a moment and then nodded.

"I don't believe he was actually trying to get help," Hickok said.

"No," she said. "The church was too far away for anyone there to do much."

"Exactly. And as it was, the gleaners managed to put it out themselves just fine."

Beth nodded. As terrible as the fire had been, the gleaners had kept it from spreading even before she and Hickok had arrived.

"So," she asked, "what did he say?"

"Well, he didn't come right out and say it, but he was scared. He was running because he's a coward."

"He was afraid of a fire?" Beth furrowed his brow. "No, wait. That doesn't make sense." Realization dawned. "He saw the wight! He was running from the wight!"

"He wouldn't admit it," Hickok said.

"He wouldn't."

"But that has to be the truth. He only went back when we were with him."

"And he's staying here tonight?"

"Unfortunately." Hickok sighed. "One more thing to deal with in the morning."

Beth found Rose had returned to their room while she'd been out with Hickok. Her friend sat on her bed combing her hair. She smiled before dipping the comb into a washbasin on the small nightstand. Beth blinked when she realized Rose's hair was wet.

"I apologize for being late," Beth said. "Things... happened."

Rose nodded, her acceptance, and then chided good-naturedly, "You missed the bath. It was lovely."

"Margaret's doing?" Beth sank onto her own bed. She realized how much her muscles ached. Weariness had started to set in.

"Mmm hmm. It's not too far from the kitchen so we were able to heat plenty of water."

"Now I'm jealous," Beth grinned. "Hickok and I spent too much time out in the cold."

"We heard about the fire. Were you there?"

Beth filled Rose in on what'd happened. As she did, Rose's smile slowly faded to a frown. She didn't stop fixing her hair until it was perfect, though. Then she offered the comb to Beth.

"I... I couldn't. I'm too dirty." Beth still smelled the smoke in her clothes.

"You can and you will," Rose said. Her tone was firm. "You need it. And tomorrow, we get you a bath, too."

"I really don't—"

"I'll even help heat the water."

Beth sighed. "Hickok's got a lot for us to do in the morning."

"I'm sure some of it can wait."

"He won't be happy."

"Well, then he can deal with me."

Morning came early and cold. Beth woke to find her feet had slipped out from under the blankets. They felt like icicles. The morning light only peeked through the curtained window, but Rose was already gone.

Beth pulled her feet back under the covers. Then she sat up and wrapped the blankets around them and rubbed them as best she could. When they finally felt lukewarm, she looked for the rest of her clothes.

As expected, she found Rose with Margaret preparing breakfast. Rose pulled potatoes from a large tub and diced them into small pieces. Margaret stirred of big bowl of biscuit batter. Meanwhile, a large kettle sat on the stove.

"You have coffee?" Beth sniffed, but only smelled the smoke of the stove's fire.

"No." Margaret sounded forlorn. "What coffee we get around here goes to the Barracks."

"That's for your bath," Rose said. "Breakfast won't be for a while, so now's a good time."

Beth shook her head. "We need to go look for the wight's lair."

"There's time," Margaret admonished. "The menfolk likely won't be up for another hour. And even if they are," Margaret nodded toward her bowl, "they're not going anywhere if they want breakfast first."

"Hickok skips breakfast regularly." Beth eyed the kettle again. "Maybe later?"

"Mmm," Rose said. "After you've been out in the cold all day and want to warm up?"

Beth laughed. "You know me so well."

"I need to get some eggs," Margaret said. She gestured at Beth. "Can you take over the biscuits?"

"They won't be as good as Rose's," Beth joked. She washed her hands and then set about getting the pan loaded with biscuits for the oven.

She'd barely gotten the second row dropped out when the kitchen door opened. Margaret's return, she guessed, but then she heard a male voice clearing its throat. Hickok stood in the doorway. He had on his warm outer coat and hat and hadn't taken either off despite being inside.

"Let's go," he said.

"I'm in the middle of cooking," Beth plopped the next spoonful of batter onto the pan.

"Let's *go*." He used his stern voice, the one he used to use when he was lecturing her on gun safety.

She paused and stared at him. He gave her a pointed look in reply. His jaws and shoulders were tight and tense. The room had fallen quiet other than the crackle of the flame in the stove. Beth sensed Rose watching them.

"If we don't go now," he said more quietly, "we'll have to deal with Sergeant Chalmers. None of us want that."

"Um, no." She couldn't see the sergeant walking on his own to the Barracks through an area where wights had attacked before. He'd either harangue Hickok until he went with him or invite himself to join them.

"Now, now," Rose said. "You need some food before you leave." She smiled at Hickok. "Perhaps you can stay here in the kitchen until it's ready? I'm sure between Margaret and me we can keep the Sergeant safely in the parlor."

"How are you going to do that?" Hickok asked.

"Keep a man where I want him?" Rose's eyes twinkled. "Why, Mr. Hickok, I do believe you underestimate me."

He blinked and his jaw moved as if he couldn't decide whether to be amused or in disbelief.

"Can you get these biscuits in the oven?" Beth asked Rose. "I need to get my gun and coat."

"I'd be happy to. And Mr. Hickok, I have just the job for you…"

Beth quickly slipped out of the kitchen before Rose finished or Hickok had a chance to protest.

———

Beth strode quickly through the light dusting of unexpected snow that had fallen overnight. Hickok slowed enough for her to keep step, but not by much. Scant clouds promised a clear day. With only the crunch of their footsteps, it felt as quiet as the woods instead of an actual city street.

They slowed once they'd passed the cemetery. Hickok began looking around. He walked carefully down the very middle of the street. His boots scuffed the snow.

"No footprints," Beth observed.

"No." He looked up at the cloudless sky and then back down at the road. "This might melt soon. Let's check the rest of the area first."

They walked down all the streets three blocks in each direction. The snow lay undisturbed everywhere.

"We're going to have to check the buildings," Beth said.

"Mmm hmm."

"You check that side and I'll do this one."

"No. We can't cover each others' backs that way."

She put her hands on her hips and stared at him. The cloud of his frosty breath faded quickly.

"There's nothing out here," she said. "We killed the wight."

"It could still be dangerous."

"Then why'd you suggest we come?"

"To get away from Chalmers. Besides, we need to wait until it's warmer to dig anyway. And you might be right."

"About something in this area?"

"Yes. The wight probably had a den or something like it. Remember the express station?"

She shuddered as the images of the bloody bodies came back to mind.

"If anything was going to attack us," she said, "it would've by now." Neither of the wights had shown an ounce of guile.

"Fine." He turned toward the nearest building. "I'll check this one." Then he strode toward it.

Beth stood there, feeling her annoyance grow. He'd clearly been humoring her. When she'd called him on it, he'd just walked away.

So she strode hard to burn off the energy. The first house was barely that. Just a crumpled set of walls. She didn't need much time to confirm there was nothing there.

The next building lacked a ceiling and the back wall. It was bigger and took more time to look through, but again there was nothing.

When she emerged, she saw Hickok also coming out of the building across the street. He waved to get her attention and then shook his head.

They didn't find anything in any of the buildings on that block. Or the next one. Or the one after that.

By then, Beth's annoyance had long since dampened to coals. The search made her weary, too. Every time she approached a possible ambush spot, she tensed up. More than once, she drew her gun. Then when the spot was empty, it took time for her pulse to slow.

Meanwhile, the sun rose higher. The snow melted and turned the ground to mud. Where it hadn't melted, it dazzled brightly. Beth took to shielding her eyes.

After the fourth block with no sight of anything that could be a wight's den, or anything else of interest for that matter, she trudged into the middle of the street. Hickok saw her and met her halfway. He walked as weary as she felt.

"Still nothing," she said.

"Me too."

"I don't know how much more we should check."

"I don't either." He pushed his hat up on his head and ran his fingers through the hair on the side of his head. He glanced around. "Most of this is rubble."

"Except the way we came." Beth pointed past his shoulder to a mostly intact stone house she'd searched in the past block.

Sun glinted on something. Next to a stone wall. Too high to be snow.

She tackled Hickok to the ground just as the gunshot rang out.

NINETEEN

THE SOUND of the gunshot echoed off the ruins. No second shot came. Beth and Hickok disentangled and rolled apart. Beth popped to one knee. Her Colt was already in her hands. She pointed it where she'd seen the glint. Nothing. Nothing she could've hit it. Her heart raced too hard and her arms shook.

Instead, she scanned left and right, looking for the gunman.

"Let's get out of the open," Hickok growled.

She nodded.

"The ruins to my left. I'll cover you."

They'd done this drill before. Beth dashed to the nearest stone wall and then dropped back to one knee. She pointed her gun down the street and waited. As she did, she steadied her breath. Then she nodded her head.

Hickok jumped to his feet and ran. Something moved down the street, beside one of the buildings. Beth didn't wait for a clear look. She fired. The movement disappeared.

The gunman had ducked back behind the wall.

Hickok came up behind her. His gun pointed down the street. He breathed hard, but appeared unhurt.

"Keep him pinned down?" he asked. When she nodded, he added, "I'll go around and come up behind him."

"Good."

She heard him run off, but kept her eyes on the gunman's hiding spot. Her breath calmed as nothing happened. Eventually, she shifted her stance when her arms began to ache. The wait dragged on.

She decided to creep forward. Even if she couldn't get a good shot, at least it worked the stiffness out of her legs. Nothing moved as she did. She kept to the ruined wall, though it wasn't much protection. It'd make her hard to see more than anything. She settled in to wait.

"It's me!" Hickok's voice rang out from down the block. She eased her finger away from the trigger. A few moments later, he stepped out into the street. He had his hands up high just in case she mistook him for a threat.

Beth holstered her gun and went to join him.

"He's gone," Hickok said.

"Dang."

"Too bad the snow's melted."

"There wasn't much." The thin dusting might not've shown footprints anyway.

"I think we should stop." Hickok slowly scanned the area. "We know something's here now, but I don't want to get shot looking for it."

Beth nodded. "Let's go look at Ellen Lemp's grave."

———

It was going to take most of the rest of the morning to get everything organized. Hickok hadn't argued when Beth said they shouldn't dig up the grave without Father O'Neill. Since the priest had morning service, they had to wait. Hickok used the time to track down the gravediggers Father O'Neill had said he'd recruit. Beth went in search of Rose.

Beth found her friend in the kitchen cleaning pots. Rose was alone, which surprised her until she remembered that Margaret served soup at the church after the morning service.

Rose scrubbed hard on something stuck in one deep pot. She grimaced, but looked up and smiled when she saw Beth.

"How did your morning go?" Rose asked.

"Someone shot at us." At Rose's look of alarm, Beth continued, "It was just one shot and whoever did it ran off." She then filled Rose in on the rest of the details.

"So they got clean away," Rose said when Beth was through.

"Mmm hmm. We didn't even get a good look." Beth picked up a towel and started to dry some of the pans Rose had finished and set to the side.

"So what are you going to do?" Rose asked.

"I want to go back and find what he was trying to stop us from finding."

"You think that's why he shot at you?"

"Why else?" Beth put the dried pan on the shelf.

"Maybe he just didn't like you?" Rose smirked. "Well, then he'd be shooting at Hickok. You're much more likable than he is."

Beth rolled her eyes. "I still want to go back."

"Why not ask the gleaners to help?" Rose suggested. "You could search the area much more quickly, and they're good at finding hidden things."

"I like that idea." She frowned. "Of course, but Hickok might not."

"Why not?"

"It'd put innocents at risk."

"Would it?"

"During the day?" Beth said. "With a lot of people around? Maybe not. Mmm… yeah. I think it'd be safe."

"So now convince Bill."

Beth snorted. "I'm not sure he'd listen."

"Oh, honey." Rose paused in her washing to look Beth straight in the eye. "Your opinion matters just as much as his does."

"I know." Beth sighed. "But he's my mentor. He trained me."

"So?"

"I'm used to following his lead. I just don't want to anymore."

"And why should you? It's not like he's your father or your commander." Rose looked suddenly amused. "That'd be something. You in the Army, reporting to Captain Hickok. You'd probably look good in the uniform."

Beth rolled her eyes.

"Your opinion matters just as much as his," Rose repeated emphatically. "You should tell him so."

"It's not that easy," Beth protested. "He's Wild Bill Hickok! He's… he's a legend!"

"And you're not?" Rose arched her eyebrows which made it clear she was serious even as she smiled. "You did fight a dragon."

"Yes, but—"

"He's just been in the papers more." Rose tapped her lips like she was thinking. "I wonder if we know any writers who'd be interested in your story? Maybe… Sam Clemens in San Francisco?"

Beth squawked but before she could form words, they heard footsteps in the parlor. Hickok poked his head in.

"I've found the gravediggers," he said without preamble. "We're going to the cemetery, but we'll wait there for you and Father O'Neill. Bring him as soon as you can."

Beth nodded, and Hickok ducked out.

"Not a 'please,'" Rose mused. "Not a 'thank you.' He even phrased it as an order instead of a request."

"Yeah," Beth conceded. "But..." she shook her head. "Is he ever going to change?"

Rose gave her a shrug in return.

Beth and Father O'Neill arrived at the cemetery to find Hickok and the two burly gravediggers clustered at the foot of Ellen Lemp's grave. They stood close and shuffled their feet to keep warm, though the morning wasn't as cold as it had been. Beth couldn't see her breath anymore. Still, enough clouds hung on to give the day a gray, pallid feel.

They'd spread a large canvas tarp alongside the grave. Shovels stuck in the ground next to it.

Hickok greeted them and thanked the priest for joining them. The gravediggers muttered similar words. Hickok waited for a pause before he spoke.

"We've inspected the other graves," he said. "None have been disturbed but this one."

"Not even Laura's?" Beth asked.

"The witch still rests in peace," one of the gravediggers answered. He immediately crossed himself.

"The Lemps have given us permission to exhume the body," Father O'Neill said, "though they do not wish to be present." He paused and looked expectantly at the others, who just nodded.

"Let us have a prayer and a blessing before we begin," Father O'Neill said. "Please bow your heads."

Beth did, and she tried to pay attention to the priest's words, but her mind kept drifting to what Hickok had said. Why had only one grave been disturbed?

After the prayer, the men got to work. They'd only brought four shovels and Father O'Neill took the last one. Beth gave Hickok a pointed look when she caught his eye, but he just shrugged.

Despite there being four of them, it looked like it would take several hours to get down to the coffin. Even though it wasn't packed hard, there was quite a bit of dirt to remove. The pile on the tarp grew slowly.

Without much to do, Beth wandered the cemetery. She found Mr. Melville's fresh grave. The dirt had already settled across most of it, though it was obviously still new. She found Laura Masterson's next. The dirt here had sunk and solidified. She reached down and poked it. Hard and cold, it clearly hadn't been dug recently.

After a bit, she wandered to the little herb garden where Ellen Lemp had died. The sun had gotten higher, but the low wall surrounding the garden still shaded wide swaths of dirt. She recognized a rosemary bush along one side, sticking out of the thin veneer of snow. She didn't recognize the other dead plants scattered around. She idly wondered who planted the annuals each year.

When she returned to the men, they hadn't made much progress. Hickok took a momentary break to lean on his shovel and nod at her. Father O'Neill drank deeply from a canteen he'd brought. The other two gravediggers had shed their coats but didn't stop work. The sounds of their shovels didn't let up.

Two young teenage boys now leaned against the low wall at the cemetery's entrance. They wore long oversized coats with the sleeves rolled up and ill-fitting caps. The skinny one with dark hair elbowed the shorter brown-haired one when he saw her looking.

Beth walked over. "Hi."

"What they doin'?" The dark-haired one gestured toward the diggers.

"Digging up the grave, dummy," the brown-haired one replied.

"Yeah, but why?" The dark-haired one looked at Beth.

"They need to." She didn't think explaining to these kids was a good idea.

"Seems like a lot of work."

"It is." She looked back at the men. The dirt pile was higher, but not by much. "It's going to take them a while."

"Usually does." The brown-haired one nodded knowingly.

"You've seen people dig up graves?" She watched the boys' faces but both were plain without guile.

"Nah. Just dig 'em in the first place. Sometimes Father O'Neill will give us some food if we help."

She nodded and turned back to watch the men. She supposed the boys could help. It'd certainly go faster with more hands. Except they didn't have enough shovels.

She paused.

If it was going to take four men several hours to dig up the grave, how long had it taken to dig it up before?

Too long for one man to do it at night.

Her heart started to race. She glanced at the boys.

"Do you come by here regularly?" she asked. By now, the brown-haired boy was watching her out of the side of his eyes more than he was watching the diggers.

"Yeah," he said. "Best pickings are that way." He gestured west.

"They are?" she asked encouragingly.

"We find a lot of good stuff. Jewelry. Good clothes." He straightened up and looked her right in the eye. "You wanna buy a necklace? Maybe a nice dress?"

She chuckled. "Do I look like I would wear a dress?"

His face fell as he looked her up and down. "You never know." He shifted uncomfortably, leaned back against the wall, and stared out at the gravediggers.

Beth suppressed a grin. She looked back at the men herself.

Whoever had dug up Ellen Lemp's grave the first time had done it without anyone noticing. They couldn't count on the boys or other gleaners not wandering by. Which meant they'd had to do it at night. And it also meant that there'd had to be more than one man doing the work.

The army didn't have one traitor. It had several.

The gravediggers uncovered the casket by early afternoon. The day had warmed and the clouds thinned but it still felt somber. Beth's thoughts kept drifting to the dead girl. Had she been happy? Had she enjoyed her short life?

Rather than try to bring the casket up, the two gravediggers had dug around the sides and created small spots for a person to stand at the casket's head and another at the foot. Hickok climbed down into the spot at the foot while the others stood on the edge. He looked up at Beth.

"Ready?" he asked.

She nodded and drew her Colt. If there was a wight in the casket, Hickok would be trapped, unable to climb back out of the grave before it attacked him. She'd have to shoot fast.

"The latch is broken." Hickok pointed at the fastener. "I don't see anything else." He knelt down, grabbed the bottom of the lid, and flipped it open.

The casket was empty.

Father O'Neill muttered something under his breath and one of the gravediggers swore.

Beth squinted. Then she gestured toward the underside of the lid.

"Are those scratches?" she asked. She pointed at several stained streaks about two-thirds the way up.

"I think they are." Hickok motioned to one of the gravediggers. "Give me a hand and let's lift this up."

A few minutes later, they wrestled the wooden box up high enough for the other gravedigger and Father O'Neill to take it out completely. Without a corpse, they moved it easily. As soon as it was set down, Beth bent over the spot she'd seen before.

There were indeed gouges in the wood. They weren't wide, but there were several of them. Dried blood stained them all. Then she gasped. One of the deeper gashes held the tip of a fingernail.

"What is it?" Hickok had climbed out of the grave.

"These are claw marks," Beth said. "She—it—was trying to get out of the coffin."

His face hardened. "They wouldn't have buried her alive. She must've been turned into a wight."

"Yes," she said. "And it *did* get out of the coffin. But I don't think it could've dug all that dirt off the top."

"If it had, it wouldn't have reburied the coffin." Hickok scowled and furrowed his brow. "That would take a lot of work."

166

"By several men. They had to dig it up and put it back in a single night." Beth gestured toward the boys. "Otherwise some of the gleaners would've noticed."

"So we've got several traitors." His scowl deepened.

"Yes. And worse… they can control the wights."

TWENTY

HICKOK'S MOUTH DROPPED OPEN, which made Beth suppress a smile. She didn't surprise him often. The gravediggers and Father O'Neill just stood in the cold looking confused.

Hickok recovered quickly. He bent down and ran his own fingers over the rough wood. Then he stood up, put his hands on his hips, and looked away in thought.

"I don't understand," Father O'Neill said.

"The people who dug up the coffin wouldn't have broken the latch," she said. "They'd just undo it."

"Unless it was broken before it went in the ground," Hickok said.

"Uhh...," one of the gravediggers said, "we'd've remembered that."

"That's what I assumed," Beth said. "So the wight broke it, pushing from the inside."

The gravedigger furrowed his brow and then bent to examine the latch more closely. "That looks like what happened."

"I still don't understand." Father O'Neill crossed his arms and tilted his head, his brow knit together.

"With a broken latch," Beth explained, "the wight would've been able to get out of the coffin as soon as they uncovered it. The grave's a deep hole and you had to climb down into it to finish the digging."

"Yeah...," Hickok said and his eyes brightened with understanding.

"Mmm hmm. Whoever was down there wouldn't have been able to get out fast enough."

"It would've torn him apart," Hickok added, "unless he could control it."

"They," Beth corrected. "One man couldn't have dug up the grave by himself overnight."

Father O'Neill's face clouded and his eyes narrowed.

"They still might've been able to get out," the priest pointed out. "We don't know when the latch was broken. The wight could've broken it after the men were well away."

"True," Hickok said, "but that's an awful risk. Like untying a bag with a rattlesnake in it. Would you do it if you thought you might get bit?"

"They might've dug it up," Beth added, "and then run away when it got free, and then doubled back to re-bury the coffin, all in the same night. But that seems awfully unlikely."

"They knew it wouldn't hurt them." Hickok's tone was emphatic. "Which meant they could control it."

Father O'Neill's face clouded and then filled with rage.

"I thought of the wights as monsters," he said through gritted teeth. "But the men who control them... *they're* the monsters."

"May they rot in Hell," Hickok agreed.

"They might," Beth said. When Hickok gave her a

look, she added, "We don't know for sure where the souls go after they move on. The ghosts don't know, either."

"Heaven or Hell," Father O'Neill asserted. He stared at the coffin for a moment and then looked at Hickok.

"We should save the ghosts' souls, if we can." The priest turned his gaze to Beth. "But we must also help Miss Lemp's soul move on. If anyone deserves Heaven, that sweet girl does."

Beth could only nod in reply.

Refilling the grave went substantially faster than digging it up had. Hickok shed his outer coat as he dug. The two boys drifted away, and after a bit, Father O'Neill took his leave. Beth happily took over his shovel. One of the gravediggers gave her a disapproving look, but didn't say anything. She ignored him and helped move the heavy dirt.

They were two-thirds done when a soldier hurried through the cemetery gate. He looked young and his uniform jacket hung loosely on him, though his cap was tight. He pulled up short when he saw them, straightened up, and marched over. His eyes remained on Hickok. He paused a few feet away and saluted.

"Good afternoon, Captain Hickok, sir," the soldier said. "Colonel Philips has requested you report to him at the Barracks."

"Requested?" Hickok brushed the dirt off his hands. "Or ordered?"

"Ordered, sir." A shadow of fear crossed the young soldier's face. "He said we were short of paper and so to just tell you. Sir."

"Well, we knew this was coming." Hickok glanced down as his filthy pants. "Your name, soldier?"

"Private Jacobson, sir."

"Well, Private Jacobson, tell Colonel Philips I'll be along as soon as I'm presentable."

"Sir, yes sir!" The soldier snapped to attention and saluted. After Hickok gave him a casual return salute, the soldier spun on his heels and marched off.

"Can you two finish up?" Hickok asked the gravediggers. When they nodded, he turned to Beth. "Let's go."

At the Soulard Inn, Beth changed into her second set of clothes while Rose fixed them a late lunch. Not that the new clothes were much cleaner. Rose clucked when she saw Beth and offered to do some laundry and mend her torn pants while they were gone.

"I know you don't dress like a girl," Rose said, "but you can at least look nice in what you do wear."

Beth settled into the a chair in the parlor. Rose's potato soup smelled heavenly and tasted divine—just salty and creamy enough to make her wonder if the Inn had a cow somewhere. They probably did. Her arms felt sore after shoveling the dirt, but it'd certainly been better than just wandering around with nothing to do.

Hickok arrived in his full army uniform. He'd trimmed his mustache and combed out his hair. His eyes lit up at the sight of the soup and Rose had a steaming bowl in front of him before he'd sat down.

"If you'd come earlier," she said, "we'd have had some bread, but there were more mouths to feed at the church today."

"The gleaners?" he asked. "How're they doing?"

"Most are fine," she said. "A few breathed a little too much smoke last night."

He nodded.

"Margaret's out with the others looking for more blankets and coats to replace those that burned."

"Margaret's out gleaning?" Beth had trouble imagining the woman grubbing around some ruins.

"Organizing, mostly." Rose grinned. "Oh, dearie, you should see the way those men follow her around. You'd think she was the Pied Piper."

Beth wrinkled her brow. She barely remembered the old tale. Of course, she hadn't done much reading since she'd started training with Hickok. For a moment, her gut felt hollow as she wondered what else she'd missed.

"So you'll come with me to the Barracks?" Hickok asked her.

"I was hoping to continue looking for the wight's lair, but..." Beth turned to Rose. "Do you think you could ask Margaret to get the gleaners to look for it? In sufficient numbers, they could watch for each other and stay safe. Maybe tomorrow morning? I'll describe where she needs to look." Beth looked back at Hickok. "Are we going to stay the night?"

"It depends on whether we want to come back after dark."

"Let's see how late it is."

They rode to the Jefferson Barracks instead of walking. Margaret's brother had taken good care of their horses. Beth's actually seemed a little frisky, like he wanted to gallop instead of walk. Still, they went slowly. Hickok wanted to drill her on spotting potential ambush locations.

At first, she'd balked at his suggestion, but quickly realized it was a good idea. If they did ride back after dark, she'd want a sense of the land. So they clopped down the weed-filled stone road with her pointing out all the places an enemy could hide.

Hickok didn't point out many that she'd missed. Maybe two in the first half hour. It took another fifteen minutes or so for Beth to realize he wasn't paying complete attention. He kept staring off, lost in thought.

"What are you thinking?" she asked.

"Huh?" He started and sat up straighter.

"I intentionally skipped three possible sharpshooter blinds and you didn't say a thing."

He grimaced. "I've been thinking about the traitors and trying to guess who they might be."

"Any good guesses?" They slowed, but Beth kept looking around for ambush spots.

"Well, one of them intercepted that messenger at the express station. So they had to have known what he was carrying. I figured that meant an officer with the express riders, but now I'm not so sure."

"Why not?"

"I poked around yesterday. Either those officers are innocent or one of them's a real smooth liar. I'm pretty good at knowing when someone's bluffing."

"I thought you gave up poker years ago."

"I did, but I haven't lost the skills," he grumbled. "Colonel Philips's office would know about the orders, of course, but they don't make sense as traitors either."

She furrowed her brow, but then nodded. "Because they could make the order disappear before it got to the express rider."

"Or rewrite it. Tell Congress and General Sanborn everything's fine. That's what I'd've done."

She could see that. Hickok could be devilishly devious when he wanted.

"Maybe the stables," Hickok continued, "but there's no reason for those men to pay more attention to an express rider than anyone else."

"Maybe, maybe not." Beth thought of Rose, who knew everything happening in town, despite being a hotel maid. She had a way of getting people to tell her things. It wasn't hard to imagine a stablehand with a similar gift.

She fell into her own thoughts and Hickok didn't disturb her. After a bit, she realized she wasn't looking for ambush spots. They were just too numerous. The road was wide, which helped, but any marksman with time to wait would have no trouble picking off a rider. Heck, she could do it with her Colt instead of a rifle if she chose the right spot.

Finally, after about two hours, they saw activity ahead. Despite the fading light, it wasn't hard to make out soldiers drilling in front of a thirty foot high wall. The wall itself was a mismatched mix of stone and wood. As they closed, Beth saw that the soldiers were a similar mishmash of ages, sizes, and even colors. Most wore something resembling a uniform, but that was a generous description.

"New recruits," Hickok said when he saw where she was looking. "Nearly every able-bodied man within a day's ride has been drafted in case the trolls attack."

Beth started. She'd completely forgotten about the trolls.

"They should be training with rifles instead of drilling," Hickok grumbled. "Shoot the trolls when they're in the boats."

Beth shrugged. "Maybe."

Before they could continue the conversation, an aide hurried out the open gate on foot. For once, he wasn't too old or too young, but a fit man in his thirties with long blond hair and a sharp pressed uniform. He waved to get their attention. Then he stood and waited for their approach.

"Captain Hickok, sir!" When they were close enough, he saluted. "Corporal Preston. I'm to bring you to Colonel Philips."

"Let me get my horse stabled." Hickok dismounted and nodded at Beth to do the same.

"Never mind that, sir." Corporal Preston reached for the reins. "I'll take care of it."

"Miss Armstrong," Hickok said, "will you please accompany the Corporal? And then, Corporal, we will require overnight accommodations for myself and Miss Armstrong. Will you please see to it? Separate rooms of course."

"Sir, yes sir."

Beth gave Hickok a curious look. Didn't he want her to meet Colonel Philips? Hickok responded by brushing his nose and pointedly looking at Corporal Preston. Of course. He considered Corporal Preston a potential suspect.

"I can lead my own horse," she said when the corporal reached for her reins. "So where are we headed?"

Jefferson Barracks was more a fort than a true barracks. She supposed it'd been enlarged since Saint Louis had been reclaimed. Cannons dotted the river-facing wall and rifle-toting sentries stood watch everywhere else. Wooden buildings crammed the space inside the walls, which explained why the new men were drilling outside the gate. As they headed to the nearby stables, Beth idly wondered how many people the barracks held.

The stables themselves were large, though surprisingly not full. The musty, earthy smell filled the air even though all three dozen or so horses were in the front stalls. A few men clustered around some hay bales a ways down, using them as a makeshift table for their dinner. Beth waited until they'd handed their horses off to a stablehand to ask Corporal Preston about them.

"They sleep here." He took Hickok's and her personal bags from the stablehand before she could object. "We didn't build as many of the regular barracks before because we didn't need them until now. But with the trolls gathering their strength…"

"Do you think they'll attack?" She felt dumb asking a question she knew the answer to, but it worked for Rose.

"Oh, it's just a matter of when," Corporal Preston answered. "We'll see it coming, though, so you have nothing to worry about, miss."

She raised an eyebrow. So he was one of *those*. Her trousers and blouse and guns didn't stop him from seeing her as a woman, and a helpless one at that. She wished Rose were along. She'd already have him eating out of her hand.

Maybe she could use some of Rose's methods.

"Oh, I'm so glad to hear that," she said, "I really want to be safe. Do you think my room will be safe?" She tried not to listen to her own words. She wanted to throw up.

"It will be, miss. You can be sure of that." He smiled indulgently. "Besides, it would take a horde to get across. They don't have guns, you see. So they need overwhelming numbers to be a worry at all."

She forced herself to nod instead of snapping at his condescending tone.

"Here," he said, "let me take you to to your room."

The corporal led her out of the stables, across a very small yard, and to a taller wooden building. This one looked new, with thick planks forming the door and walls.

They went up some outer stairs, onto the second level, and then down a short hall. The corporal paused in front of two doors, one on the left and one on the right.

"This is the most secure room in Jefferson Barracks." He indicated the door to the right. "The door is sturdy and has a very sturdy lock. The window is high and too small for a man to crawl through. I think you'll find it perfectly safe."

"Thank you." She smiled her best Rose-imitation smile and nodded toward the door on the left. "And this one?"

"It will be Captain Hickok's, but it looks out over the stables and, well, the smell..." He wrinkled his nose in demonstration. "You wouldn't like it."

'Why, thank you. And then will Captain Hickok meet me here...?"

"I'll make sure to speak to him about it. Let me just put your bags in your rooms."

"Thank you."

Her room contained a bed, a small wardrobe, a chamber pot, and not much else. The high window was as the corporal had described—maybe a foot tall and three feet wide. Rough blankets covered the bed and an oil lamp sat on the top of the wardrobe. She didn't see matches. It certainly wasn't going to be as comfortable as the Soulard Inn.

She'd just finished looking around when Corporal Preston stepped back in. He held up an iron key.

"For you, miss."

"Could I have Captain Hickok's too?" she asked. "I'd like to get his things laid out the way he likes before he comes back."

"Why of course." He fished in his pocket for another key and handed it to Beth. He then bowed. "If you need anything else, just ask."

"Why, thank you."

And then he was gone.

With a sigh of relief, Beth waited a count of twenty until she was sure he'd left the building. Then she crossed the hall to Hickok's room.

It mirrored hers in almost all ways except for the window and the fact that it had matches. The window was square, three by three, and could easily be raised. With it closed, she couldn't smell much. She walked over to it and stared out.

Below the window, a sloping roof jutted out from the building and hid the courtyard below. The shingled stable roof was immediately beyond that and nothing about it looked out of the ordinary.

She opened the window and looked down. The drop to the first floor roof below was only a few feet. In a pinch, she could climb out.

She'd learn a lot more about the Barracks on her own at night than Hickok would. She needed to switch rooms.

TWENTY-ONE

HICKOK ARRIVED to find Beth sitting on her bed cleaning and oiling her Colt. She'd left the door open and he leaned against the frame. With the sun down, she'd lit the oil lamp, which brightened the room some. Outside the window, the clangs and shouts of barracks life had quieted. He crossed his arms and waited for her to snap the barrel back in place.

"They have a shooting range," Hickok said. "You wanna go in the morning?"

"Maybe. Right now, I'd like some food."

He nodded. "Then let's go get supper."

The mess hall was a longer walk than Beth had expected. The building itself was half wood, half tent, and crowded. Somehow they found a table and consumed a very thin soup and over-baked rolls. They didn't linger and soon found themselves on the walk back to their rooms. They stayed silent until they'd reached their rooms and then Hickok motioned for her to follow him into his.

"Did you learn anything in the stables?" He leaned against the far wall under the little window.

"I didn't have time." She sat on the edge of the bed. "Well, there are some soldiers bunking there."

"So plenty of people could've known about the express riders." He frowned.

"Did you learn anything?"

"Colonel Philips wasn't very helpful."

"What'd he want?"

"My report on the wight attack." He scowled. "And to know why I didn't come back with Sergeant Chalmers."

Beth rolled her eyes.

"I told him we suspected more than one traitor, but I don't think he listened."

"Why wouldn't he?"

"He said 'I'm sure they're in Soulard.' As if that wasn't part of his command." Hickok crossed his arms across his chest.

"Ugh!"

"Mmm hmm. He's just too focused on the trolls. We were interrupted twice by worthless messages from the watch towers."

"Worthless?"

"No changes. You don't need to send a messenger to say nothing's changed."

She nodded to that.

"Anyway, there's an officers' canteen. I thought we might go there and see if we can learn anything." He shrugged. "Their beer's good."

"I'll just drink water."

———

The officers' canteen felt surprisingly subdued. The room itself wasn't much bigger than the parlor back at the

Soulard Inn, but with worse lighting and the smell of stale hops. Two burly officers in dirty uniforms sat at one table in the back. The bartender wasn't out front, but could be heard banging around beyond a door behind the bar.

"Well, still as dull as ever," Hickok drawled. "Maybe that table there?" He pointed to one nearby the officers. "I'll go get our drinks." He stepped to the bar and pounded a fist on it.

Beth made her way to the table. The two officers broke off their conversation and stared at her. One spat to the side.

"Gentlemen." She nodded and slid into a chair with its back to the wall.

The bartender appeared. A minute later, Hickok turned. He noticed the officers and glared at them. They stood and left without a word. Hickok sank into the chair opposite Beth.

"What was that about?" she asked.

"They were here last time." He raised his beer. "They didn't care for some of what I said."

"Which was?"

"I was having a discussion with Corporal Preston. I may have implied that there were too many shirkers and drunks here."

"And they took offense?"

"They may not have been sober at the time." He smirked and took a sip.

"I'm surprised they didn't fight you."

"I outrank them. They'd be court-martialed for striking a superior officer." He leaned back in his chair and the smirk grew.

"Is that what you wanted?" She wouldn't put it past him, but he shook his head.

"I was trying to make a point to Corporal Preston."

"Which was?"

"These men are not ready for a battle." He grimaced in frustration and drank some more beer.

"Surely Colonel Philips is doing his best."

"Colonel Philips barely knows what he's doing. And he won't listen to my advice."

Beth nodded and suppressed her own smirk. She suspected the latter was Hickok's real issue with the commander. No point in saying anything, though.

The door opened, letting in a blast of cold air. Corporal Preston swept in. He spotted them and waved.

"Ah, Captain Hickok, may I join you?"

When Hickok nodded, Corporal Preston went to the bar, which was once again deserted. He scowled, then ducked around the bar and disappeared into the back. A moment later, he emerged with two mugs of beer.

"I bought you one, Captain, if you don't mind." He set it in front of Hickok and turned to Beth. "Would the young lady like one as well?"

"No, thank you," she said.

Corporal Preston nodded. He sat and turned to Hickok. "Our conversation during your last visit was rudely interrupted before you could tell me what you would do about the trolls."

"Ah, yes. That was rude of them." Hickok grimaced and took a sip of beer.

"So what would you do?" Corporal Preston put his elbows on the table. His eyes were wide, his face eager.

"Watch for the feint, for one. The trolls aren't going to attack the obvious place. They'll fake an attack somewhere to draw our forces out of position. Then the real attack will start."

"Colonel Philips says they're not that smart." Corporal Preston took a swig of beer.

"Nine out of ten aren't that smart," Hickok countered. "But somewhere across the river is number ten. I'm sure of it."

"Why?" Beth asked.

"The last time the trolls crossed the river—in Cherokee Territory last year, remember?—the Indians saw the boats along the shore weeks before the attack. Whoever's leading these trolls is keeping the boats hidden."

"So we can't be sure when the attack is coming." Corporal Preston nodded several times in eager agreement. "So they feint north and attack south."

"Maybe." Hickok took a drink and then gave the corporal a knowing smile. "I'd feint an attack in the middle, so the main attack could be either north or south."

"Of course." Corporal Preston nodded again. "Keep the defenders guessing."

"Even better, the attack in the middle pins down units so they can't move north or south."

"But there are ways around that." Corporal Preston leaned forward on his elbows, his expression eager.

"True," Hickok said. "You have to be patient and wait to commit your forces until you're sure. It can be hard. There's always some officer who's too eager to get started and they attack too early."

"Chalmers," Preston snorted.

"He'd attack?" Beth asked. She didn't quite believe that.

"Sometimes cowards do that," Hickok said. He raised an eyebrow and looked at Preston, silently daring him to argue.

"Thankfully, Chalmers won't be at the front line,"

Preston said. "I'm more worried about others. What do you think we should do if the feint isn't in the middle?"

The two men fell to detailed discussions of logistics and troop transport. Beth followed for a while, but soon her mind drifted. They were deep into options that probably would never happen.

Instead, she watched the portly bartender. He'd brought a keg into the main room and was moving it onto a shelf behind the bar. About the time he'd wrestled it into position, another thinner man in an apron came in from the back. He helped the bartender get the keg positioned and the tap inserted, but he kept glancing toward Beth's table. He did so often enough to raise the hair on the back of Beth's neck.

Beth tried to draw Hickok's attention to the man without interrupting. He didn't notice, and then the man and the bartender returned to the back room. A few minutes later, the bartender appeared and brought fresh beers to the table. Hickok thanked him. Then Hickok and Corporal Preston drank and talked for several minutes before the subject turned to the trolls' ability to build boats.

"They're really poor carpenters," Hickok explained. "They usually rely on slaves."

"Slaves?" Beth said. "I thought they ate humans."

"They do," Corporal Preston explained. "But only the ones that don't work. You don't work..." He drew a finger across his throat. Then he grinned like he'd made a joke.

"Oh." Her voice was so frosty that Hickok blinked.

"Well, perhaps we should be going," he said.

"Might as well finish your beer first." Corporal Preston nodded to Hickok's half full glass. "We can talk about something else." He gave Beth an apologetic look.

"That's quite all right." Hickok picked up his glass and

chugged the rest. Then he stood. "Good evening, Corporal."

The corporal curled his lip in frustration but rose. "Yes sir, Captain Hickok." He managed something resembling a salute, which Hickok returned.

"Well, this was a waste," Hickok muttered to Beth as they headed out the door.

———

Hickok stumbled on the bottom step of the stairs to their rooms. He caught himself on the handrail. He took a deep breath and shook his head. Then he looked up at Beth, a few steps ahead of him.

"Didn't think I drank that much." He shook his head again, as if trying to clear the fuzz from his mind.

"You didn't." She'd counted. He'd had three beers, which wouldn't've been enough to affect his aim, much less his balance.

"Must be tired." He took a deep breath and slowly, deliberately climbed the next step.

"How early do you want to leave in the morning?"

"Before Corporal Preston passes on my suggestions to Colonel Philips."

"Agreed."

———

Sleep came hard. She'd abandoned her idea to sneak out because too many soldiers remained awake, even in the darkest of the night. Despite the closed window, enough noise still filtered in to make her jumpy. She kept snatching for her Colt with every muffled yell. The room was too cold as well. She kept her clothes on and tucked the blanket around her as best she could, but still only slept fitfully. After an indeterminable and insufferable time, she heard a scrape of wood on wood.

Her eyes flew open but she didn't move. She lay still in the dark, but then slowly slid her hand under her pillow. She wrapped her fingers around her Colt.

The scrape came again. Then cold air.

Someone was opening the window.

Beth tensed. She peeked out of the corner of her eye, but she faced the wall.

The scrape came once more. She tried to figure how much the window had moved. Was it fully open yet?

Another scrape, and then another. Then a third. She inched her Colt out from under the pillow. Another scrape and then some bumps and thumps.

They were climbing in.

She snapped upright and whipped her gun around. The dark shape of a man filled the window, half in, half out.

"Freeze!" She cocked her Colt.

The shadow moved and something flew by her ear.

She fired.

The shot reverberated through the room, almost deafening her. The dark shape slumped, and then fell into the room. Beth kept her gun trained on it, despite breathing hard. Twenty heartbeats later, there was pounding on her door.

"Beth!" Hickok called. "Beth!"

"It's okay!" she yelled back. "I'm all right." She threw back the blanket and edged to the door without taking her aim off the fallen figure. She unlatched it and then stepped aside as Hickok shoved it open.

He'd brought an oil lamp. His other hand held his gun. He held the lamp up so they could see.

A soldier in a dirty uniform lay sprawled by the

window. One foot remained caught on the sill. Blood oozed in a big puddle under his torso.

Shouts and cries filled the air outside. They must've heard the shot.

Hickok swung the lamp and looked around the whole room. A knife stuck in the wall above the headboard.

"He tried to kill you," Hickok murmured.

"No." She let out a deep sigh as the nerves began to drain away. "He tried to kill you."

TWENTY-TWO

HICKOK STARED AT HER. He looked pale and a sheen of sweat covered his brow. The cries of other soldiers became louder and she heard the thumps of someone pounding up the stairs.

"I switched rooms," she said. "This was supposed to be your room."

Before Hickok could reply, they heard a shout.

"Captain Hickok!" Corporal Preston called from the hall. The light from his lamp shone across Hickok's back and the wall behind him. "Captain Hickok, are you alright?"

Hickok stepped into Beth's room. Despite looking sick a moment ago, he now pulled himself together.

A moment later, the blond corporal appeared out of breath. His eyes immediately fell on the dead man.

"Oh, no." He hurried to the corpse's side. "Lieutenant Lloyd."

Hickok's eyes widened in recognition, but he didn't say anything. It took Beth a moment, but then she too, started in surprise. She'd seen the dead man in the canteen earlier.

Corporal Preston turned back to Hickok. "What happened?"

"Attempted murder." Hickok strode over to the bed and yanked the knife out of the wall and held it up. "Too bad his aim was off."

Corporal Preston's eyes widened as he looked from the knife to Hickok and back to the body.

More footfalls and then two more soldiers appeared at the doorway. They looked as shocked and confused as Corporal Preston.

"I imagine Colonel Philips will want to hear about this immediately," Hickok drawled. "Corporal Preston, perhaps you should notify him? We'll meet him in his office shortly."

Corporal Preston remained frozen for a moment as he looked at the body. He looked one more time at Hickok and then at the men behind him.

"Sir, yes sir." Corporal Preston gestured to the new soldiers. "Privates, please take Lieutenant Lloyd to the mortician's and keep an eye on the body until I arrive."

"Until *we* arrive, Corporal." Hickok's eyes were flinty, his shoulders tight. He then stepped aside to let the privates in. "In fact, Corporal, why don't you go with them and meet us at Colonel Philip's office?"

"Yes, sir." The corporal didn't look pleased, but he did salute before joining the other soldiers in getting the corpse out of the window.

Beth waited, tense, on the balls of her feet until they'd all gone, privates, corpse, and corporal all. Only then did she relax. To her surprise, Hickok's steel strength faded faster. He sat down on the bed and put the knife next to him. Then he put his face in his hands.

"What?" she asked.

He took a deep breath and looked up at her.

"Someone put poppy juice in my beer," he said with the flat tone as if this was a normal occurrence. "Not enough for me to taste and not enough for it to knock me out, obviously. But enough to disturb my innards." He gave her a feeble smile. "I've spent most of the night purging myself."

"You think they wanted you sound asleep?" A knot in her gut appeared.

"I do. I think they got the dose wrong."

She nodded. If she hadn't been mostly awake, she might not have heard the window open. And then... she suppressed a shudder.

"I suspect," he said, "that we will find one of the bartenders has also disappeared during the night."

"He will once Corporal Preston warns him," Beth said. "If he hasn't already."

"Corporal Preston?" Hickok's fatigue faded and was replaced by a look of intense curiosity.

"Mmm hmm. He arrived just a little too quickly. And he was the one that assigned you this room."

Hickok nodded. "It's not enough to accuse him, but..." He took a deep breath. He stood, took his own knife out of its sheath and replaced it with Lieutenant Lloyd's. He set his knife on Beth's pillow and turned to her. "We need to keep it safe."

She nodded. It was probably Army issue, but why chance it going missing?

"And now," Hickok said, "we need to go see Colonel Philips."

Colonel Philips, a worn, bald man with a fuzzy brown mustache, was not happy to see them. The half dozen lamps that blazed in his office made him look pasty, too. He sat behind a desk the size of a piano covered with neat stacks of papers while Beth, Hickok, and Corporal Preston stood in front. The corporal kept his jaw clenched. Hickok was more relaxed, as he explained the facts.

"That's a serious charge, Captain Hickok," Colonel Philips intoned. "Just why would Lieutenant Lloyd try to kill you?"

"I'm not entirely sure why, sir," Hickok answered. "But the facts do point that direction. He only failed because Miss Armstrong couldn't sleep."

Colonel Philips frowned as he looked her over, but then nodded.

"I feel responsible, sir," Corporal Preston said. "I, um, may have conveyed to Lieutenant Lloyd that Captain Hickok had a low opinion of him after the captain's last visit."

"Oh?" Colonel Philips looked only mildly interested. "What exactly did you say?"

"Sir, I, ahem," Corporal Preston shot a nervous side-eyed glance at Hickok. "I may have told him that Hickok had called him a 'yellow-bellied skunk and two-bit coward unfit for any military in the world, much less the U.S. Army.'" The corporal started to tremble.

"Captain?" Colonel Philips raised an eyebrow as he turned to Hickok.

"I don't remember my exact words, sir, but the sentiment's correct."

"I see." The colonel looked back at Corporal Preston. "And Lieutenant Lloyd had been drinking?"

"I saw him in the officers' canteen," Beth volunteered.

"I see." Colonel Philips stroked his chin as he regarded

them. "It sounds like we have a simple case here. Lieutenant Lloyd, under the influence of drink, found the courage to try to take revenge for Captain Hickok's insults. He, of course, failed, much to all our relief and his own loss."

"Sir, I'm afraid it may not be that simple—" Hickok stopped when the colonel waved a hand of dismissal.

"This is unfortunate." Colonel Philips's voice caught. "We have a dead officer, when we shouldn't." The colonel squared his shoulders. "But we have bigger issues than one drunken man, Captain. The scouts returned tonight and have reported hundreds of small boats hidden in the trees on the troll side of the river north of here. I will be shifting some of our forces to oppose them first thing in the morning."

"What about the ironclads from New Orleans, sir?" Hickok asked.

"Still no word."

"But—"

"Captain!" The colonel's eyes flashed. "The patrol I sent—at your advice I might add—has not had time to get to New Orleans."

Hickok frowned, but before he could say anything, Colonel Phillips continued.

"We did receive reports that the southern lookout stations are undisturbed."

Hickok rocked back in surprise.

"Now, I have work to do. Dismissed."

Beth walked quickly to keep up with Hickok and Corporal Preston. She'd wanted to argue more with Colonel Philips about the case, but had taken her cue from her mentor. Had that been a bad idea? She wasn't in the chain of command and she'd found sometimes that gave her latitude to do things soldiers couldn't. Being a woman helped, too. Sometimes men just answered because they were so surprised at her boldness in asking.

And the colonel's theory just didn't make sense. Cowards might become bold when they were drunk, but drunks couldn't throw a knife as well as the dead lieutenant had. Drunks also didn't drug drinks ahead of time and someone had drugged Hickok's drink. Hickok had known that perfectly well, but hadn't pushed it when the Colonel cut him off.

They reached the mortician's office to find far too many men hanging around. The soldiers talked quietly among themselves and parted to let Corporal Preston, Hickok, and her through. They found Lieutenant Lloyd's body on a thick wooden table, but he'd already been stripped down to his unmentionables. His clothes were folded in a stack nearby, with his holster and gun on top.

"What's this?" Corporal Preston barked. He looked around until he spotted one of the privates who'd removed the corpse. "I thought I told you to keep an eye on the body."

"We did," the soldier whined. "It's right there."

"Well, this is no use," Hickok grumbled. "Any evidence in his pockets is long gone." Still, he pawed through the lieutenant's clothes. "Nothing." He turned to Corporal Preston. "It's been a long night. Let's continue this in the morning."

"Yes, sir. Reveille?" Corporal Preston looked both worn and wary.

"After breakfast. We'll meet you in the mess hall."

"Yes, sir. Unless…" Corporal Preston's brow furrowed. "Unless Colonel Philips has orders for us to deploy, sir."

"Of course. Now good night."

"There's something I don't understand," Beth said as they walked back to their room. "Why did he use a knife instead of his gun?"

"A gun would make a lot of noise."

"Which wouldn't matter once I woke up. He saw I was awake. So why'd he throw the knife?"

"Maybe he couldn't reach his gun. He was only halfway through the window."

She shook her head. "It still doesn't make sense."

They fell silent until they'd reached the rooms. Hickok reminded her of his knife in her room. After she lit the bedside lamp, he picked it up and looked briefly at the blade.

"I wonder if Lieutenant Lloyd's knife would've disappeared if I'd left it," he mused. "I suppose nothing's been disturbed."

Beth looked around. She couldn't see anything different. Someone had mopped up the blood while they'd been gone, leaving the room very much like it had been before.

"What the…?" Hickok had drawn Lloyd's knife and held it in one hand but was staring at his sheath. "It's wet."

"Let me see." She held out her hand and he passed her Lloyd's knife and then started undoing his belt to extract his sheath.

She held the knife up close to her face. In the flickering light from the lamp, it was hard to see, but there was a thin oil coating the blade.

Then she gasped. Small bright red threads ran through the oil, like lace or a spider's web. They had a familiar fuzzy shadow she'd seen before. The shadow of something that'd come through the rift from Jotunheim.

"What?" Hickok's tone was sharp.

She held the knife toward him. "Can you see the red?"

He took the knife from her and moved it into better light. Then he shook his head. She held out her hand and he passed it back.

She double-checked. The threads shifted, slid, and moved within the oil. She narrowed her sight a bit more and yes, the same gray film that surrounded ghosts was there, too.

"What are you seeing?"

"This knife is coated with something that came through a rift," she said. "The oil's not of our world. And... it's the same red as in the wights."

"The wights? What do you mean?"

"The wights' souls are bound to their bodies by what look like red cords. At least to me. This... this is the same stuff." She gingerly set the knife down on the bed. Her heart raced, but she was sure she was right.

"You sure?" Hickok slowly eased his hands away from his wet sheath.

"I'm sure." She took a deep breath and then looked him straight in the eye.

"I don't think Lieutenant Lloyd was trying to kill you," she said. "I think he was trying to turn you into a wight."

TWENTY-THREE

HICKOK'S JAW DROPPED. The lamplight played across his face and heightened both his fatigue and his look of surprise. He stared at Beth and then his eyes fell on the knife. He grimaced and held out his hand for it. He took extra care to not touch the blade as he accepted it.

"So it's a type of poison." He held the knife up and stared at the edge intently.

"It must be," she said. "Remember Ellen Lemp?"

"Mmm hmm."

"They said she only had a small scratch on her when she died, and we think she became a wight."

"Then this must be handled with care." With a grimace of distaste, he slid it back into his sheath. He glanced at his own knife on the bed. "We'll get a sheath for that from stores before we leave in the morning."

"I thought we'd continue our investigations here." She didn't know how, but surely they could?

Hickok shook his head. "We need to be gone before Colonel Philips issues his redeployment orders, or I'm likely to be stuck wherever he sends me."

"I thought he wasn't in your chain of command."

"But he still outranks me."

"Okay…"

"It wouldn't be hard from him to justify it in a way that would be difficult for me to avoid." Hickok looked grim. "Yeah. We should leave at dawn."

"Back to Soulard?" She was already looking forward to the inn's bed.

"I think so. There's no point in going anywhere else."

She nodded. Then she turned to look at the room. "But I don't want to sleep in here." She nodded toward the blood still stained the floor.

"You can have my bed. I'll find somewhere else. Meet you back here at dawn?"

Beth nodded. She needed some time to think.

———

Hickok's room felt surprisingly warm. His blanket was thicker, too, and very soft. She stretched out and pulled it over her. Then she tucked her Colt under the pillow. Only then did she take a deep breath and try to relax.

The Barracks trip had been frustrating. Instead of being on her own, she'd just trailed in Hickok's wake. In Soulard, he'd at least listened to her. She'd also learned a great deal without him.

She didn't know how to deal with soldiers or sniff out traitor officers. She needed to be looking for wights. That was what she was good at. The question was—how?

———

Beth snapped awake in the dark room. She lay still, her heart beating. Then she heard the knock on her door again.

"Beth?" Hickok's voice.

"Just a minute." She slipped out of bed and unlocked the door. He came in, looking just as worn and disheveled as he had earlier.

"Ready to go?" He held up a small burlap bag. "I've got some bacon and bread from the mess hall. I've refilled our canteens, too."

"What about bullets?"

He grimaced. "They're real short, and I'd have to talk to the quartermaster to get them."

"That's not good. That they're short."

"I know." He looked as unhappy as she felt.

She quickly gathered her things while Hickok nervously watched the hallway. They quietly made their way to the stables. Even at dawn, they passed handfuls of soldiers hurrying here and there. None gave them more than a passing look.

The stables, too, were coming to life. Men carried feed to the stalls. Others led a large piebald out of his stall and began to saddle him. Even the men who apparently slept there were up and about. A couple of them paused what they were doing and stared at Hickok and Beth as they talked to a groomsman about their horses.

Beth tensed. She recognized one of the staring men— the bartender's assistant the night before. As soon as he realized she'd noticed him, he turned back to the horse he was tending. When the groomsman turned to lead them to their horses, she nudged Hickok and nodded toward the man.

"Well, well," Hickok murmured. But then Hickok deliberately ignored the assistant bartender.

Beth kept her attention on the man without looking directly at him. He seemed to be returning the favor— watching them without trying to look like that's what he was doing. But then he turned and disappeared into a far stall.

Hickok stopped at the stable's entrance and turned to the head groomsman.

"How are the roads south, Private?" Hickok asked loudly. "Think we can ride fast?" He gave Beth the slightest of warning glances.

She clamped her jaw rather than ask.

The groomsman muttered something about clear roads and good weather. Hickok exchanged a few more words with him and then motioned for Beth to mount her horse.

"Well thank you, Private." Hickok's voice easily carried through the stables. "We should be back the day after tomorrow." With that, he urged his horse forward.

Beth kept quiet until they left the fort's gate. She still glanced around to make sure no one was close enough to overhear.

"Still going to Soulard, I presume?"

Hickok gave a curt nod. He snapped his reins. "Let's ride."

They went south for a ways before turning and taking a wide loop back north. They reached Soulard just before the church bells announced the morning service. Small scatterings of heavily-bundled families trudged toward the church doors as Beth and Hickok slowed their horses to a walk. Margaret and her younger brother emerged from the Inn wrapped in their own coats, but then the brother saw the horses and hurried over.

"Stable them for you, Captain Hickok?"

Hickok nodded and dismounted. When Beth had done the same, the boy eagerly grabbed both reins and hurried off. Margaret chuckled once he was out of earshot.

"Pa pays him by the number of horses he cares for," she said. "He'll end up running the Inn when Pa's had enough."

"Or more than just the Inn," Hickok said. "Ambitious boys can go far these days." He glanced at Beth. "Or girls."

Beth frowned. She wasn't a girl anymore. Still, it wasn't worth an argument, so she changed the subject. "Where's Rose?"

"Out with the gleaners." Margaret gestured in the general direction of the cemetery. "She said you wanted an area searched."

Hickok's eyebrows shot up. "And she's out there alone?"

"Hardly alone. She has a dozen boys and a few women."

"I want to join them." Beth turned to Hickok. "I didn't tell Rose exactly where to look."

"Father O'Neill did." Margaret smiled and pointed at the church. A spindly old man was holding the door open and looking pointedly at their little group, which was the last on the street. "Now if you'll excuse me."

"I," Hickok said, "need to sleep. I didn't get any last night."

"Even in the barracks?" Beth asked.

"No beds, so I went nosing around." He shrugged. "Didn't find anything."

"So you sleep, I'll help search."

His face tightened into a pained look. He lightly bit his lip and then nodded.

"Just stay safe," he said.

"It's broad daylight. I'll be fine."

Beth found Rose standing in the middle of the street about a block west of where she and Hickok had been shot at. Boys and the occasional girl ran back and forth from various ruins to her. Each shouted out and held up something they'd found as they did. Rose exclaimed with delight and was examining the most recent treasure when Beth got within earshot.

"It is the most beautiful brooch, John," Rose said to a skinny boy of about ten wearing an adult's fur hat. "See how pretty the blue is? But we're looking for signs that someone has been living there recently. Did you see any?"

The boy shook his head and held out his hand. Rose returned the brooch and the boy took off at a run to the next building.

"These children are quite amazing," Rose said to Beth. "They've made some wondrous finds."

"But no sign of the dead wight's lair?"

Rose shook her head. "But there's still time. We've barely just begun." She broke off to tell a little girl that her broken rock was pretty but not what they needed. When the girl ran off, she turned back to Beth. "So how was the Barracks?"

Beth filled her in on the assassination attempt. Rose shuddered when Beth got to the part of the oil on the knife and perked up at the part about the troll boat sightings.

"We'd heard those rumors," she said, "but they were so garbled..."

"The scouts' reports weren't that clear either," Beth said. She paused. An older woman was marching down the street toward them.

The woman strode with purpose and fire in her eyes. She wore an oversized gray wool coat that hung well down below her knees where bunches of thick skirts swished as she walked. Fierce eyes sat in a wrinkled face and she didn't slow until she was almost on top of Rose and Beth.

"Found something." She gestured back the way she'd come. "Old blacksmith's shop. There's ashes in the furnace."

"That's strange, Mrs. Hardaway." When Rose saw Beth's furrowed brow, she continued. "Margaret says the blacksmith for Soulard lives a block behind the church."

"That's right," Mrs. Hardaway said, "and this one's been cleaned. No cobwebs." She turned and gestured for them to follow her.

She led them to a small building with an overgrown corral. The weeds had long since died, leaving husks that had been crushed by earlier snows. The shop itself had the customary collapsed roof and broken walls, though a brick chimney still stood. Mrs. Hardaway led them down a winding path through the debris. When they reached the chimney, they spotted an anvil, some torn bellows, and empty racks for tools.

Mrs. Hardaway pointed at the open door to the furnace. "See? Those are fresh."

Beth bent closer. While soot blackened everything, the bottom of the furnace contained the flaky remnants of a small fire. She poked them with a finger and watched them crumble. These had to be no more than a few days old.

"Let's look around," she said as she straightened up, but Rose was already doing so.

Most of the clutter came from the broken walls and ceiling remnants. Someone had cleared a place around the anvil. Mrs. Hardaway found a broken hacksaw blade, but no other tools.

"If they took all the tools, why didn't they take the anvil?" Beth asked.

202

"Too heavy to move," Mrs. Hardaway said, "at least for one man. Most gleaners work alone."

"Still, it'd be valuable."

Mrs. Hardaway shrugged. "Mr. Hollister and the Army already have anvils. Who would you sell it to?"

"What's this?" Rose held up a small curved piece of shiny metal.

Beth furrowed her brow and reached for it. She held it up to the light and looked at it from each side.

"It's the trigger guard for a Colt .45," she said. "It looks like it's been cut off."

"Why would anyone do that?" Rose asked. "Wouldn't that make it more likely to shoot your foot off?

"I wouldn't want to holster one without the guard." Beth looked around. "Where'd you find it?"

"In the corner over there, under that plank."

"You looked there?" The old woman's eyebrows rose.

"I used to be a maid," Rose's cheeks dimpled. "We cleaned everywhere."

"Used to be?" Beth mused.

"Now, now," Rose chided. "When was the last time I cleaned a room? Weeks at least."

Beth laughed, and the old woman just looked confused.

Their merriment suddenly cut off as a scream ripped through the air.

TWENTY-FOUR

BETH RAN. She wound her way through the courtyard back to the street. The scream had come from the south. She raced that way as fast as she could. She sensed the other women following, but falling behind.

She listened for another scream. Nothing.

She ran.

She couldn't see anything, so at the next street, she headed west, back to the street with the other gleaners.

And promptly found the whole mob running toward her. The teenaged boys raced ahead. One woman picked up a young girl and carried her. Shouts went up when they saw Beth. She slowed and tried to look beyond them.

Then they parted enough for her to see.

A creature—it had to be a wight—in a tattered girl's dress shambled down the street. It didn't look injured, but it wasn't running either.

Beth drew her gun but held it by her side until the mob fled past her. She strode forward. The gleaners circled around behind her and their yells faded to a general buzz.

The wight kept coming. Part of her was surprised. It

wasn't night. The wight shouldn't be out. But that didn't matter. It was here.

It walked straight. Its gaze—what there was of it—locked on her. With a start, she realized who it was.

Ellen Lemp.

The skull showed through the girl's face. One arm was similarly skeletal, with only thin tendons holding the bones together. As it shuffled, Beth realized one foot was half gone.

But it came on, slowly and steadily. Without the rush of the other wights.

Beth peered deep, trying to see the ghost within. In the gray daylight, she just couldn't.

When the wight closed to about ten feet, she raised her Colt.

The wight stopped.

"What do you want?" Beth called, as loud and as clearly as she could.

The wight swayed for a moment, and then sank to its knees. It clasped its hands as if it were begging.

Beth took two steps forward. The wight just watched her.

"Ellen," Beth called. "You're Ellen Lemp."

The wight nodded its head. As it did, loose flesh from its scalp swayed. Beth's stomach churned at the sight.

Still, she took two more steps forward. A loud murmur rose from behind her, but she ignored it. If this was a trap, Rose had her back.

The wight remained still with its—her?—hands clasped. Beth slowly strode forward, never lowering her gun.

"What do you want?" she repeated when she was only a few feet away.

The wight slowly unclasped its hands. It pointed one finger at the gun.

"You want me to use this?" Beth said. "You want to move on?"

It nodded.

"But I have so many questions." Beth bit her lip. Could she really deny Ellen Lemp the release from this horror because she was curious?

Inspiration struck.

"Rose! Go get Father O'Neill!"

"On my way!"

Beth turned back to Ellen. "We'll wait for Father O'Neill. He'll bless you. We'll make sure you go to Heaven."

The wight collapsed into a heap. Beth was sure it was sobbing, if that was possible. She fought the urge to step forward and comfort it. Or to lower her gun.

"He'll be here soon," Beth said. "This will all be over soon."

Ellen continued to shake.

Beth sighed. She lowered her gun but stepped back, just in case.

"It will be okay," Beth soothed.

Ellen continued to sob.

"Whatever they did to you will be over. And they will pay for it."

Ellen's head snapped up. She scowled.

"They...," Beth looked for the words. "They turned you into this. With poison."

The wight's hands formed into fists.

"We know some of them are soldiers," Beth continued.

The wight's fists tightened.

"One of them is already dead. A Lieutenant Lloyd."

The wight's mouth moved like it was trying to speak, but no words came out. It shook its fists instead.

"But we don't know why they did this to you," Beth said. "Did you find something? Something they didn't want found?"

Ellen nodded.

"What? Where?"

It pointed behind itself, south. Then it lowered its head again and the sobbing started all over.

Beth asked a few more questions, but Ellen didn't respond. After a bit, Beth gave up and turned to scan the crowd. A few of the gleaners remained. They stood wary, several yards behind her. All their eyes remained on Ellen, even as some of their expressions were grim.

She turned back to the former Ellen Lemp and waited.

Eternity seemed to pass before Father O'Neill and Rose arrived, both out of breath. He took one look at the wight and his chin dropped. With wide eyes, he slowly strode to Beth's side.

"Miss Chamberlin said you needed a blessing."

"Yes. And then I'm going to need to shoot her. Several times." She shuddered at that thought. It felt like murder to shoot someone who just knelt there.

"Several?"

"I need to sever all the points where her soul is tied to her dead body."

"Oh." Father O'Neill blanched.

"It won't be easy."

The priest nodded. Then he ducked his head and took off the cross that hung around his neck. He held it out at arm's length and began to chant. It wasn't English—Latin she guessed—but it seemed to help. Ellen slowly stilled.

Beth took a deep breath. She stepped forward and tried to recall where she'd seen the red lines on the other wights.

Pelvic bone. Base of the skull. Center of the chest. She hoped that was all.

She moved to the wight's side and took another deep breath. It didn't strike out. She knelt down and placed the barrel of her Colt against its skull, right where the spine joined the head. She wrinkled her nose and tried not to let the smell of the decayed flesh overwhelm her.

"Everything will be fine," she murmured.

Then she pulled the trigger.

The loud shot reverberated and the wight collapsed forward. Beth stepped back, aimed at the pelvic bone and fired again. She put a third shot through its back where its heart would be.

"Is she free?" Father O'Neill asked. Beth looked up to see unshed tears in his eyes.

"I won't know until it's dark." She gestured at the body. "Let's take Ellen back to the church and keep an eye on her. We can bury her again in the morning."

Beth trudged back toward the church and the Soulard Inn with Rose and Father O'Neill walking slowly at her side. Some of the gleaner boys had known where to find a wheelbarrow and they were bringing the body, which Beth kept a close eye on.

Her limbs hung heavy as she walked. She'd killed men before. She'd even killed wights. But shooting Ellen Lemp —it felt like murder. Like a cold-blooded execution. She'd never just walked up and shot someone before. It felt... wrong.

But Ellen would be at peace now. Surely she'd made it to Heaven. From all accounts, she'd led a good life. And the fact that she'd ended up like this... she hadn't deserved it.

And that made the bile rise in her gut. The more she thought about the men who'd done this, the more she balled her left hand into a fist and the more her right kept drifting down to her gun.

Ellen's wight raised so many questions. Why hadn't it tried to kill her? Or anyone else? Why had it appeared in the daytime at all? And where had it come from?

It didn't make sense.

Yet as her brain whirred, her feet kept moving and soon they were back at the church and the Soulard Inn.

"Let me get you something warm to drink," Rose said quietly to Beth.

"Yes," Father O'Neill added. "Rest, my dear."

Beth slowly acquiesced with a nod.

"I will send for you when we are ready for Ellen Lemp's, um, second funeral."

Beth nodded and followed Rose.

They found Hickok in the parlor, dressed and washed, eating eggs and ham. He wore his full Army uniform, with the hat on the table by his food. His shoulders still hung low and the circles under his eyes were as dark as a raccoon's. He gestured for Beth to join him. Rose murmured something about tea and slipped into the kitchen.

"I thought you were sleeping." Beth slid into the chair next to him. He drooped, but forced a smile.

"I was. Until Sergeant Chalmers showed up with my orders." He set his fork down on his plate.

"Oh, no."

"Yes, that is the right sentiment."

"So…?"

"I'm to immediately take command of the southern forces, since I am so convinced that the attack to the north is a feint." He snorted. "That's a near quote, by the way. Apparently the colonel's heard me, even if he refuses to listen."

"You need to take someone you can trust." She tried to think of the Army men she knew.

"I've already thought of that. I've asked for Private Johnson—remember him? From the watch tower?—anyway, I know he can't be mixed up with the traitors. So I asked for him as my aide de camp."

"He'll be pleased." Beth could already imagine the private's awe-filled face.

"As long as he's willing to stay awake when I sleep. I can handle myself except for that." He grew more somber. "But I'm worried about you."

"Why? I can handle myself." She leaned back. From his expression, he was serious.

"Both of the wights nearly killed you." He grimaced.

"But they didn't."

"True. But what happens next time?"

"I can handle myself," she repeated and emphasized it with a glare.

He snorted and looked away.

"I'm fast," she said. "I'm careful. I know when to run. I'll stay safe. And I just did, by the way."

She briefly filled him in on the encounter with Ellen Lemp. While his eyes widened and his jaw clenched, he only asked a few questions.

"Well," he said when she'd finished. "I don't know what to make of that, but you handled it well."

"And I'll handle the next problem, too."

"You better." He looked back at her, his flinty stare back. "Because I'm not going to explain to your ma what happened if you don't."

"Yeah." Beth sighed.

"I mean it."

"Oh, I know. If Ma had her way, I'd stay home wrapped in blankets in case I fell." She leaned back, crossed her arms, and glared back at him.

His stare didn't let up. "This is different. Someone out there is actively trying to kill us."

"*You.* Kill *you.* I'm only in danger around you."

He put his hands on the table and pushed himself up so forcefully, his fork rattled on the plate. His eyes still burned, but he kept his jaw clenched.

"Excuse me," he finally said. "I have to report to my unit."

He strode out and Beth blinked. Had she gone too far?

The kitchen door swung open and Rose entered with a pot of tea. Her brow furrowed in confusion.

"He left." Beth gestured toward the door.

"And without finishing his ham?" Rose tsked. "What a shame."

Beth sat in the parlor drinking Rose's herbal tea for some time. She couldn't help comparing Hickok and Ma in her mind. She knew that both wanted what was best for her, but she wasn't a little girl anymore. Hickok seemed to know that, most of the time. But lately? He wasn't quite as bad as Ma. Yet.

But Hickok was more infuriating. He *knew* what she could do. He'd trained her. He knew all about what she'd done in Yellowstone. He hadn't been there, but—

That was it. He'd never seen her in an actual fight until the wight at the express station.

She snorted softly. They'd won that fight. And the one against the second wight. And he'd been in as much danger as she was.

She was mulling over what to do when Margaret hustled into the parlor, flushed and all out of breath. She saw Beth and relief swept over her face.

"Father O'Neill wants you, Miss Armstrong. Can you come to the church?"

"What's wrong?"

"He doesn't think Ellen Lemp's soul has moved on."

TWENTY-FIVE

MARGARET LED Beth through the church to a small, windowless back room not much bigger than Father O'Neill's office. Fancy paintings of crucifixion scenes covered the walls along with an ornate tapestry of Christ on the cross. In contrast, the furniture was surprisingly simple. Ellen Lemp's body lay on a long wooden table while a basin of water sat atop a small cupboard off to the side. Something burned in a small brazier next to it, which filled the room with a sweet scent and masked the stench of decayed flesh.

Father O'Neill stood by the head of the table. He wore stained gloves and a workman's apron over his robes. He'd been leaning against the edge of the table but stood when Beth and Margaret entered.

"Thank you for coming, Miss Armstrong," he said.

"Margaret said you think she's still here?" Beth glanced at the body.

"Yes. I cannot be sure…" He looked a bit abashed. "… but sometimes I can sense these things. Laura could see ghosts during the day if it was dark enough, so I thought that maybe…?"

Beth blinked. She'd always assumed the ghosts just came out at night, but maybe they were always there, but too faint to see.

"May I?" Margaret reached for the door. After Father O'Neill nodded, she pulled it closed. Then Father O'Neill put out one of the lamps.

Beth sucked in her breath. Sure enough, the ghostly glow of Ellen's soul filled her body. Enough of the head was now gone so Beth could see the face quite clearly. The ghost's eyes were closed and she lay still. If her chest had been moving, Beth would've thought she was asleep.

"She's still here," Beth murmured. She bent over for a better look.

The thin red spiderweb of threads filled Ellen's chest and shoulders. None of the red lines extended into her skull, and they were a mishmash around her broken hips and chest, where Beth had shot her. They ran down her legs and into her feet, one of which was severely mangled, with the heel missing. In the same way, the red strands flowed down her arms to her wrists.

Beth started. That was strange. Ellen's hands were completely free of the red threads.

Beth moved to look at her wrists from a different angle, and Father O'Neill shuffled out of her way. He looked at her with an unasked question.

"She's still bound," Beth said. "Caught. We need to destroy more of her body, I'm afraid."

"What do you recommend?"

"Cremation, actually. But… perhaps a good carving knife?"

Margaret paled and sucked in her breath.

"Miss Benton?" Father O'Neill said. "If you would be so kind?"

"Yes, Father." She slipped from the room and quietly closed the door behind her.

Beth slowly scanned the body. It wasn't as bad as she thought. She spotted knots of red at the major joints. If they cut those, most of the threads should become untethered. The arms would fade when they cut the wrists and shoulders. The legs, when she finished with the hips and knees. To her surprise, there seemed to be another abdominal node where Ellen's liver would be. That, too, would have to be cut.

At least her aim had been good at the heart and hips. If she squinted, she could make out where the nodes had once been.

But, confusingly, the threads didn't even extend up to the base of Ellen's skull where Beth had shot her. They stopped at the base of her neck, right at her—

"Is she wearing a necklace?" Beth asked.

"I'm sure she is," Father O'Neill said. "Here, let me." He reached under the dead girl's collar and pulled it out. A small silver cross on a silver chain hung around the corpse's neck.

Beth quickly checked Ellen's wrists. She had silver bracelets around both.

"These are pretty nice," she said, as she examined one more closely.

"The gleaners find quite a bit of jewelry in the ruins," Father O'Neill said. "More than anyone with modesty can wear, actually."

"Well, maybe the silver stopped the infection." Beth stepped back and looked at the whole of Ellen's body. "It certainly looks like it did."

"We have a great deal of silver," the priest said. "I will spread the word."

"I wonder if we should wake her up," Beth mused. When she saw Father O'Neill's confused look, she added, "She looks like she's sleeping."

"Do you think we'll hurt her?"

"I don't think so." Beth looked closer at the red lines.

He waited for her to continue.

"The other wights didn't flinch when we shot them. Come to think of it, she didn't either."

"I'd prefer to let her rest. But... is there perhaps something you need to know...?"

Beth paused. There was, actually. There was so much she still didn't know. She took a deep breath.

"Ellen?" she asked. "Are you there, Ellen?"

The ghost didn't respond.

"Ellen?" Beth raised her voice. "Could I please speak with you?"

Ellen's ghost opened her eyes. She looked at Beth and then Father O'Neill and furrowed her brow.

"We need to do a bit more to release you," Beth said. "But soon. Very soon. I promise it won't hurt."

"Heaven awaits, my child," Father O'Neill said. "It is just a bit delayed."

The ghost's eyes went wide. She looked at Father O'Neill, but he didn't respond. He couldn't see her, after all. Just her corpse. Beth steeled herself.

"Do you know who did this to you?" she asked. "Do you know their names?"

Ellen's ghost frowned. Her mouth moved as if she were speaking.

"I can't hear you," Beth said. "Just nod your head."

The ghost did so, though only slightly. The flesh didn't

move, but then Beth remembered the top of the spine had been destroyed.

"Do you know the names of who did this to you?" Beth repeated.

Ellen's ghost hesitated and then nodded. She lifted her hand and held up one finger. Then she slowly lowered her hand back to the table.

Father O'Neill jumped back. To his credit, he only paled and didn't cry out. His eyes darted to Beth. Then he took a deep, calming breath.

Beth took one herself before looking back at the ghost. "You know one name. Was it Corporal Preston?"

Ellen's ghost furrowed her brow in confusion.

"Sergeant Chalmers?"

The ghost nodded. Beth's eyes widened and she turned to Father O'Neill. "He's not a coward! He's a traitor!"

Beth forced herself to calm down. She took several deep breaths and willed her heart to slow. She couldn't do anything immediately. At least not about Sergeant Chalmers. What she needed to do was take care of Ellen. Poor, poor Ellen, still trapped on this side.

Sergeant Chalmers had killed her and turned her into a wight. But why?

Ellen had said she'd found something. She needed to know.

"Ellen," Beth asked gently. "What did you find? What were they hiding to do this to you?"

Ellen's ghost paused. Then she held up a hand with a single finger. She began slowly moving it in the air.

Beth watched for a moment before she blinked in recognition.

"Letters! You're drawing letters!"

Ellen's ghost nodded and continued.

"N..." Beth repeated the letters out loud and the ghost nodded. "I... G... H... T... S... H... A... D... E... Nightshade!"

"Nightshade?" Father O'Neill said. "That's very poisonous."

"It grows around here?" Beth asked.

"Sometimes. It looks like blueberries, which leads to accidents sometimes."

"Where did you find it?" Beth asked Ellen's ghost.

It pointed.

"You found it south of here," Father O'Neill said, and Ellen confirmed it with a nod.

"Nightshade," Beth mused. "Why would they kill her for finding nightshade?" She paused. "It'd have to be because they were using it for something special... something like..." She looked at Ellen again. "Maybe part of the poison that turned her into this. A part that didn't come through the rift."

Ellen's ghost had closed her eyes again. She appeared to be quietly sobbing once again.

"Is there more?" Beth gently asked.

The ghost ignored her.

Just then, Margaret returned carrying a large carving knife. She held it out to Father O'Neill, who gingerly accepted it. He turned to Beth.

"So where do I cut?" He shifted his grip on the knife but still clutched it tight.

"I'd better do it." She grimaced and held out her hand for the blade.

"Are you sure?"

"I'm the only one who can see where the threads are."

"So what do you want me to do?" he asked.

"Wipe away any blood or gunk." She moved to Ellen's shoulder. The ghost had closed its eyes again.

"Thank you, Ellen," Beth said. "You resisted these evil men, which was so brave of you. You'll have peace soon."

Beth raised the knife.

It's just like butchering back at the Astor, she told herself. She took a deep breath and started cutting at the bundle of attached threads. When she'd severed it, the red lines faded. When she cut the wrist, they disappeared completely.

"It's working," she said. Ellen's ghostly cheek had a tear on it. Her eyes remained closed.

Beth watched the ghost's face as she sliced through the other nodes. When she cut the last one, a gray-white disk opened above the body. Ellen's ghost floated up and into it. Then it closed.

"She's gone," Beth said quietly.

"Mmm?" Father O'Neill said.

Beth nodded. "She's passed on."

Father O'Neill said a quiet prayer and both he and Margaret crossed themselves. Beth just sagged against the side cabinet in relief.

A surprisingly large crowd attended Ellen Lemp's second funeral. Word had spread through the Soulard and gleaner communities and it seemed that everyone wanted to see and hear what had happened themselves. It certainly wasn't the draw of food. Margaret had spent the afternoon helping Father O'Neill prepare the body while Rose had continued to organize the gleaners' search. Everyone had converged on the church at dusk and filled the pews.

Ellen's mother sat in the front row. Father O'Neill had

decided to spare her the sight of her daughter as a decayed wight, saying she'd suffered enough, but she was here for yet another funeral. Beth couldn't help but admire her strength.

Rose and Beth picked seats by the aisle halfway down just before the service was to start. People shuffled and coughed as they waited for Father O'Neill to ascend the lectern.

"Brothers and sisters," he began, "we gather to celebrate Ellen Lemp's ascension into Heaven. She led a good life, and we know, beyond any doubt, that she has risen to be with our Lord Jesus."

A murmur ran through the crowd and several people looked over at Beth.

"Miss Lemp suffered horribly upon her death," Father O'Neill continued, "but like our Lord, her suffering has brought good to us, good to the world. She has shown us the path to salvation."

That drew a similar hubbub.

Father O'Neill held up his crucifix. "She wore a silver cross upon her chest! Held by a chain of silver! Both blessed by our Lord!"

The hubbub grew.

"She did not succumb to evil," he continued. "She retained her mind. Until it was time for her to take her final step into our Lord's care. Amen."

This time, the crowd was only shushed by Father O'Neill lifting his Bible and then beginning to pray. Beth bowed her head, but couldn't help wonder. Was it the cross, or the silver chain, that protected Ellen's mind?

She let out a deep breath. She suspected the silver chain, but she wouldn't argue that with the crowd. Besides, she had other problems to solve. And she would need help.

After the service, Beth asked Rose and Margaret to join her in the Soulard Inn's kitchen. A few of the gleaners had decided to pay for rooms rather than sleep in the church. Beth wasn't sure the parlor would be private enough, but was confident they wouldn't enter the kitchen. Besides, the stove would keep the room warm. Warm was good.

She quickly caught them both up on what she'd learned from Ellen's ghost. To her credit, Rose took it all in stride, though she did ask a dozen questions before she was satisfied.

"We need to warn Hickok about Sergeant Chalmers," Beth said. "Is there any way we can send him a message?"

"Hmm." Margaret pursed her lips. "Sergeant Chalmers delivers most of the messages between Soulard and the Barracks. There were others, but—" Her face went white.

"But of course," Rose shook her head sadly, "they were the first victims of the wights."

Margaret nodded in agreement.

"Can we send a gleaner?" Beth asked. "Or one of the local boys?"

"Where?" Margaret asked. "If we just send them to the Barracks, we don't know who they'll talk to. It might be one of the other traitors."

Beth sighed and nodded in agreement.

"Do you know where Captain Hickok is deployed?" Rose asked.

"Just to the south."

"If a gleaner shows up at the Barracks asking for Captain Hickok, it's going to be suspicious," Rose added. "I can't imagine they'd tell him where to find the captain without a great deal of questioning first."

Beth grimaced. Rose was right.

"Are there any soldiers you know we can trust?" Margaret asked.

"Not really," Beth mused. "Well, Private Johnson, from the watchtower. But Hickok was gonna take him as his aide."

"Matthew?" Margaret's eyes lit up. "Matthew's with the captain?"

"He was the one soldier Hickok was sure wasn't involved," Beth replied.

"Then," Margaret said with obvious relish, "I know just what to do."

TWENTY-SIX

BETH MARVELED at how simple Margaret's plan was. And how Beth never would've thought of it, even with all the time in the world. Margaret would ride down to Jefferson Barracks and tell them that she needed to see her "beau," Private Matthew Johnson. She'd be insistent, but only hint as to why. With a few well-timed tears, the soldiers would surely tell her at least where he was stationed. Rose was completely convinced it was a great plan. Beth just shook her head in amusement.

"Will that really work?" Beth wondered aloud.

"Oh, dearie, you're too direct," Rose told Beth. "Men shuffle away when you ask them things."

"Not all men," Beth protested.

"True." Rose smiled and patted Beth's hand. "But the men that can stand up to you aren't going to slip and admit where Captain Hickok is, now, are they?"

Beth grumbled and nodded.

"Now I'll take care of the Inn and the suppers for the church folk," Rose said to Margaret. "What else do I need to do while you're gone?"

"We'll talk to my brother before I leave," Margaret said. She'd already started packing up food and filling a canteen. "He can handle the other chores."

"What about your father?" Beth asked.

Margaret chuckled. "Oh, you can leave him to me."

Just then, a loud knock came from the door to the parlor.

"Margaret?" her father's voice called out. "There's a boy here to see Miss Chamberlin."

"My, what timing." Rose's eyes twinkled.

Margaret opened the door. "Papa? Could I have a word?" She slipped out and then a skinny boy of about ten with a mop of brown hair came in.

The boy held his hat in his hands in front of him and his eyes widened as he looked at Beth. They darted to the gun at her hip and he swallowed. Then he turned to Rose.

"Miss Chamberlin?" He swallowed hard. "We, uh, found something."

She smiled warmly. "Hello Joseph. What did you find?"

"Some, uh, chains. In a basement. And, uh, part of Miss Lemp's foot. At least we think that's what it is."

"Can you take Miss Armstrong to it?" Rose asked. She looked at Beth. "I need to start on tonight's soup."

The boy nodded vigorously, and then motioned for the door. "C'mon. Let's go."

Two other scruffy boys, obviously gleaners, joined them as they walked north into the ruins. At first the boys were quiet, but after a few blocks they started asking questions. Most were about the wights. When she described killing the first one, Joseph's jaw dropped.

"You shot it?" His eyes stayed wide. "And hit it in the chest? From across the road?"

"Yes..."

"You must be really good."

"Well, yeah..." She wondered how much modesty she should have.

"My Pa lets me shoot his gun sometimes and I could never do that."

She smiled. "I've had a lot of practice."

"You must practice all the time! Every day! All day!"

"She can't practice that often, Joe," one of the other boys in an oversized thick wool coat said. "She's gotta do other stuff too."

"That I do." Beth picked up the pace. Her legs were as long as the boys' and if they were walking fast, the questions would slow. "So how far are we going?"

"Just a bit more," Joseph said.

They wound their way through the streets and even an alley before the boys led her into a completely ruined building. Not a single wall stood more than three feet high. In one corner, a ramshackle stack of thick planks sprawled next to a large hole. Stairs led down into the darkness.

"Uh..." Joseph looked pensive. "Did you bring a lamp?"

"No one said anything about needing a lamp." She gave him a firm look.

"I got some matches!" One of the other boys started fumbling in his pants pocket. He pulled several out and passed them to Beth.

"So who's going with me?" she asked.

The boys shot nervous looks at each other and then Joseph grimaced and stepped forward.

"Why don't you use these?" She passed him some of

the matches and then drew her Colt. "I'll be right behind you."

"We been down there before," Joseph said, but his shoulders still relaxed when he looked at her gun.

He edged ahead of her and slowly crept down the stairs. She followed two steps behind. At the bottom, Joseph struck one of the matches. The flickering light illuminated a large room cut out of the ground. Stone lined the walls, and some of it looked natural. Fist-sized rocks littered one corner like they had fallen from the scratched wall beside them.

"What is this?" Beth asked. It was far bigger than any root cellar she'd seen.

He furrowed his brow and tilted his head as he looked at her. "Uh, a basement, Miss Armstrong."

"Oh." She'd heard of basements, but Golden City didn't have any. They were too much work when land was plentiful.

"Over here." He gestured toward a dark corner. As he got close, the match started to burn out so he dropped it and lit another.

There were indeed chains on the floor. They twisted around what looked like a pipe and were fastened with a sturdy lock. The ends were curled into loops like makeshift manacles. One contained a hunk of decayed flesh that looked like it might've been from a foot. The mild stench wasn't horribly strong, but was clear.

The second match started to flicker and fade, so Joseph lit a third. Beth looked quickly around. She spotted smudges on the pipe and stains on the floor where Ellen had obviously sat. Then she saw that the pipe had broken near the bottom, which must have been how Ellen had escaped. Other than that, the basement was bare.

"Only got a few more matches," Joseph said.

"We'll save the rest." Beth lightly tapped her pouch where they were. "There's nothing else here."

"I s'pose not," Joseph agreed.

"Let's go." Beth grimaced. This had been a good place to hide a prisoner, but why?

The answer immediately clicked into place. Because Ellen hadn't gone crazy like the other two. They'd chained the wight up because that was the only way to control it.

So how did they control the other wights? Or did they?

By now, the shadows had grown quite long. The boys stood around nervously. Joseph kept fiddling with something in his pocket. She smiled at them.

"Let's go. We can be back at the church before dark."

Beth found Father O'Neill in his little office. The priest's face was ashen, with dark circles under his eyes. He still managed a partial smile. He gestured her in and offered her the little chair, but she shook her head.

"I want to look at the map again," she said. "Ellen said they'd killed her because she'd found something. I'm hoping to figure out where."

"By all means. I hope it helps." Then he frowned. "I'm afraid I won't be able to assist you tomorrow, though."

"Oh?"

"I must report to the Barracks."

"Really?" She blinked in surprise.

"Like all men, I have been drafted and ordered to report to Jefferson Barracks tomorrow. I do not agree with the orders, but I will not shirk them."

She nodded and waited for him to go on.

"I will ask to work with the medics. I have a bit of skill in that area."

"Who's going to take care of the church?"

"Miss Benton, I hope. Though some of the other ladies will help, I'm sure. Perhaps...?" He raised a questioning eyebrow.

"I'm sorry," she said, answering his implied question. "We still have the wights out there."

"Yes." He nodded. "That's true." He gestured to the map. "If you find something worth investigating, please let me know. I will return in a few minutes."

After he left, Beth stepped up to the map. Father O'Neill had already marked the spot to the north where they'd encountered Ellen Lemp's wight. He'd also moved the pencil line to show the surrounding area had been searched. Beth found the basement where the wight had been chained. Everything around it now fell into the searched area.

She frowned. Ellen's ghost had said she'd been killed because she found something to the south. But everywhere between where she'd been and the church had now been searched. She supposed the gleaners could've missed something, but she suspected they were pretty thorough.

Her eyes drifted further south, toward the Barracks. Her gaze settled on the rash of dots down near the breweries, where the first deaths had occurred. Where the witch Laura had been killed.

Certainty settled into her gut. The answer had to be there. She'd have to look in the morning.

———

Beth stood in the main hallway of the Soulard Inn and stared down at the mirror at the far end. Rose had already retired for the night, which made the hall the best place to practice. With the four oil lamps she'd lit, her reflection was clear. She let her right hand hover over her holster.

Then she drew.

Her gun snapped up and level. Her left hand met it to steady it. From the feel, more than the reflection, her aim was good.

She mentally counted "forty-nine" and then holstered her gun again.

Mr. Benton's raised voice came from the front room. Beth turned and cocked her head as she strained to listen. She couldn't make out any words. She quietly walked toward the commotion.

"I will not!" Mr. Benton protested. His back was to her, but he was shaking his fist at—

—Sergeant Chalmers.

Beth's heart skipped.

The sergeant shifted his weight forward. His thick shoulders were tense and his right hand hovered near his holster. His eyes narrowed to almost a squint and he seemed to bite back a sneer as he watched Mr. Benton rant. Then he caught sight of Beth and he straightened up and forced a smile.

"I'm sorry, Mr. Benton, but those are the orders. Every able-bodied man or boy is to report to the Barracks."

"Except for those providing food and supplies! Food and supplies! Good Lord, is there something wrong with your hearing?"

"I'm sorry, sir. That's no longer an exception. We'd be drafting the women, if we could." He looked pointedly at Beth, but then switched to a mask of innocence.

Mr. Benton followed his gaze and turned around. His glare only softened a little.

"Well," he snapped at Sergeant Chalmers, "not every

woman is Miss Armstrong. But you'd be far better off with her than me. I have a trick knee!"

Beth edged her way into the room so she could see both men's faces at once. Mr. Benton's was nearly purple and a vein in his forehead throbbed. Sergeant Chalmers shifted to parade rest, though his eyes kept darting between Mr. Benton and her.

"I cannot go!" Mr. Benton said. "I just cannot."

"Orders are orders." Sergeant Chalmers shrugged and held up a paper. "I'm authorized to confiscate the goods of any man who does not report by sundown tomorrow."

"What!" Mr. Benton's eyes bulged. "What? Why, that's an outrage!"

Beth's gut tightened. She couldn't imagine the Army supporting such an order. Certainly not Colonel Mosby back in Golden City. But she bit her lip. She didn't need Sergeant Chalmers's attention.

"They're my orders." Sergeant Chalmers turned to leave. "We'll see you at the Jefferson Barracks tomorrow, Mr. Benton. Your son, too."

"My son?" Mr. Benton yelled. "My son!"

Sergeant Chalmers ignored him. Instead, he tipped his hat to Beth. "Good day, Miss Armstrong."

Mr. Benton was so spitting mad, he couldn't form words. Sergeant Chalmers ignored him and strode out. When Mr. Benton finally regained enough composure to use words, he turned to Beth.

"It's always been food and supplies!" he spat. "Always!"

"Did he say why it'd changed?" she asked as evenly as she could. Rose said that being calm herself help calm upset men.

"Something about the trolls," he fumed. "It's a load of nonsense!"

"But they're threatening to invade." She furrowed her brow. "They've built the boats and everything."

He waved a dismissive hand. "They do that every two to three years. They never make it across the river and then we sink all their boats."

"Really?"

"Yes! Colonel Philips would know that if he'd been here two years ago. Chalmers certainly should." Mr. Benton glared at the door Chalmers had departed through.

"Maybe it's different this time," Beth suggested.

"Why in the world would it be?" He threw up his hands. "At least the Inn's empty but for you ladies."

"I thought one of the gleaners was here."

"He skedaddled right after he talked to Chalmers." Mr. Benton snorted. "Smart man. So it's just you ladies. I trust you'll be all right with all the men gone." He glared at the door again.

Beth followed his gaze and nodded. Then she caught herself.

"Wait a minute," she said. "Sergeant Chalmers isn't staying here?"

"I wouldn't let him even if he'd asked," Mr. Benton grumbled. "I need to go find my son. Good evening, Miss Armstrong."

He headed into the hallway while Beth stared at the outer door.

After they'd fought the wight by the gleaners' camp, Sergeant Chalmers had been "too afraid" to ride back to the Barracks after dark. Or at least that's what he'd said. But if he wasn't staying at the Inn, where was he staying?

She needed to find out.

TWENTY-SEVEN

BETH SLIPPED OUT of the Inn into the cold night. She pulled her coat tight and glanced around. The street was still and quiet. Even the few lights from the church seemed weaker than she remembered from the night before.

She sighed. She'd given Sergeant Chalmers too much of a head start. She walked to the middle of the street and peered in all directions. She didn't catch sight of him.

She briskly headed to the church. The child who opened the door for her said they hadn't seen the sergeant. She briefly considered asking around anyway, but decided against it. She didn't want to call too much attention to the fact that she was looking for him.

The gleaners had abandoned their camp after the fire. She briefly considered whether Sergeant Chalmers had gone there, but couldn't come up with a good reason. Would he go to the basement where Ellen Lemp had been kept? Or maybe the blacksmith's forge they'd found?

Neither made sense. Both had clearly been abandoned.

He could've ridden back to the Barracks, she supposed. His "fear" about taking that ride, which he'd confessed to

Hickok, had probably been a lie. But the ride would still take a couple of hours and it was already late. No, he had to still be around, but where?

She tried to imagine Chalmers riding through the dark streets to the Barracks, but then caught herself. She'd never seen him on horseback. Did he even have one?

Hickok had asked to borrow her horse for Private Johnson. She suspected there weren't many left in Soulard, but that didn't mean Chalmers didn't have one.

She needed to talk to Margaret's brother, Jack.

She found Jack in the stables. He wore a work overall and had rolled up his sleeves. His back was turned as he packed some saddlebags. When he heard her, he scooted away from them and turned to reveal a guilty look on his face.

"What're you doing?" she asked.

"Uh... packing, Miss."

"Going some place?" She strolled up to the bags and peeked into them. A shirt sleeve spilled out of the top one.

"Um, uh." Then in a rush, "Pa wants me to take a message to the Addisons. Pa wants me to tell them we won't be needing any bacon soon, on account of the Inn being closed by the Army. He wants me to go tonight, because, uh, they need to know, in case uh, they're planning to send us some, uh, soon."

"Mmm." She smiled, which didn't seem to calm the boy. Sweat beaded on his brow and he kept shifting his weight from foot to foot. She decided to throw him a lifeline.

"And given how late it is, you'll have to spend the night, won't you?"

"Uh, yes, Miss!"

He'd probably spend more than one night, she suspected. The Addison farm had to be beyond Sergeant Chalmers's reach. Speaking of which...

"I was looking for Sergeant Chalmers," she said. "I thought he might keep his horse here."

"Sometimes," Jack said, "but he came and took it a little while ago."

"Did he say where he was going?"

"Yes, Miss. Back to Jefferson Barracks."

"Oh."

"But he said he'd be back in the morning."

She frowned. A two hour ride south followed by another two hour ride back the following morning? No, Sergeant Chalmers was somewhere nearby. But where?

She was missing something. She glanced at Jack but he continued to hurriedly pack.

"Did Sergeant Chalmers say anything else?" she asked, "Or do anything unusual?"

Jack paused and scratched his head. "No."

"You sure?"

"Well... he looked real nervous. And he asked for some lamp oil."

"Lamp oil?"

"Mmm hmm. He said he wanted to make sure he could see any problems early on the ride back."

"That doesn't make any sense." She shook her head. "You can't ride and hold an oil lamp without it spilling."

"Yeah. He probably should've taken a torch." Jack smiled and cinched one of the saddlebags. "He had a big lamp, too. It'd be hard to hold."

A big lamp? That really didn't make sense. It wouldn't help him see into all those nooks and possible sniper's blinds she'd spotted on her own trip to the Barracks. A big lamp would only be better than a torch for shining light long distances…

She sucked in her breath. She knew where he'd gone.

Beth decided to jog to the river. She might not be able to keep up with Sergeant Chalmers if she found him, but it'd be easier to hide in the shadows. She was sure he and his friends had tried to kill Hickok. If he caught her alone…?

She followed the street that they'd taken into Soulard from the river eastward. She had enough moonlight to see that she didn't get too close to the ruins and other houses. She passed one that was clearly inhabited, from the light peeking out from under its shutters. It was quiet, though, so she just kept on.

The street finally ended at the big north-south road that paralleled the riverbank. Beth still hadn't seen a hint of the sergeant. She moved closer to the shore, past the low ruins there, until she could see the nearest watch tower, some five hundred yards to the south.

Where there was a light. Which flashed off and on. Then did it again.

She jogged toward it. She tried to keep her steps light. Half her attention was on the ground so she wouldn't trip. But out of the corner of her eye, she caught another flash. This one came from across the river.

Her blood went cold.

Beth paused and watched the flashes. While they were a mix of long and short, it didn't quite look like Morse code. The long flashes had wildly different lengths. Then they all stopped and went dark. She started running again.

As she did, she peered at the watch tower. Despite being silhouetted against the lighter sky, she couldn't make out any details. She continued to run as best she could over the uneven ground.

When she was a hundred yards out, she spotted a dark shape descending from the tower. She slowed enough to draw her Colt and then kept moving. The shape hit the ground and disappeared into the shadows.

She sped up. She could now see what had to be a horse, and a moment later, a rider on it.

"Stop!" she shouted.

The horse startled and its rider jerked its reins. He turned and fired a gun.

Beth dropped to the ground. The bang of the shot rang through the air, but it didn't even come close. She climbed to one knee and saw the rider was already galloping away, further south.

She fired. Then a second shot. Then a third. The rider didn't fall or slow.

She grimaced. Maybe she should have looked harder for a horse for herself.

Beth hurried the rest of the way to the guard tower. A second horse remained tied beneath it in a small protective lean-to, a little sturdier than the horse shelter at Private Johnson's watchtower. She briefly considered riding after Sergeant Chalmers—it had to be him, she was sure—but thought better of it. She needed to check on the tower's original guard.

Beth carefully climbed the ladder in the dark. At the top just before the platform, she paused and listened. Nothing. Not even the slightest stirring. She took a deep breath and poked her head through the platform opening.

She spotted the sprawled body immediately.

Nothing else moved, so she climbed into the watchtower. She knelt next to the fallen soldier. Blood pooled around his chest and he wasn't breathing. She put her fingers on his neck to feel for a pulse, and his flesh was already cooling. There was no ghost.

She stood. Even with her eyes having adjusted and the bright moon, she couldn't see much. Whatever was across the river remained completely in shadow.

She looked around the tower. She'd hoped for a horn or drum or some way of making noise, but if had been there one, it was gone. Her eye fell on a large unlit oil lamp. The cloth hanging on the side was warm to the touch. A crazy idea came to her. She fumbled in one of the pouches at her belt until she found a match. She checked the wind—the breeze was light from the west. She lifted a fabric flap on the lamp and used it to shield the match before she struck it. She managed to light the lamp on the first try.

Beth faced the lamp across the river. Then she lifted the flap and let the beam of light shine. After a count of three, she closed it. Another count of four, and she opened it again.

She couldn't remember the patterns she'd seen, so she started opening and closing the flap at random. She watched the far side of the river for a return signal, but none ever came. After a couple of minutes, she gave up.

Maybe she'd at least confused them.

Beth knelt by the dead soldier again but with the lamp open this time. He lay on his side, his eyes bulging open. He'd been stabbed in the chest and his blood soaked everything. Like Private Johnson, he was young, with only a scraggly beard to mark that he wasn't a boy. She closed his eyes and then stood.

She looked back across the river. She still couldn't see what was coming, but if Chalmers had been willing to leave a body behind, it had to be soon.

Beth panted hard when she reached the church. Her legs ached and her chest hurt from breathing. The church was dark, but she pounded on the door until she saw a small light through the window. A face appeared at the glass and peeked out at her. A moment later Joseph, the skinny boy who'd shown her the basement, cracked the door open.

"We've got trouble," she gasped. "Is Father O'Neill still here?"

"Yeah." Joseph stepped back to let her in.

A few candles on the altar softly illuminated the large sanctuary. Blankets and clothes hung over several pews. Beth guessed there had to be fifty or so people camped out in here. Other than Joseph, most were still in bed, barely stirring.

"He's in the back." Joseph pointed. "Dunno if he's awake."

"Let's go find out."

Joseph shook his head. "I gotta stay at my post." He indicated the door, and then Beth realized he had a gun belt on.

"You do that," she said. "Whatever you do, don't let Sergeant Chalmers in."

"Huh? Why?"

"Just don't." She waited for him to nod before she hurried toward Father O'Neill's office.

She found Father O'Neill carefully packing a haversack in his office. He was holding a worn shirt up and inspecting it, as if looking for stains. He moved slowly, and when he turned, the dark circles under his eyes made him look aged and worn. He furrowed his brow when he saw her.

"Sergeant Chalmers is working with the trolls!" she blurted. "He signaled them!"

"What? When?" Father O'Neill set the shirt down. "No, start at the beginning."

Beth told him about her encounter with Sergeant Chalmers in the Soulard Inn and her guess that he'd gone to the river. When she told him about the encounter there, he asked if she'd been able to get a really good look at the rider.

"No. But it had to be him," she said. "The lamp was the same one Jack Benton saw him with."

"Same one? Or same type?"

She grimaced, but he motioned for her to go on. When she told him about the dead lookout, he muttered a prayer and crossed himself. But the his face grew grim. As she continued, his shoulders tensed. His eyes narrowed. His fatigue fled.

"We need to warn the Barracks," she said when she'd finished. "The attack must be tonight—he wouldn't have left the body otherwise."

Father O'Neill gritted his teeth. "The attack will surely be across the river here, where there is no longer a sentry to give warning."

She grimaced. She was sure he was right.

"Did you signal the other towers up and down the shore?"

Her gut sank. "No. I didn't think of it. I don't know how, anyway."

"I believe young Joseph out there may. His brother served in one of the watch towers and he used to spend the day there."

"It's worth trying."

"Yes, because a signal will be far faster than sending a rider."

"Mmm hmm. Besides, Chalmers will ambush any rider." When Beth saw the priest's surprise, she added, "It's what I'd do. Or... kill the sentries in the other towers as well."

"Then we must try both." Father O'Neill dropped the shirt he'd been holding and looked around until he spotted his coat. "Which would you prefer?"

"Signaling should be safer." She grimaced again. "So I'll take the road."

"Are you sure?"

She firmly nodded. "Take Joseph and stay alert. The trolls could already be in the boats." She glanced back toward the sanctuary. "We should get Rose to organize the people here. I don't know if the church can be defended..."

"She can get them into the caves," Father O'Neill said. "They should be safe there."

Beth's chin dropped. "Caves? There are caves under the city?"

"Of course. Didn't you know?"

TWENTY-EIGHT

BETH'S HEART raced as she stared at Father O'Neill. Her thoughts tumbled so fast that she couldn't think of what to ask first.

She finally settled on, "Where are these caves?"

"Why, all over. The city's built on limestone and there are many natural caves."

"All over?" She couldn't believe it. "Like... one big cave?"

"No, though some have been widened and connected. I think the nearest one connects to the inn's cellar."

"Oh, that explains it," Beth said. "Margaret said it had two rooms, which seemed huge to me. But there are others?"

"What are you thinking?" His forehead creased in alarm.

"Where there's caves, there could be tunnels, right?"

"I suppose—" His eyes widened in alarm. "You don't suppose the trolls...?"

"It's a long way under the river, but I bet they could do it." Beth's mind continued to race and the words spilled out. "Hickok said they'd launch a feint but their real attack would come somewhere else. What if the *boats* are the feint, and they're coming through a tunnel?"

"You think they'd do that?"

"I'm sure of it." She turned to the map on Father O'Neill's wall. Her eyes quickly found the cluster of black dots around where the witch Laura had died.

"You said these used to be mostly breweries, right?" She jabbed the spot with her finger.

"Yes, they were... and most of them stored their beer in the caves."

"Did anyone search them?"

"I thought so, but..." He shrugged. "How many men would go into a dark cave after a wight?"

"None." She jabbed the map with her finger. "I wouldn't be surprised if those caves run a long way toward the river."

"So what do we do?"

"We need to check the breweries." She sucked in her breath. "I can do that."

"Are you sure?"

"Yes. If there's nothing there, I can go on to the Barracks. You should still signal the Army." She gave Father O'Neill an apologetic smile. "I could be wrong. The boats could be launching right now."

"I'll get Joseph and set out right away." But then he paused and stared at the map. After a moment, he shook himself out of his thoughts. "Excuse me, Miss Armstrong."

After he'd hurried out of the room, Beth turned back to the map. Her eyes drifted back to the cluster of dots. She had a bad feeling they were running out of time.

———

242

Beth quietly cracked the door open to the room she shared with Rose before she realized that was silly. The whole point was to wake her friend up. She pushed the door hard and raised her lamp.

Rose stirred immediately. She sat up and rubbed the sleep from her eyes as Beth strode in.

"The trolls are coming," Beth quickly said. "We need your help."

"What do you need?" Rose pushed her blankets down.

"Protect the people in the church."

"How?"

"Father O'Neill's gone to warn the Army. He says there's a cave attached to the cellar."

"There is." Rose swung her feet onto the floor. "What's happening with the trolls?"

Beth briefly explained what had happened at the signal tower while Rose got dressed. When she got to the tunnels, Rose's face went pale.

"You don't suppose our cellar...?" Rose asked.

"It's small enough to search, right? Did you see anything that could be a tunnel?"

Rose shook her head and let out a relieved breath. Then she grew pensive. "Do you think the trolls will come into the cellar?"

"They might," Beth admitted. "But you've got your gun, right? You should be able to defend the cellar door."

"Until the ammunition runs out," Rose grumbled. "Maybe the gleaners have some."

"You'll figure it out," Beth reassured. "You're the most resourceful woman I know."

Rose's cheeks dimpled. Then she paused.

"I... do have something for you." She opened the nightstand drawer and pulled out two silver chain bracelets and a thin silver chain necklace.

"The gleaners couldn't find a necklace that was solid silver." Rose passed the jewelry over. "I hope this is enough."

Beth held up the necklace. While the links were thin and delicate, they'd been artistically wrought.

"It's… it's beautiful," she said.

"I wish it were thicker, like the bracelets."

"The necklace should work just fine." Beth slipped it over her neck. "Besides, I'm not planning on getting poisoned."

"See that you don't." Rose's tone was so firm that Beth smiled.

"I'll do my best." She slid the bracelets on and then pushed them as high as she could. She really didn't need them flopping around loose when she was trying to shoot. "I'm going to check out the breweries before I go to the Barracks."

Rose nodded. "I'll tell Hickok if I see him."

"You won't."

"Then you take care of yourself, you hear?" Rose's smile was gone, her expression all business. "Now let's go. We've got people to save."

Beth strode down the dark street. She silently grumbled as she did. Someone had taken all of the horses out of the Inn's stable while she'd been at the river. She mentally berated herself for not having ridden to the river in the first place, even if it'd been a "borrowed" horse.

She picked up her pace. The ruined buildings created deep wells of darkness where the moonlight couldn't reach, but she marched on. For once, she wasn't cold.

She counted the blocks down the main road to the

Barracks until she was one short of the first black dot on Father O'Neill's map. If Chalmers had an ambush planned, that'd be a good spot. She turned west, away from the river, and went three blocks before again turning south.

She briefly considered jogging. She'd get there faster, but a bit more winded. Except she needed to be alert. That's what mattered.

She slowed when she passed a building that had once had a large porch out front. The low stone wall surrounding the patio had been smashed in the middle and most of the building wrecked. Still, it looked like a place folks might gather to drink beer.

She was confident the breweries were close.

After the next block, she caught sight of familiar landmarks. She figured she was about a block west of where Laura had been killed. Beth moved to the shadows along the side of the street. She hadn't seen Sergeant Chalmers yet, but he was around. He had to be.

Or if not him, another wight, guarding the tunnels.

She eased her way forward. With each step, she looked left and right as well as ahead. From time to time, she looked back. She followed the uneven pace Hickok had taught her. Rhythmic moves caught the eye. Irregular were harder to see.

Beth approached the stone brewery with the porch where Laura had died. Approaching from the west, she couldn't see the entryway where they'd found her body, as the intact wall blocked her view. The hair stood on the back of her neck. She had an open courtyard full of scraggly bushes and dead weeds to cross, which would leave her exposed.

She took a deep breath and raised her gun. Slowly she moved her way through.

Nothing came out. Nothing fired at her. Most of the

way across the courtyard, she stepped to the side to avoid a bush that still had some small dead berries hanging from it.

She froze. Nightshade. She'd found Ellen's nightshade.

She still didn't know why it'd been worth killing her, but here it was.

But she didn't have time to figure it out. The trolls could be in a tunnel. And there had to be a tunnel. It was the only thing that made sense. The river attacks were a feint. The tunnel was the real attack.

It had to be.

She put her back to the wall and eased up to the edge. She couldn't hear anything. Slowly, she peeked around the corner.

The gray ghost of a young girl sat on the blood-stained step. The ghost's hair hung in braids, making her look quite young. She wore a winter dress and short boots and seemed to be staring out at the street. But then her head turned and her eyes went wide.

She'd seen Beth.

Beth scanned the area and didn't see anything else of note. She stepped out into full view of the ghost and lowered her gun.

"You must be Laura," Beth said.

The ghost nodded and its mouth moved. Beth held up an open hand.

"Stop. I can't hear you, only see you."

The ghost pursed its lips in a frown.

"I need to stop the trolls," Beth continued, "and the wights. Can you help?"

The ghost tilted its head and regarded her. Then it put its hands on its hips and stared at the building for a moment before turning back to Beth.

"Is there a wight in there?" Beth asked. "Nod or shake your head."

The ghost nodded. Then it held up two fingers.

Beth's chest tightened. One was bad enough, but two?

"Do you know where they are?" she asked.

The ghost pointed at the doorway beyond her. Then it grimaced and shrugged its shoulders.

Beth looked closer at the ghost. Laura had been a plain girl in life. She had a pointed nose and sallow cheeks. Her messy hair had mostly escaped her loose braids. She wore a heavy wool dress, which reminded Beth it'd been only a month or so since her death.

But before she could consider anything further, the ghost gestured for her to approach. Beth took a few steps and scanned left, right, and up toward the roof as she did. She saw nothing out of the ordinary.

The ghost led her to the doorway and then waited. It looked back at her and made sure it had her attention. Then it disappeared inside.

Beth paused at the entryway. She couldn't see a thing in the pitch black. Not enough moonlight made it in, and she couldn't even see a hint of the ghost. She kicked herself for not bringing a lamp.

Then she remembered she'd kept some of the matches after she'd explored the basement with the boys. She holstered her gun and poked around until she found one in her waist pouch.

When she struck it, the flames illuminated a small room that seemed completely empty. It'd probably been a small storefront or cloakroom. The ghost stood at the far side, though, with its arm halfway through a wooden wall. It looked back at her and gestured with its free hand.

"Is that a door?" Beth asked.

The ghost nodded.

And then the match blew out.

With a grumble that was almost a curse, Beth struck another. She didn't have many left.

When the new match flared up, Beth quickly studied the floor. She was going to have to move fast—

She paused. Even if she made it to the shadowed door, she'd still end up stuck in the dark with wights around. This was a bad idea.

She needed a lamp. Or a torch.

The match died with the ghost still gesturing her forward.

She backed up a few steps up and looked around. Given the light snow of the recent days, all the wood she could see was wet.

She didn't see a way in. She rolled her eyes at the irony. She wasn't being held back by a wall, a door, or even an enemy. She was being held back by the dark.

Still, the ghost wanted her to see something.

Beth lit another match. The ghost still stood at the wall. Once again, it gestured for her to come forward.

"Come out," Beth said. "I don't have enough matches to go in there. Come out so we can talk where I can see you."

The ghost paused.

"Come out!" Beth gestured to the ghost.

Then the match's flame died.

Beth took several steps back from the doorway. If there were wights nearby, they could've heard her. She drew her gun and backed up a little further.

She watched the door and waited. As she did, she strained to listen. Other than the sound of her own breathing, she heard nothing.

And then... footsteps. But not from the door. From around the corner of the building.

She turned just as a wight burst into view.

TWENTY-NINE

THE WIGHT MOVED FAST despite a hitch in its step. One arm hung low, like it was broken. Otherwise, in the low moonlight, the wight almost looked human. It just didn't move like one.

Beth fired when it was twenty feet away. It stumbled as the bullet tore through it, but then kept coming. She aimed more carefully and put her second shot through its skull.

The wight didn't stop.

Beth turned and ran.

She sprinted east, down the middle of the open street. The rough ground was easier to see. After a hundred yards, she turned.

The wight hadn't been able to keep up, but it was still coming. It was now about thirty yards behind her.

She took long, deep, steadying breaths. She raised her gun and held it with both hands. She aimed for the middle of its pelvic bone where she'd seen red thread anchors on the other wights.

She fired.

It jerked and fell, but her shot wasn't on target. Slowly,

it rose to its knees. But then it paused and just stared at her.

No. Stared *past* her.

She spun and dropped just as the gunshot rang out. The bullet brushed her shoulder, but didn't pierce flesh. She rolled and popped back to her feet as a second shot rang out. That one missed by a wider mark.

She spotted a dark shape—man-sized—down the road. She shot once and dropped to the ground again.

The shape cursed—definitely a man's deep voice. The wight now stood again.

Beth scrambled up and ran for the nearest ruins. The human's gun barked but the bullet missed her. She scrambled over a low broken wall and landed with a thud on the scrabble on the other side. She banged her shin on a large brick and grimaced. Then she turned and peeked back over the wall.

The wight shambled toward her. It didn't run this time —more of a steady walk. The man had disappeared.

Was it Chalmers? Or someone else? Where'd he gone?

To encircle her, she realized.

Beth immediately ducked and scrambled sideways, down the length of the wall. She kept completely under cover until she was more than ten feet from where she'd originally hopped the wall.

She poked her head up. The wight still ambled forward, though toward where she'd gone rather than where she was. She didn't see the man. She ducked back down and quickly reloaded.

When she looked again, the wight was nearly at the ruined wall. The man remained missing, but she was out of time. She shifted to her knees, raised her gun, and steadied it. She was close enough to aim for the wight's chest.

She fired.

A second shot immediately echoed hers. A bullet smacked into the top of the wall, showering brick shards all around her as she ducked.

She dropped to the ground and then scuttled on her hands and knees another five feet. She was running out of wall, though. With a deep breath, she shifted to a crouch, and then ran toward a gaping doorway in another smashed wall, away from the road.

No gunshots.

Rubble filled the far side of the doorway. She scrambled over it and bumped her knee as she did, but bit her lip to avoid crying out. Free of the ruin, she ran north for about a block before ducking into the shadows of an old destroyed house. There, she paused to catch her breath.

She'd found the correct spot, all right. The tunnel entrance had to be there, inside the building, if both wights and a human were guarding the place.

She reloaded again. She was only down one bullet, but better reload now than need one more bullet later. Then she turned and headed west. Best to circle around the brewery and make it harder for the gunman or wight to spot her.

Still... she was sure she didn't have much time.

She jogged around the brewery in a large circle while always watching where the wight had been. She didn't see it or the human. When she figured she was about due south of the brewery, she slowed to a walk. Maybe the brewery had a back door. She slowly picked her way through the fallen masonry and tall dead weeds until she reached the brewery back wall. Sure enough, there was a doorway. The door itself was gone, revealing only blackness beyond.

She walked up quietly. With her gun out, she slid against the wall next to the doorway. Then she edged over to the opening and peeked around.

She couldn't see a thing. Not even the far walls, if there was indeed a room there.

She sucked in her breath. Did she want to walk in, and look for the tunnel, with the wight and the gunman still around and chasing her?

Finding them first would be smarter. It'd make it easier to avoid them.

But she didn't want them coming out this entrance and getting behind her. The wights didn't seem to have any problem with the dark.

She glanced around for a board or a long stick that she could use as a makeshift tripwire. Nothing. She cursed quietly in frustration. The gleaners had been too efficient at scavenging wood.

But there were plenty of rocks around. She found a few and scattered them across the doorway. Hopefully if something came out the doorway, it'd at least kick one and give her some warning.

Then she started working her way east along the brewery's back wall. When she reached the end, she knelt and brought her gun up. Then she peeked around the edge.

Nothing. Not a thing was moving. She waited and listened as hard as she could. Still nothing.

She slowly turned the corner to the east side of the building and hurried north to the next corner. Now she had a good view of the street where the gunman and wight had attacked her before, but they were gone. She couldn't see them anywhere.

She looked again, more carefully this time.

Nothing.

No, not nothing. There were two gray figures by the doorway where she'd met Laura's ghost. The first and brighter one stood in the center under the overhang where Laura had died. At this distance, it had the height and slimness of the girl. Beth couldn't make out its features.

The second, dimmer gray figure stood a few feet away from the first. It nestled against the wall in the deep shadows. It didn't actually look complete. The glow came from where the head and hands would be, with spots here and there for the rest of the body. Combined, the spots were clearly human shaped.

The wight. It had to be. If it'd been human, there'd have been no way for her to see it. It had to be a trap.

So if the wight was some sort of sentry, the man was likely inside.

Beth briefly considered chancing the back door, but remembered the ghost's raised fingers. There were two wights. The second one was unaccounted for.

She needed to get rid of the one in front of her. But how?

It had its back to the wall, which meant she couldn't sneak up on it. She could circle around and get closer to it before she had to break cover, but she wasn't sure that was a good idea. If it was a sentry, it surely had a way to warn the gunman and maybe the other wight. Besides, while it hadn't had anything it could throw at her before, it certainly could now, like the first wight back at the express station had done.

Her shoulder twinged at the memory of the axe flying through the air. She resisted rubbing it, but then paused.

When she'd been wounded in Yellowstone, she'd been on the roof and the dwarf had climbed up behind her.

Up.

She looked above the wight. The wall broke off into crumbled spires on the second floor, which looked like it'd been largely wrecked. The porch overhang remained completely intact. If she could get up there…

She backed away from the edge and checked the brick wall. Any potential handholds were too high to reach. She went around to the back, where the wall remained smooth. When she arrived at the back door, she paused.

If the brewery was anything like the Astor or any of the two-story buildings back in Golden City, it'd have a stairwell near the back door.

She took a deep breath. It'd be dangerous, but entering that back dark room now seemed like the best choice. She felt into her pocket. She had two matches left. She took one out struck it.

She steeled herself as the match sparked into flame. Nothing leapt out at her.

Instead, the dark revealed a small room with a doorway on the far wall and— yes!—wooden stairs leading up to the left. They ran straight, with an iron railing. The first step had been broken off but that was it—apparently stealing them for the wood had been more work that it was worth.

She quickly glanced around the room and spotted nothing else. Whatever it had contained had been removed long ago.

The match burned down to her fingers and she had to shake it out.

Beth carefully stepped into the blackness.

In the complete darkness, she made her way by feel. She moved slowly, casting about, until her hand hit the iron railing. She shuffled her feet until her shin hit the now-bottom step. She bit her lip as the pain briefly lanced through her. Then she shook it off and started to climb.

She took each step slowly, letting her toes drag up the side until she found the top of the next step. She listened for movement after each step but didn't hear anything.

Finally, finally, she spotted faint light above. Well,

"less dark" was a better description. She guessed it was moonlight from its diffuse grayness. A few more steps and she was sure. The stairs ended on a landing with two walls and half the roof missing. When she reached it, she peered out over what had once been the second floor.

The remains of crumbled walls stood on two sides—the north and west. Dark patches scattered here and there in the floor hinted of gaping holes. Above was just the moon and stars.

She listened carefully. Still nothing. She slowly stole forward, toward where the porch overhang had to be. When she passed a large hole, she looked down, but couldn't see anything other than blackness. She paused frequently so that her steps wouldn't be obvious to anyone listening below, but the floorboards still creaked at times. She briefly wondered if they'd rotted in the weather, but it was too late to do much about that except hope for the best.

Once she reached the porch overhang, she knelt down. She listened again. Still nothing. Then she inched forward until she could look over the edge.

She spotted the glow of the wight below and off to the left. She couldn't see Laura, and so guessed she must be on the porch proper, underneath Beth. She listened for movement, but didn't hear any. The wight remained still as well.

Beth slowly and carefully brought her gun up. She grimaced. She could see the red thread at the base of its skull, but not the ones lower down. The angle was wrong. She looked over at the roof above the ghost. Dark holes. It wouldn't support her weight.

She turned back to the wight. Maybe, if she was lucky, destroying the skull would be enough to immobilize it. She doubted it, but... what else could she do? She carefully sighted down her barrel.

And fired.

The gunshot echoed off the nearby walls as the wight's skull exploded. The wight staggered and turned, looking this way and that. Enough flesh had fallen away that she could now make out its ghost face—an angry young man with a bushy beard. It took a few steps forward and peered to its left, toward the corner of the building.

Which exposed the red threads in its arms. She aimed at the node in its right shoulder and fired again.

This time the wight stumbled forward, but then turned and stared up. Its right arm hung uselessly by its side. It raised its left hand in a fist when it spotted her.

"Where is she?" Chalmers's voice. Directly below her through the porch roof.

The wight pointed at her.

She fired at the node in its left shoulder. The wight staggered again.

Another shot rang out, below her, accompanied by a loud smashing sound from the wood to her right and splinters flying through the air.

Oh God, Chalmers was shooting through the roof!

She scrambled left and moved off the little porch area as a second shot tore into the wood. It didn't come close to her, and she couldn't tell if it'd made it all the way through. It could if the wood was thin enough—Hickok has once shown her that with some scrap boards. She scrambled to the side and backed further away from the edge.

He didn't fire a third time. Instead, she climbed to her feet, her heart beating furiously.

"You can't win, you know," Chalmers called out. "And all you're doing is making me mad."

She held still and tried to guess where he stood so she could shoot back.

"Just give up," he called again. "I'll let you live if you do. And if you don't…"

She forced her breathing to steady. She still couldn't tell where he was standing. She didn't see the point in blind shooting. She slowly shifted her weight, and breathed a little easier when the board she was standing on didn't creak.

"Give up!" His voice was louder. "You don't want to make me mad. There are things worse than death!"

Like becoming a wight. She bit back the urge to argue with him and quietly stepped toward the stairs.

Chalmers stayed quiet.

Beth slowly stole along the roof and took care with every step. No rhythm. If a board started to creak, she stepped ahead or behind it. She focused on listening as much as moving.

And then she heard a muffled thump from the stairwell. Like someone or something banging into something.

The broken step. Someone had run into the broken step.

Someone, or some thing, was coming up the stairs.

THIRTY

THE DARK NIGHT suddenly felt cold. Beth glanced around—there wasn't any good cover on this broken second floor. She was about ten feet from the porch over-hang and a good thirty feet from the western edge. With the scattered holes in the floor, she didn't think she could make a run for either.

So she had to make a stand.

She shifted to the side so whoever was coming up the stairs wouldn't see her immediately, and then raised her gun. She kept it pointed at the stairs and forced herself to calm her breath as she waited.

More bumps. More creaks. Whoever was coming up the stairs wasn't making an effort to be quiet.

"Hey!" Chalmers called again, still from the porch area. "You gonna surrender or not?"

She cocked her gun as a dark shape came into view up the steps. While mostly dark, it glowed gray around the head and hands.

Another wight. She didn't have a good shot at its head or legs, so she aimed for the pelvis and pulled the trigger.

The wight wobbled as the bullet slammed home. She fired a second shot into the same spot, but the wight just turned her way and reached for something at its waist.

She dropped to the floor just before something went whizzing overhead. A knife she guessed. She rose up just enough to fire again. Whether she missed or hit, she couldn't tell.

The wight started walking her way.

She scuttled back and then stood. A loud shot rang out from below, followed by the crackle of wood as the bullet smashed into the floor to one side of her. She couldn't help skittering away.

The wight kept coming. She quickly shifted so that one of the larger holes was between them. It paused, staring at her.

She raised her Colt and fired. The bullet smashed into its skull. She saw a trace of red lower down, so she fired again at its torso. To her shock, the wight collapsed. It dropped to its knees and then its face. One arm hung off the edge into the hole.

She quickly dashed around the hole, holstering her empty pistol as she did. The wight still moved, trying to get to its feet, but its head and most of its guts were missing. The ghost within couldn't lift the rotted body. She knelt and shoved it forward.

It started to fall.

Then it lashed back with one arm.

She lurched back, but it wasn't trying to grab her. Another knife slashed across the back of her left hand as the wight tumbled through the hole.

She pressed down on her left hand with her right. Pain seared from the cut, but she could wiggle her fingers. Blood still poured freely. She took a break to fumble for a handkerchief and pressed it on the wound. As she did, she glanced down into the hole. All was dark—she didn't see any gray.

Light flickered behind her. She swiveled just in time to see Chalmers emerge from the stairs. In one hand, he held a lantern. In the other, a Colt, which he leveled at her.

"Well, well," he chuckled and lowered his gun. "If it isn't Miss Armstrong. And all along, I thought Hickok'd be the problem."

"He'll be coming for you," she snapped.

"No... no, I'm quite sure he won't."

She turned so she could see his face. Despite the flickering shadows from the lamp, she could see enough of his cold, narrow eyes to wonder how Hickok had ever considered this man a coward.

"I suppose you're working with the trolls." She edged a bit closer to the hole as she continued to hold her wounded hand. "Using your pet wights to help them."

He laughed. "I have no need to tell you all of my secrets." He nodded his chin toward her hand. "At least not yet. In three days, maybe. After you've turned."

"That's in three days."

His muscles were tense. His shoulders tight. His eyes narrowed further.

She tensed, preparing to spring.

"Nothing says you have to be *alive* for those three days," he snarled. He raised the gun again.

She jumped down the hole.

The shot passed over her head. She kept her feet under her as she fell but landed on something uneven and tumbled to her side. She tucked her head and half-rolled, half-flopped until she banged hard into the wood floor. She scrambled up to her knees and tried to ignore the new pain in her shoulder and hip.

What she'd landed on writhed. She looked closer in the

dim moonlight and realized she'd dropped onto the wight. There was gray there—how she missed it before, she didn't know. It wasn't crawling toward her though—just moving its arms.

The boards above her creaked.

Beth scrambled backwards, away from the hole. Blood from her left hand smeared everything and she clamped her right back over the cut.

Chalmers's footsteps stopped. Light from his lantern played through the hole. When it illuminated the wight, Beth's stomach turned. The wight's broken spine jutted out from its back.

"You alive, Miss Armstrong?" Chalmers called.

She held as still as possible.

"Well, if you are, it's just for a little while. You didn't have to be so much trouble, you know? You could've done just fine when we take over."

She tried to quiet her breathing.

"'Course, you are a bit skinny for my tastes. Rose is more what I like. But there's men that wouldn't mind you. Not at all."

The rage welled up in her gut, but she held still. The cut on her hand still throbbed and she focused on that rather than his voice.

"Enjoy the last few minutes of your life, Miss Armstrong. I've got things to do."

The boards creaked as he walked away from the hole and the lantern light faded. After a dozen breaths, Beth was plunged into near darkness again. Only the gray glow of the wight gave her any light, and it wasn't enough to do much.

Still, it was a start. She listened for a bit longer. When she heard nothing beyond the wight's useless clawing at the floor, she quickly pulled a second handkerchief from her pocket and used it tie the first to her hand in a makeshift bandage. As she did, she mentally thanked Rose for insisting that "a lady" should always carry two, so that one was always clean.

Also, thankfully, the bleeding had slowed. She wiggled her fingers again, which hurt, but they moved. She'd most likely be able to use her hand again, unless it'd been badly poisoned.

Her heart skipped at that thought, but then she shook her wrist until she felt the silver bracelet against her skin. She smiled at Rose's preparedness.

The wight slid on the floor. It'd managed to lift its torso off the ground and was pulling itself along with its hands. Fortunately, she was closer to its feet and it had to turn around before it'd be able to reach her.

She desperately wished for a good hunting knife. Shooting the remaining red tie points would be too loud and she wasn't sure she could hit them all anyway. She didn't like leaving it, well, "alive" wasn't quite the right word. Leaving it a threat. Even if it wasn't very mobile, it was still a threat.

Her hand throbbed. The pain spiked every time she rotated her wrist. Maybe her injury wasn't as clean as she'd thought.

She needed to get out of the room. But which way?

The gray light from the wight didn't illuminate the walls well enough for her to make out anything more than dark or really dark patches. It was too bad she couldn't "turn him up" —

—maybe she could.

First, though, she needed to reload.

She scooted away from the wight until her back touched a wall. The she pulled her Colt from its holster and set it in her lap. Her bullet pouch was on her left hip and her left hand flared with pain as she fumbled with the clasp. She gave up and reached across with her right.

Loading all the chambers one-handed took agonizingly long, but if she kept the fingers of her left hand bunched together and slightly curled, she could ignore the pain. After she managed to get the first two bullets in, she pulled the makeshift bandage up slightly over her knuckles. She briefly wondered what she could use to tie her fingers together, but nothing came to mind.

One bullet dropped on the floor. Thankfully, it made no noise—or at least nothing louder than the clawing and scrapes of the wight. The monster had managed to turn itself about a quarter of the way around.

Finally, finally, she had the gun loaded. She holstered it and felt around on the ground for small rocks, broken bricks, or dirt clumps. When she had a handful, she pushed herself to her feet and looked the wight over again.

Its torso was a mess of broken flesh and bone. The rotted flesh looked more like slaughtered meat than a human body. The legs barely moved as it twisted around, trying to reach her. Most of the skull was missing. The ghost's face that showed through glared at her. Another young soldier, from the cut of his mustache and the sallowness of his cheeks.

She threw the handful of debris into its face.

The ghost flashed white as the debris passed through it or bounced off of what remained of its skull. Then its eyes flashed and it silently yelled at her before raising one fist and shaking it. But as it did, it remained bright.

It worked. Angry ghosts turned white.

Now she could see the red threads that bound it to its body more clearly. The nodes in its pelvis and the base of its skull were severed. The shoulders remained, though those would be hard to reach. She still needed a knife.

She knelt and picked up another handful of debris. Then she surveyed the walls of her little room. The west wall was completely gone and opened up into another dark space. Rubble blocked the bottom of an open doorway to the south. The east was solid to the ceiling. She had her back against the north wall, which had a dark opening to her right, the size of a door.

So north it was.

She edged her way to the opening while watching the wight the entire time. When she peeked around the corner, she let out a soft sigh. The next room was missing enough ceiling for the moonlight to illuminate the floor. Even better, most of the west wall lay in rubble. She could make out more moonlight beyond.

The wight scrabbled a bit more behind her. It still glared at her and still glowed white hot. She briefly considered saying something, but caught herself. Chalmers was still around, as well as the first wight.

So instead, she gave the wight a casual salute and stepped through the doorway.

This new room was much like the last, but with more fallen bricks and broken boards. She picked her way through it to the gaping hole in the west wall. A light cold breeze brushed her face as she peered out into the little yard with all the tall dead weeds. Nothing else moved.

She surveyed the hole. With a little bit of care, she could climb through, back to the outside. The trick was doing so without using her left hand. It still throbbed, though she'd managed to keep her fingers pretty still. She tucked it into her chest just in case and started to squirm through the gaps in the brick.

She only banged her elbow once before she managed to drop to the ground on the other side. She landed in a cluster of old dead vines with some berries on them. The leaves stung when they slapped across her wrist. She got to her feet and looked at them.

More nightshade. It had to be. Dead or dormant from the winter cold, but alive just a few months ago. Only a few of the poisonous berries remained, frozen and misshapen after having over-ripened in the fall. Some of the plants had been stripped, though, as if the berries had been harvested.

Of course. They'd killed Ellen because she'd found this patch, either for the nightshade itself or its location next to the tunnel. But this was it.

Her hand itched. Was there nightshade in whatever had coated the wight's knife?

His knife! She mentally kicked herself. She hadn't spotted it in the room with him, but it had to be there. If she found it, she could sever the last of the red nodes!

But that wight wasn't going anywhere. She needed to find the other one. Before it found her.

THIRTY-ONE

BETH CHECKED herself for other wounds besides her hand. Various bruises from her fall ached, particularly one shoulder. She had some scratches here and there, but nothing serious. The cut on her hand had stopped bleeding, though it still stung.

She took a deep breath of the cold, crisp air. For a moment, she considered running for reinforcements, but then she caught herself. If there was a tunnel, the trolls had to be at least halfway through it by now. If she could block it up before they emerged, she had a chance—after that, it'd be too late.

So she steeled herself and strode back toward the brewery.

When she reached the corner near the porch, she paused and listened carefully. She couldn't hear the wight around the corner, but it had to be there. Instead, she heard... low booms, like thunder. Coming from the river.

Oh, God! Cannons! The trolls were crossing!

Which meant they had to be in the tunnels too!

She took a deep breath, knelt down, drew her gun, and peeked around the corner.

She blinked from the blazing white light. Laura stood on the porch a few feet from the wight. The ghost glowed furiously and had her hands on her hips. Her mouth moved, her anger directed at the wight.

The wight leaned against the wall, turned three quarters away from Beth, and stared at Laura. Its skull was missing—apparently her earlier shot had been on target. The ghost within the wight didn't wear the military cap as so many of the others did. From the ragged hair, she took it for a gleaner. Most of the body showed deep rot. The right part of its torso was a particular mess. That was probably where she'd shot it the first time. Too bad she hadn't severed the spine.

Could she do that?

It'd be a very difficult shot, and she wasn't sure she'd get more than one.

She'd have an easier time taking out its knees. She'd still need a bit of luck, especially since she couldn't steady her grip with her left hand, but it was her best bet.

She studied the wight a bit more. It remained distracted by Laura and occasionally held up a long knife in its left hand. The right arm hung slack and Beth couldn't see a red node in it. Strips of decayed muscle had fallen off the right leg, leaving part of the bone above the knee looking white against the dark flesh.

Beth raised her Colt and steadied herself against the wall. She took careful aim at the knee...

...and fired.

The shot echoed off the building as the wight collapsed. Beth jogged forward.

Laura stared at her, mouth open and eyes wide.

"Hold him down!" Beth urged. She spotted the wight's knife in the dirt where he'd dropped it.

The ghost looked confused. Meanwhile, the wight tried to push itself up with its hands.

"Hold him!" Beth kicked the knife away before the wight could grab it.

The ghost furrowed its brow. After Beth pointed at the wight, the ghost took a few steps forward and then shoved down on the wight's ghostly head. It clawed up at the ghost's arms and Laura pulled back.

Still, it was enough to let Beth pick up the knife. She took care not to touch the blade, and then moved behind the wight, which had managed to rise to its left knee.

"Again!" Beth called to Laura.

Laura blinked and hesitantly stepped closer to the wight. It grabbed for the ghost again. Beth rushed in and stabbed the node in its left shoulder. The wight whirled wildly, but Beth had already danced away.

She'd severed the node! Now the left arm hung limply by its side.

"Push it to the ground!" Beth said.

To her credit, Laura quickly nodded and did so. She knocked the wight forward and sat on its back.

Pinned by the ghost, the wight wiggled on the ground like a stuck bug. Beth stabbed the nodes in its legs. She cut a few smaller nodes before stepping back and looking it over. While the wight still tried to move, the only remaining large node was its heart.

"Don't move," Beth said. "I'm going to go through you." She knelt by the wight's side and plunged the knife into its back. As her arm passed through Laura, the cold shocked her flesh, even through the sleeve of her coat.

And then it was over. The last of the red threads unraveled. A small gray disk appeared and then the wight's soul floated up and into it. Beth watched until the portal faded away.

Laura watched it go as well. Her eyes were wide, like she was about to cry, before her face tightened with resolve.

"He's better off," Beth said.

Laura nodded, and then slowly began to fade to a duller gray.

"No!" Beth cried. "Stay angry!"

The ghost tilted her head and regarded Beth.

"When you're angry, you shine and I can see. Think about the evil that Chalmers has done, and then show me what you wanted me to see before."

Laura furrowed her brow. Then her eyes narrowed. The gray color fled as white took over. She turned and floated back into the old brewery.

This time, Beth could clearly see the full, bare room. Pits and gouges scarred the wooden floor and scrapes covered the walls, but they were solid and strong. A gaping door stood open at the spot where the ghost had previously pointed. Beth didn't have to guess where Chalmers had gone.

"Is that the tunnel?" Beth asked.

Laura frowned and then held out her hand, palm down, before waggling it in a so-so gesture.

"Oh, it's sort of the entrance to the tunnel," Beth said.

The ghost nodded.

"The entrance is through there, but that's not all that's through there."

The ghost nodded more vigorously.

"Anything dangerous?"

Laura furrowed her brow, and then slowly shook her

head. Then she turned and floated toward the open doorway.

"Wait." Never leave an enemy behind you. So where exactly had she left the other wight? Beth tried to figure out the layout of the brewery. She thought she could get to the other wight by going through this door, but wasn't sure.

"There's another wight," she told Laura. "It can't move, but it's somewhere in there." She pointed in the correct general direction. "I need you to lead me to it so we can release it."

The ghost nodded, and then floated through the wall.

Beth caught her breath as darkness filled the room once again. Moving by feel, she reloaded her Colt. She ran her fingers over the bullets in her ammunition pouch as she did. She had two dozen left, more or less. She took another deep breath and stilled her nerves as she waited.

After a few long minutes, the room brightened as Laura floated back through a wall. She went toward the doorway and gestured for Beth to follow.

The wight was only two rooms away. It had pulled itself a few feet closer to the doorway Beth had left through, but that was all. It glared at her as it rose up on the ends of its arms.

"I'm sorry this happened to you," Beth said, "But I'm going to release you."

The wight swiped at her, but its clawed hands didn't come close enough for her to even jump.

Beth turned to Laura. "Can you hold this one down, too?"

The ghost's eyes went wide and she swallowed. She started to float toward the wight, which then tried to grab her. Laura skittered back.

"Go up." Beth gestured with her hand. "You're not bound by gravity. Float up!"

Laura did a double-take. Then she grinned. She flapped her arms and rose several feet in the air. Then she drifted above the wight and sank back down. When her feet touched the wight, Laura's "weight" shoved the wight flat to the ground.

Beth drew her captured knife. With the wight immobilized, she made quick work of cutting its red nodes. When she'd finally cut the last one, she stepped back. A gray circle opened as she'd expected and the wight's soul passed through.

Laura held her hands together as if in prayer. She stared at the fading circle, her eyes full of longing, until it faded.

"You want to pass on, don't you?" Beth asked quietly.

The ghost nodded. She looked like she was about to cry.

"Then show me what's keeping you here."

Beth's skin prickled as much with nerves as from the cold. Laura led her back one room and then toward a hole in the wall blocked with fallen rotted boards. At first, it looked like they made the hole impassable. When she reached them, though, she realized they were too orderly to be debris. Also, the ceiling above remained intact. She gently moved them aside as Laura hovered nearby. When she could step next to the hole, the ghost floated into the room beyond.

She'd found the brewing room. Smashed barrels and the remains of what had to be fermenting tanks lined the far wall. Two large copper pots sat in the middle—obviously too large and heavy to move. Beth guessed they'd once been used for brewing beer. Laura floated to the nearest and pointed into it.

Beth shifted the boards a bit further so she could climb through the hole. Her left hand twinged and ached as she did. Actually, it felt more numb than painful.

That didn't seem like a good sign.

Despite the numbness, she managed to scramble through the hole without giving herself any new scrapes. She headed to the pot and peeked inside.

A thin layer of colored ice filled the bottom of the pot. It looked almost black with a bluish tint. Two large stirring spoons rested inside, their handles on the edge and the tips encased in the ice.

She looked at the ghost. "What is this?"

Laura held one fist up and made a slashing motion through the air. She repeated the motion a few times and then pointed at Beth's hand.

"Ah. This is the poison that makes the wights."

The ghost nodded.

"So what do you want me to do?"

Laura said several things but Beth shook her head in confusion. Then the ghost clenched her fists and stamped a foot in frustration. Which amused Beth since it was floating a foot above the ground.

"Write it in the air with your finger," Beth suggested.

Laura looked at her in surprise, but then smiled. She started tracing letters in the air with big strokes.

"D...," Beth said. "E... S... T... R... O... Destroy it. You want me to destroy it."

The ghost nodded vigorously and bounced up and down.

"Okay. But how?"

The ghost started tracing her finger in the air again. B... U... R... N...

"Burn it," Beth finished. She wasn't sure how the ghost knew that, but it made sense. How else could they completely destroy a liquid?

She glanced around. The rotted wood that had blocked the hole was cold, but dry. It might catch. She could certainly throw it in the kettle and use one of her last matches...

But would it be enough? She didn't have any tinder, which she really needed.

"Is it flammable?" Beth asked.

Laura shrugged, but then she pointed to something on the floor on the far side of the pot. Beth hurried around and almost laughed in delight.

An oil lamp. Chalmers had left an oil lamp in his poison-making room. Even better, it looked full.

"I'll destroy it," Beth said. "But will you stay around until we stop Chalmers? Otherwise he'll just make more."

Laura frowned, but then slowly nodded.

Beth wrestled the dry wood into the kettle. It cracked the ice, and black goo oozed out. It was a thick sludge, so she hoped it'd burn rather than just extinguish the flame.

Once she had the last of the wood piled into the kettle, she doused it with half of the oil from the lamp. She set the lamp down and pulled out one of her last matches. She exchanged a grim look with Laura.

"Let's hope this works," Beth murmured.

She struck the match and dropped it on top of the oil soaked wood.

The flame caught, and quickly spread. When it reached the poison, the black ooze sizzled. After a moment, enough of the wood had caught for Beth to let out the breath she'd been holding.

Then she heard the distant rumble of cannons. They didn't have much time.

"We can let this burn," she said. "We need to find Chalmers. So which way'd he go? Where's the tunnel?"

Laura pointed back into the main room, through the hole. Beth grimaced. She rubbed her left hand as best as she could without disturbing the bandage. The numbness wasn't much worse, thankfully.

She briefly considered lighting the lamp, but paused. The lamp would give her position away. The white ghost would not. She decided to keep the lamp in reserve.

She set the oil lamp down on the far side of the hole in the wall. Then, with a deep breath, she climbed through. As she did, she put a little weight on her bad hand and pain shot up her arm. Once she was through the opening, she shook it out. Now her forearm hurt as well.

Below the bracelet.

She sucked in her breath. Then she gestured to Laura.

"Come here," Beth said. "I need to see." She slowly peeled the bandage back.

The wound was raw, but didn't bleed. The scratch was longer than she'd thought but thankfully not deep. She hadn't cleaned it well, as it looked both red and black in the low light.

No... the red was more than blood. The soul-tying scarlet threads were forming, anchored to her wrist, just above the silver bracelet. None of them extended past it.

So why was she in pain beyond the bracelet?

She took stock of her body. She was breathing hard, harder than she expected. Her pulse pounded.

The nightshade poison—the bracelet wouldn't stop it. She'd never heard of an antidote, so all she could do was hope she hadn't gotten much. But the wrist... she looked more closely.

Some of the red threads had snaked past the bracelet and up her arm.

Whatever the second half of the poison was, the soul-trapping part, it wasn't completely stopped by the bracelet.

Her heart pounded. How long until the nightshade killed her and she turned into a wight herself?

THIRTY-TWO

A CHILL SWEPT THROUGH BETH. She stood in the small room with the hard stone under her feet, the white light from the ghost flickering off her skin. As her mind raced, she was sure her pulse was fading, though it felt strong. Maybe her breathing was off?

She forced herself to take several deep, calming breaths. Panic wouldn't solve anything. She needed to get the threads out.

She grimaced. She knew how to do that.

"I need your help," she said to Laura. "I need to cut the spot where these threads are attached. There should be one in my wrist."

Laura furrowed her brow.

"I... I can't see into my own flesh to see where it attaches. But you can. You can touch my soul but pass through my skin."

The ghost's eyes widened and she shook her head wildly while waving her hands.

"What?"

It wasn't hard to read the ghost's lips: No, no, no, no.

"If I cut the binding point," Beth said, "I won't become a wight."

Laura paused and then raise a single finger. She started tracing letters in the air. Beth repeated them out loud to make sure she got them.

"C...u...t...t...i...n...g..."

Laura paused and then nodded.

"Cutting." Beth watched as the ghost started again. "Separates..."

The ghost shook her head up and down before she continued.

"soul....from....body..."

Laura stopped and Beth's jaw dropped.

"If I cut it," Beth said, "I'll separate my soul from my body?"

The ghost held her hand flat and then rocked it back and forth.

"Sort of," Beth interpreted. "If I cut the node, I'll separate my soul from part of my body."

Laura nodded again.

It made sense, Beth realized. At death, a person's soul detached from their body. The nightshade poison killed the person. The wight poison, whatever was in it, stopped the soul from departing...

...and she was very glad there were more nodes than just the one in her wrist.

But that didn't fix things.

"So how do I stop the poison?" she asked. "The wight poison." The nightshade part, she'd just have to endure and hope she'd gotten too little in the scratch to kill her.

Laura pointed to the bracelet, and then to the one on her other wrist. The ghost mimed moving them together.

Beth grimaced. If she wrapped the two silver chain bracelets together, there wouldn't be the gaps between them and her skin. But it also meant her right hand wouldn't be protected.

But if she lost her right hand, she wouldn't be able to shoot so she'd be dead anyway. She fumbled with the bracelets until both were wrapped tightly around her left wrist. Her left hand was going to be worthless for a while, and maybe forever, but she could live with that if she didn't become a wight.

Now she just had to stop Chalmers.

She waited until the pain had subsided enough to no longer feel faint. Then she turned to Laura once again.

"Let's find the tunnel entrance."

Laura led her south to another room that had to be against the back wall of the brewery, if Beth had her directions right. This room had holes in the ceiling that let in low moonlight, but the ghost's brightness was still her best "lamp." She thought again about turning up the oil lamp, but that'd give her away as much as it'd help her see. Better to save it.

Most of the walls of this room were intact. Only the one on the west where she'd entered lay in shambles. The floor consisted of mostly planks but she could see underlying rock in the gaps between some of them. She stepped carefully around some fallen mortar to where a large wooden hatch had been pushed aside. An iron ladder bolted to the stone wall and disappeared down into the hole below.

Beth sucked in her breath. She'd be defenseless climbing down. But did she have to?

"Is this the only entrance to the tunnel?" she asked Laura.

Laura shrugged.

"Great," Beth muttered. There was no way to tell how many breweries in the area were using the same cave.

"Can you go first?" she asked. "We need to make sure Chalmers isn't lying in wait."

The ghost nodded and floated down into the hole. Beth set the unlit lamp down by the entryway and peered over the edge. She watched as the ghost's light illuminated more and more of the room below. The walls gave way to a largish space, and the ladder ran all the way to a rough cut stone floor.

Beth gasped.

Another wight stood sentry at the bottom of the hole. This one was new—barely decayed at all. The ghostly gray of its soul only peeked out around the hands and face. Its full soldier's uniform looked no more tattered than any soldier's at the Barracks. It stood straight, with a rifle at its side.

And then it looked up, first at Laura.

And then at Beth.

She leveled her Colt at the wight. Out of habit, she clasped it with both hands and then winced with the pain. The wight dove out of sight before she could fire. She shifted her grip to just her right hand and waited.

A deafening shot rang out. She ducked, but the bullet hadn't come close. Instead, Laura flared brighter—almost blindingly bright. Beth scrunched her eyes shut and backed away from the hatch. Then she opened her eyes.

Laura floated at the lip of the hole. She shook her fist and glared down the shaft. The ghost seemed to be shouting things, but for once Beth was glad she couldn't hear. She wondered if the wight had shot at the ghost instead of at her.

Beth slithered forward on her stomach to the edge of

the hole. She couldn't see the wight at all. Three sides of the shaft were visible, which meant the wight had to be hiding under the lip of the fourth. There wasn't a good angle to fire blindly into that corner. She might hit its feet at best. Of course, that meant it couldn't shoot her, either. If she spotted the rifle barrel, she'd know where to shoot.

Laura continued to silently yell and wave her fist as she glared down the hatch. That gave Beth an idea where the wight was, but it didn't change much. Laura might be able to point out the wight's exact position, but the angle was the real problem. There just wasn't a good sight line to where the monster had to be.

The monster. She snorted softly. Just another poor kid murdered by Chalmers with his special poison. From what she remembered, the wight had stood with a slump, much like Ellen's wight had done.

Beth blinked. Ellen hadn't been mad with the desire to kill, like the first two wights. She just wanted release so she could move on. This soldier was a new wight. Maybe he was wearing a silver necklace, too. She knew some Catholic men wore crosses that way. Maybe…

"Hey, Private," Beth called. "We don't have to do this. You don't have to follow Sergeant Chalmers's orders."

She waited, but there was no reply.

"What he's done to you is evil," she said. "Truly evil. Murder is evil, but not to let the victim's soul go on to Heaven…? Truly evil."

She heard a small shuffling from below.

"I can help you move on," Beth called, a bit louder this time. "I can cut the bonds that bind you to this world. That are keeping you from Heaven. From the reward that you deserve. Chalmers won't let you move on, but I can help you."

She paused again, her heart racing. She heard a little more movement, but still didn't see anything.

"I promised Laura I'd help her move on," Beth called again. "I helped Ellen Lemp. You don't have to exist like this. It's just... wrong."

Silence.

"Do you want to serve a man who'd do this to you? Or do you want to go to Heaven?"

Still silence. Though the light had dimmed. Laura looked at her with curiosity and now shone an alabaster white instead of blazing like a small sun.

She took another deep breath. "I'm coming down. Don't shoot me. I'll show you what I can do."

Laura ghost's eyes widened and she turned and started speaking rapidly toward the dark opening. Then she looked back at Beth and nodded.

Beth shifted around so she could put her foot on the ladder. She grimaced. With only one good hand, she was going to have to holster her gun to climb and leave the lamp. She had to hope that she'd gotten through to the wight.

She got one foot on the top rung and paused. No shots rang out. Shakily, she lowered herself another rung. She stiffened, waiting for the bullet, but none came. Two rungs later, she still hadn't been shot. She let out a long breath and concentrated on climbing down while only using her good hand. It wasn't easy—she leaned into the ladder as she shifted her grip—but she made it to the bottom without a fall.

She stepped off the bottom and turned around. The wight hadn't shot her, which she took as a good sign. Even better, he stood with his rifle at his side. Laura had floated down enough for Beth to get a good look at the wight. It actually appeared to be on the edge of tears.

Beyond the wight, the walls opened up into a bigger room. Nothing moved in it, so Beth focused on the former soldier in front of her.

He was short and young, with only a hint of a beard. The flesh on his face had shrunk but not started to rot. He gave her the most plaintive look she'd ever seen, even including some looks from the down-on-their-luck miners begging for food back in Golden City.

She smiled at him. "I'll release you. I promise." She held her hands out to show they were empty.

He slowly nodded.

"I'm… I'm going to have to stab you. I need to cut the red threads that are binding you here. I don't know if it will hurt."

The wight turned to Laura and they exchanged a few words. Then it looked back at Beth and nodded again. It leaned its rifle against the wall and took a step toward her.

She took another deep breath and pulled the previous wight's knife from her belt. Then she turned to Laura.

"You'll have to guide me," Beth said. "I can't see through the flesh that well."

Laura nodded. The ghost moved close to the soldier, speaking softly as she did. The wight held up one hand, fingers wide. Then it moved to the wall and placed its hand against the stone.

"Good thinking," Beth murmured. With the wight's hand braced, it'd be easier to cut the right place. She moved up next to the wight and wrinkled her nose. Only the fact that her nostrils were mostly frozen kept her from gagging on the smell. Still, decaying flesh wasn't the worst thing.

With Laura's guidance, she severed the red node in the wight's left wrist. Then the one in the right. She suggested it lie down on the ground after that. When it did, she spotted that it indeed did wear a small silver cross on a chain around his neck.

She knelt at its side while Laura hovered right above it. To her surprise, the wight remained still as she methodically worked her way through all of the nodes.

"Last one," she told the wight as she held the knife over its chest. It just looked at her, surprisingly calm. As if it was simply waiting.

She plunged the knife in, as hard as she could. She leaned on it to give the blow additional force, since she only was using one hand.

Then she let out a sigh of relief as a gray disk formed a few feet away. She smiled at Laura.

"One soul. On its way." Beth climbed to her feet. "If Chalmers stationed a new wight like him here, that wasn't fully under his control, he must be running out."

Laura pointed up, in the general direction of the vat room.

"Yeah," Beth agreed. "He can always make more."

She looked around the little cellar. The rough stone floor was slightly sloped, with uneven patches here and there that could trip the unwary. Low moonlight spilled in through a dozen melon-sized holes in the planks above, and the air filled with dust that tickled her nose. Three separate passages led off, all generally headed east toward the river. The central one was larger than the other two, but a person could easily enter any of them without stooping or having to turn sideways.

"So," Beth said, "the question is, which way did he go?"

THIRTY-THREE

BETH STUDIED each of the three openings. Laura sensed what she was doing and floated to over to them, standing in the entrances so Beth could see better. The cellar's air was still, without a hint of a breeze that might've otherwise indicated a tunnel or chimney. It was cool, too. Not as cold as it'd been above, but not exactly warm. Nothing Beth could sense told her which passage was the right one.

"Can you go down these?" she asked Laura.

Laura frowned and then floated through the leftmost entry. Beth stilled her heart as all the light went with the ghost and plunged her into complete darkness. When the ghost returned a few minutes later, it shook its head.

"That's not the passage?" Beth asked.

Laura shook her head again. Then she raised a finger and began tracing letters in the air.

"Can... not... go... far..." Beth blinked. "Oh, that's right." Ghosts were anchored to either their body or where they died. "You can't go too far from the porch upstairs."

Laura sadly nodded.

"Was there anything down that way?"

Laura shook her head.

She couldn't go down the tunnels, then. She'd have to wait here. But...

This was where Chalmers had left a sentry. So this was the choke point. There wasn't much debris down here— just a few broken boards from what had once been shelves. But maybe they could suffice.

Unfortunately, she didn't see a good place to put them. Three or four boards wouldn't provide much of a shooting blind themselves, and she was sure they wouldn't stop .45 rounds anyway.

But maybe as an obstacle...

She surveyed the room with a more critical eye. The ladder descended into a little alcove only a few feet wide. That opened up to the larger room with the three tunnels. The wight had been standing in the alcove itself, and its body still lay at the neck between the alcove and the larger room. Standing there herself, she could see a little down the center and right hand tunnels, if the ghost was in the middle of the room. Not so with the left. There wasn't enough broken moonlight making it through the ceiling.

She took the broken boards from the shelves and piled them on the ground at the entrance to the lefthand tunnel. Then she dragged the wight's body next to them. It wasn't much of a tripwire, but maybe it'd slow the trolls down just enough. When she'd finished, she returned to the alcove and crouched along one wall.

"Check the others?" she asked the ghost.

Laura nodded and drifted into the middle passage. Beth took a deep breath as darkness descended once again.

Then she settled in to wait.

Beth moved her fingers to get some of the stiffness out. The ache in her left hand had faded, but her heart seemed to pound harder than it should. Despite the cold, sweat beaded on her brow. She waited for Laura, but before she returned, Beth spotted something else.

Firelight flickered from down the right passageway. She sucked in her breath and leveled her Colt at the entryway.

The light danced along the walls, creating shadows. It grew brighter and bigger and then...

Two of the ugliest things on two legs she'd ever seen marched out of the tunnel.

The trolls—for they had to be trolls—were furry and fuzzy with big floppy ears, pallid gray skin, and fat noses. They wore leather jerkins and the taller one carried a torch. They both looked around.

Before they spotted her, she fired.

The roar of the gun echoed in the closed room, temporarily deafening her. The torchbearer was down— she'd hit him then. She aimed at the shorter one and her bullet caught it in the chest before he could drop to the ground. The torch had rolled to one side, plunging most of the room into deep shadow.

At least until Laura emerged from the center tunnel. Beth smirked. She didn't know if trolls could see in the dark, but now she could. The ghost drifted to a spot halfway between the center and right entrances.

As her ears recovered a bit, Beth heard shouts down the righthand passage. She shifted her stance to cover it and waited. A few minutes later, she spotted movement along the walls. Trolls crept along both sides, staying pressed against the stone.

Beth took a breath and steadied her aim at the one on the right. When he reached the lip of the tunnel, she fired.

Once again, the roar of her shot echoed off the walls. But then it was followed by other shots.

They were shooting back!

Beth flinched and ducked out of habit. She looked up when the gunfire stopped. The one she'd shot was down, but another had taken its place. This one held up a Colt with its fat finger already on the trigger. Both trolls craned their necks as they looked around.

She grimaced and briefly wondered where they'd gotten the guns. Or how they were using them. Private Johnson had said their fingers were too fat.

Oh! So that's what Chalmers had been doing with the blacksmith forge. Cutting off the trigger guards so the fat fingered trolls could use them!

That made things hard. She didn't have enough cover for when they finally spotted her.

She took sight on the one on the right. Then the one on the left. She shifted her hand one more time to make sure her motion was smooth.

Then she fired two quick shots. After the second, she holstered her gun and ran for the ladder.

Climbing *hurt*. Excruciating pain shot through her bad hand every time she curled it around a rung. She fought through it and scrambled up as fast as she could. She made it to the top just before more gunfire erupted below. They were firing wildly, thankfully.

Beth crawled away from the edge of the pit and then shifted to her knees. She fumbled for her ammunition pouch. Fortunately, Hickok had long ago drilled her on reloading in complete darkness. She finished just as Laura floated up the shaft.

"Can you stay at the bottom, please?" Beth quietly asked. "You can point them out to me."

Laura nodded and sank back down. Beth dropped to

her belly and pulled herself forward to the lip of the pit. She propped herself up on her elbows and leveled her gun at the alcove where the wight had hid before.

Now torchlight shone from the direction of the tunnel. Several torches, from the way the shadows danced on the walls and floor below. Laura stood directly below her and pointed in several directions.

Beth waited.

After several dozen heartbeats, she saw a shadow of movement by one wall. Laura pointed at it, and Beth fired. Something yelped and jumped back.

"Miss Armstrong?" Chalmers's voice. "Miss Armstrong, is that you up there?"

Beth held her tongue. Instead, she scanned rapidly from left to right in case Chalmers was trying to distract her while other trolls attacked.

"You can't win, Miss Armstrong. All you're doing is making it harder on yourself."

She bit back a retort.

"Hickok can't save you, you know. Preston took care of him."

Beth's heart jumped, but she caught herself. He'd say that no matter if it was true or not. She cocked her gun, but she still didn't see a thing.

"You can't win," Chalmers repeated. "There's too many of us. All you're doing is making me mad. Which is gonna be bad for you. Bad for you and... Miss Chamberlin."

Beth narrowed her eyes and tried to focus. Rose would be fine. Rose could take care of herself. Beth needed to stop Chalmers here. Now.

"Yes," Chalmers continued. "I'd really hate to do anything to Miss Chamberlin. She'd serve me well. Can you imagine—"

Motion!

Beth fired, ignoring Chalmers's words. Then more movement to the right. She fired again. Then in the middle! They were rushing her!

She fired twice more, now completely deafened by the gunshot echoes. Some of her shots had hit. At least two trolls sprawled on the ground. But the pause didn't last long. Another pair of trolls ran forward toward the ladder. She fired at the one in front and it tumbled into the second. The tangle-up kept either of them from reaching the bottom rung.

Shots rang out from below. She ducked back as bullets flew overhead. Just how many guns did they have?

She scrambled away from the ladder. She reloaded, gasping for breath as her heart pounded. Her fingers fumbled with the bullets and she dropped one, but nothing appeared at the top of the ladder.

Her eyes adjusted to the new dimness. Laura remained below. Still, the torchlight danced on the ceiling above the hole.

She waited.

Something thrust up above the lip of the pit. She held her fire—it didn't look like a head. A block of wood. She waited and steadied her aim just below it.

A moment later, the tip of a troll head appeared. As soon as it was high enough, she put a bullet through its eye. Yells came from below as it toppled backward.

She paused. Her chest pounded. Her left hand throbbed. She hadn't counted the bullets left in her pouch, and they wouldn't last forever.

But as long as the ladder was their only way up, they'd only be able to come at her one at a time. They had to know that, too, so what would they do instead?

If the other two tunnels had paths to the surface, she

was in trouble. There wasn't much she could do about that but keep her ears open. She briefly wondered how Hickok and the Army were doing.

The light shining up from below grew, along with the sounds of voices. Was it just a matter of time before they tried again?

Laura floated up, her face filled with alarm. It gesticulated wildly and pointed down.

Beth shook her head. She started to ask a question, but then caught herself. If she spoke, the trolls would know where she was.

Which meant she should move, too. She glanced around to see where else she could crouch and then nearly slapped her forehead in disgust.

The hatch. The hole to the cellar had a cover that had been pushed aside. She'd completely forgotten it in her scramble up.

While the ghost continued to point, Beth scrambled over to the hatch cover. She holstered her gun and tried to slide the wooden disk. Made of thick oak, it was heavy and hard to move with just one hand. When she pushed with her left, the pain shot through her arm once again.

This was going to take a while. And from the way Laura was carrying on, she might not have much time.

Beth rose to her knees and pulled out her Colt. She fired blindly into the hole. Maybe that'd force them to keep their heads down. Then she reholstered her gun and pushed on the hatch lid once again.

The yells started when she got the edge of the lid over the hole. Then shots—the bullets slammed into the bottom of the hatch and one went through, but they didn't move it.

She continued to push. Slowly the hatch eased into place. The shouts increased. Then something heavy thumped against the bottom of the lid before everything went quiet. She kept pushing until the lid sealed the hole.

Except it didn't. She needed to weigh it down so they couldn't just push it up.

Shots rang and bullets thudded into the lid. One punched through the wood. She looked wildly for something heavy.

The only thing around was the lamp, and it wouldn't be heavy enough. Even if there were some big rocks, she couldn't move them with one hand.

Her gun was her best chance. The hatch just bought her time.

But time until what?

THIRTY-FOUR

BETH POSITIONED herself near the door. She watched the hatch for the slightest movement. She wished, wished, wished she'd told Father O'Neill to send Hickok word about the breweries. The best she could do was delay unless she could seal the hatch. If the trolls were willing to sacrifice some soldiers, she'd run out of ammunition rather quickly.

Her saving grace was that she was sure none of the trolls wanted to *be* the one sacrificed. There was probably a lot of debate about who climbed the ladder next.

Then the wooden hatch moved. Just a little hop, like someone had thumped it from below. She waited, and then it hopped again. It started to lift... just a little...

She fired into the crack. The lid slammed back into place but there wasn't a yell like she'd expected.

Then it started pushing up again.

She waited until she saw a fat troll hand. At this range, it was an easy shot. She put a bullet right through the palm. The lid dropped.

There was no scream of pain.

The hair went up on her neck.

The lid moved up again. This time, two hands, including the mangled one she'd already shot.

Oh, God. They had another wight! A troll wight!

She shot the good hand and then the mangled one. Like before, the wooden lid slapped back into place. A loud thump followed.

The wight must've fallen. Maybe she had a chance. With its bad hands, it would have a slow climb back up. She had a little more time. But to do what?

The hatch lid wasn't thick enough to stop bullets, so she couldn't use her own weight to keep it down. If she moved it out of the way, they could shoot her. If she didn't, the wight... or another wight?—would climb up and push it aside.

She turned to Laura. "I need to seal this for good. Any ideas?"

Laura hesitated, and then nodded. She pointed down, toward the tunnel.

"There's something down there?" Beth asked.

Laura nodded. She mimed something small and then getting large. Something... exploding.

"There are explosives down there?"

Laura nodded again. She held up three fingers and then pointed to the middle one.

"Explosives in the middle tunnel."

Laura's face lit up and her chin bobbed up and down.

Beth let out a long breath. Of course. Chalmers had probably needed them for digging his tunnel. It couldn't be all dirt to the river. He'd've needed something to deal with rock when he ran into it. And of course, the explosives would be stored nearby. If she set them off, she could seal the tunnel permanently. That'd leave the river crossing. She'd just have to trust the Army could handle that.

But to set them off—she had a whole mess of trolls, a troll wight, and Chalmers himself in between.

Even if she could get down the ladder with her bad hand, she didn't see how she could fight her way through all that. She'd have six shots at most because they wouldn't give her time to reload. She was sure there were more than six down there. Not that it'd matter. She'd be impossible to miss the whole climb down.

Maybe if she jumped, she could surprise them. She could grab some of their guns and use them...

She really needed to jump down behind them, though. That'd be the way—

She caught herself. The main room, with the entrances to the tunnels, had a wooden ceiling with holes in it.

She *could* jump down behind them!

She turned to Laura.

"I need to get to the room above the tunnels," she whispered urgently. "It should be the other side of that wall." Beth pointed toward the one opposite the entrance to the chamber. "Can you show me?"

Laura gestured for her to follow and floated quickly through the door out of the room. Beth took one last look at the hatch, grabbed the oil lamp, and hurried after.

They wound their way through a maze of broken rooms and debris that felt longer than it actually was. Finally, they arrived at a wide open room without a ceiling of its own. It'd been some sort of storeroom, judging by the broken wooden bins here and there. But what mattered was the broken planks in the floor.

"Where's the entrance to the tunnel?" Beth hissed. "Can you look?"

The ghost furrowed its brow, but then it nodded. It sank through the floor. Beth counted her heartbeats until it floated back up. It pointed toward a hole a bit further away from where they'd come.

Beth moved to the edge and looked down through the broken planks. She could hear guttural voices not too far away, but couldn't see a thing. The hole wasn't quite big enough for her to jump through. Though some of the broken edges looked rotten, so maybe she could widen it.

Except that'd make noise. If she went slowly, she might be able to minimize that. But how long would it take them to realize she wasn't at the top of the ladder?

She had to go slowly. She'd need the time at the bottom to look around. She couldn't afford to have a troll investigate the sounds of wood breaking.

Beth set the unlit oil lamp down a few feet from the hole. She grabbed the end of one of the rotted boards and pulled. She had to bring her left hand down for leverage, which caused more jolts of pain. She gritted her teeth and kept pulling.

The plank broke with a snap and she almost tumbled backward. When she caught her balance, she sat and listened. Her heavy breathing threatened to overwhelm the distant voices below.

Laura floated down through the floor. A few moments later, her head and arm appeared. She held a thumb up and nodded.

Beth grabbed the next rotten board and pulled. After it broke, she waited while Laura checked the room below. She repeated the process for another board. That gave her a gap big enough to shimmy through.

She paused and caught herself. If she did jump down, how would she get out?

She wouldn't. Instead, she'd be trapping herself with the trolls and Chalmers. If the explosives didn't work, the trolls would be loosed on the city.

She didn't even know if there were enough explosives to do the job.

So instead of climbing through, she found a sturdy section and stuck her head through a hole.

She peered into a narrow passage, not much wider than a door. To the west if she had her directions right, she heard a large number of voices and could see the bright flickering light of a number of torches. She guessed that was the troll army. She was probably twenty feet from the main underground room.

In the other direction, the passage ran about ten feet before it ended in a wall with a bunch of old barrels stacked in front of it and several stacked wooden boxes. What looked like a plank leaned against them.

She furrowed her brow, but she couldn't see clearly. She turned to Laura.

"We need to find a hole closer to the explosives," Beth said.

Laura nodded and they headed east.

The floor was sturdier here. Thick semi-rotten boards still covered what Beth thought of as part of the cellar. They'd probably stored beer in the barrels to keep it cool in the summer, and built the floor over it. When she found new holes in the floor, they were smaller than the past spot. She measured off the distance to where she thought the barrels and boxes were and found the nearest hole. Once again, she set the unlit lamp on a sturdy section and peered below.

Laura moved through the floor without being asked.

With the additional "light" from the ghost, Beth could

make out the boxes better. She squinted and then started chuckling.

Dynamite, all right. With the lid of the top box left off.

It might not be enough to collapse the neighboring tunnel completely, but it was the best shot she had.

But there was no hole directly over the box. So how to light it?

She looked at the lamp she'd been carrying. She could light that. Then she might be able to lower it through a hole and then swing it toward the box. But it'd be too easy for the flame to get extinguished in the process. And she might miss, even then.

She needed something else. Something that would already be aflame as it fell onto the box. Like a torch.

Or cloth.

She stood and quickly took off her coat. It was too big and too thick to tear. After a deep breath, she started taking off her shirt.

The cold stung her bare skin. Her chemise underneath kept the worst off her torso, but the hair on her arms froze almost at once. She quickly pulled her coat back on, but her flesh didn't warm immediately.

And her left hand stung worse. She checked it and let out a sigh of relief. The red threads weren't creeping past the entwined bracelets anymore.

She stretched out her shirt and rolled it into a long thin strip. Then she opened the oil lamp and thoroughly soaked two-thirds of its length. She lowered it through the hole nearest to the dynamite and practiced her swing.

"Check my aim," she told Laura.

Laura stuck her head through the floor and then used hand signals to help her make sure she was swinging toward the dynamite.

Beth pulled her shirt out. With trembling fingers, she struck her last match. It flared to life and she lit the shirt. Then she thrust it through the hole. She coughed in the smoke and tried not to lose her grip when the heat hit the back of her hand.

She swung once, twice, and let go.

She scrambled to her feet and ran toward the street. She ducked around a partially-standing brick wall. Laura led the way, guiding her.

The world behind her roared.

Beth stumbled and fell as the explosion sent stone and wood flying. Two large rocks slammed into her back, and a third struck her arm. She covered her head with her hands as smaller debris rained down on her. Her ears echoed when the roar finally stopped. She waited until the last of the pieces had hit the ground, leaving just the dust and smoke in the air. Then she stood.

What was left of the brewery above the cellar and tunnels had completely collapsed. She couldn't see much through the swirling mess, but from first look, she'd done it.

Still, she needed to know.

She gingerly picked her way back through the debris toward the now large gaping hole. It extended a good twenty or thirty feet in all directions. What she could see of the bottom was filled with rubble, broken stones, and burning wood.

She worked her way east around the hole. It all looked the same. By the time she stood on the southern edge, she was convinced she'd passed the tunnel the trolls had emerged from. If they were still down there, they were—

No. She could hear muffled voices. The came from the southeast edge of the crater, There, not only had the ceiling collapsed, but the walls had fallen in as well. The voices she could hear drifted up through cracks and holes, none of which were big enough for more than a mouse.

She'd done it!

She almost collapsed in relief. She'd sealed the tunnel.

A gunshot!

Then pain as a bullet slammed into her left shoulder.

Beth fell to the ground as white hot agony took hold.

THIRTY-FIVE

BETH'S ARM flared with pain. Her eyes watered and she panted for breath. She immediately clamped her right hand over the wound. It was shallow—the bullet had just winged her, passing through the outer muscle.

But it *hurt*.

And the gunman had to be coming.

She pulled herself to her feet and loped away from the direction of the shot. As soon as she could, she ducked behind part of a broken wall. Then she dashed to the next one. Behind it, she slumped to the ground.

Waves of pain wracked her body.

Blood covered her fingers. She needed a bandage—but the only ones she had were already on her left hand. She yanked them off and applied them to her shoulder, making sure to turn them around. Better the dirty side than the bloody side with possible poison. Her left hand oozed, but thankfully it didn't start bleeding hard again.

Gritting her teeth, she kicked off her right boot and yanked off her sock. She loosened her coat enough to shove the sock up against the wound and then pulled the coat tight. It wasn't great, but it'd have to do. She slid her bare foot back into the cold boot and tried not to wince at how badly her toes felt. But the pain in her shoulder soon distracted her.

She had to find the gunman.

She drew her Colt and peeked around the corner. With only the moonlight, she couldn't make out more than the dark shapes of the broken walls. Deep shadows lay everywhere. She looked around for Laura but didn't see her. She must've run too far from her death location.

One of the shadows moved. Just a little. Then a figure separated from it, running toward another broken wall.

Beth fired.

With a cry, the shadow collapsed.

She didn't wait to see what happened. She jumped to her feet and ran further east.

Footsteps followed her. She guessed that not all the trolls had been caught in the blast. She zig-zagged toward the street. When she caught sight of another running shadow, she fired at it. She didn't stop to see if she'd hit it.

She reached the main street between the breweries. She looked east toward the river—nothing. Well, maybe some firelight in the distance, but it was too far off to matter. She looked west and caught her breath.

The bright white light from Laura nearly blinded her. She stood in the middle of the street, only a dozen feet from where she'd died, but she wasn't alone. Two short creatures stood on either side of her, as if holding her. They gave off a patchy light as well.

Beth's blood chilled. Two troll wights. *Holding* the ghost. She wasn't sure how that was possible, but that's what it had to be.

A dumpy troll with a large staff stood a few feet away. Next to him—Chalmers.

She seethed. Unconsciously, she took a step forward. She caught herself and returned to the shadows.

"Oh, Miss Armstrong!" Chalmers called. "Miss Armstrong!"

She held still.

"Miss Armstrong, do come out," Chalmers yelled. "Come out before we have to do things to your friend here." He gestured in the general direction of the ghost.

The troll was more precise. It poked the ghost with the staff—and hit it. Laura writhed and the white flared brighter.

Beth gaped. How had the staff touched the ghost?

"My witch friend," Chalmers nodded toward the troll with the staff, "can send her soul to Jotunheim. Come out if you want her to go to Heaven!"

Beth took a deep breath. Her left shoulder still throbbed in agony which made it hard to think. Her hand, too. Her feet. Every part of her ached.

The range was too far. She could probably hit Chalmers or the troll witch, but it wasn't a sure thing. Not in the state she was in.

"We won't shoot you, Miss Armstrong. Just come on out so we can talk."

She took another deep breath. Then she strode into the street.

"What do you want?" she called.

"Ah. There you are. You've caused me a great deal of trouble, you know."

"Let her go!"

"Her?" He gestured back toward the ghost and the wights. "Is it a her? I can't see ghosts, unlike my friend here." He indicated the witch. "And you, apparently."

She took two steps forward. "What do you want?"

"Why, safe passage of course." He'd lowered his

voice, but in the stillness of the night, his words remained clear. "I won't be the king of Saint Louis now, but I won't be hanged either."

"You were gonna be king?" She slowly walked a little closer.

"Of course I was! With my own harem, and people to do my bidding! The trolls and me had it all worked out. But I... I underestimated you."

She smirked at the compliment and took another step forward. She now stood in the middle of the street, at the edge of her range.

"Now, now," Chalmers said. "That's close enough." He looked behind her. "Oh, Hell."

Beth swiveled around and her heart almost leapt out of her chest. The firelight she'd see was from torches! Soldiers—two dozen at least—were running toward them from the east. Father O'Neill must've passed on a message after all!

"You tell your friends," Chalmers said, "that all we want is to walk to the river unharmed. Then we'll let the ghost go so she can pass on. Otherwise Trilla here will send the ghost to the Jotunheim Hell."

Trilla poked Laura again with the staff. She tried to twist away, but failed. The two troll wights held her fast.

"How can we trust you?" She shifted her stance to lessen the pain from her shoulder.

"Why would I condemn a girl to Hell if I didn't have to?" He snorted and shook his head. "I'm not a monster."

"Beth!"

She swiveled and looked behind her. Hickok raced forward at the head of the men.

"Stay back, Captain!" Chalmers shouted.

"He's got a hostage," Beth called, "and there's trolls in the ruins."

Hickok drew up short. He said something low that Beth didn't hear and the soldiers spread out. Several disappeared into the shadows of the surrounding buildings.

"Who's the hostage?" Hickok asked.

"Laura." Beth pointed toward the wights. "He says the troll witch can send her soul to Hell."

"Well, that'd be a problem." Hickok shifted to the side. So Beth wasn't blocking his line of sight to Chalmers, she realized.

"We just want safe passage, Captain," Chalmers said. "Me and my friends. Then we'll let the ghost go."

"Are those wights?" Hickok asked. He pitched his voice so Beth could hear but it didn't carry.

"Yeah. I know how they're made now."

"Can Chalmers make more?"

"Him or that troll witch." The way the two wights kept looking at the witch made Beth sure she—he?—was the one who was the real creator.

"What'll it be, Captain?" Chalmers raised his voice. "We're not asking for much." He stared at Hickok, who stared back.

Beth watched the witch. She kept the tip of her staff tilted toward Laura, but the wights seemed to shy from it, too.

"I don't think you can send a soul to Hell," Hickok drawled loud enough for Chalmers to hear. "Souls go where they're supposed to."

"You wanna try me and find out?" Chalmers nodded to the witch, who poked the ghost again.

Laura writhed in agony.

Hickok squinted. "Sure wish I could see her."

"She's right between the wights," Beth said. "They're holding her."

"I figured that."

304

Of course he did. She shrugged. But then a wave of wooziness washed through her from her shoulder.

"Can you get the witch?" Hickok asked, his voice low again.

"Maybe. I'm in a lot of pain."

He gave her a sideward glance and his eyebrows rose in concern.

Chalmers raised his pistol. "I'll shoot you down where you stand, Captain, if I have to."

"My men will tear you apart." Hickok's hand dropped to the handle of his own Colt, holstered by his side.

"Maybe," Chalmers said, "But you'll be dead. Better to let us just get to the river."

The witch jabbed the staff closer to the ghost's face.

Hickok stepped sideways, away from Beth. He shifted into his gunfighter stance, resting his weight on the balls of his feet. Beth mimicked him, moving an additional step away and dropping her right hand to hover over her Colt.

A shot!

Hickok fell.

Beth yanked her gun up, leveled it, and fired! She sent her first bullet at the witch, her second at Chalmers. Then she dropped to the dirt.

Gunfire erupted all around her. She glanced toward Chalmers to see that both he and the witch were down, but the wights still stood. However, bullet after bullet from Hickok's men slammed into them. She could hear gunshots from the ruins where the trolls had hid as well.

She crawled to Hickok. Her left shoulder exploded in pain as she did. He was alive—grimacing and holding his left thigh. Her wooziness turned into dizziness…

…and the world went black.

THIRTY-SIX

SHE WAS WARM. As she drifted awake, Beth's first thoughts were about how wonderful it felt to be warm. She felt the blankets covering her and the heat of the room. A fire crackled nearby and she could smell the light smoke. The bed underneath her was soft, too. Her shoulder throbbed, but with a dullness that implied it'd started to heal. She could sense the tightness of a bandage wrapped around it. She stirred and slowly opened her eyes.

"Good evening." Rose smiled at her from a nearby chair.

Beth glanced around. Somehow she was in the Soulard Inn's parlor. The tables had been replaced by her bed and another nearby that was mussed but empty. Judging from the lamps, it was evening.

Her lips were chapped. She tried to moisten them and Rose immediately stood and held out a glass.

"Can you sit up?" she asked. When Beth nodded, Rose helped her slide up against the headboard. As they did, the bracelets on her left wrist jangled.

"I didn't want to take those off," Rose said, "given how your hand looks. We added a couple more as well."

Beth held up her hand. A small bandage wrapped around the scratch, but thin black lines radiated through her skin, like a spiderweb centered on her wound.

"It's the wight poison," she said.

"What's that?"

"It's nightshade mixed with something the trolls brought with them."

"Nightshade shouldn't've made those lines," Rose said.

"No. It should've just killed me."

Rose let out a long breath.

"I guess I didn't get enough."

Rose nodded. "You lived. That's what matters."

"So…," Beth asked, "what happened? The last thing I remember is facing Chalmers."

"Oh, that evil man!" Rose shuddered. "He's dead."

Beth nodded.

"The troll invasion's been turned back. The soldiers brought you and Hickok here because it was closer than the Barracks. Hickok's wound was minor—he didn't even pass out! He's around somewhere, hobbling on his crutch."

Beth nodded as it all slowly sank in. "How long?"

"It's been about a day. Are you hungry?"

Beth nodded.

"Would you like Margaret to make you some soup?"

Beth nodded again.

"Here." Rose handed her the glass of water. "I'll be right back."

Beth drank slowly as her friend bustled into the kitchen. She looked over at Hickok's bed. It wasn't hard to imagine him being a bad patient.

A few moments later, Rose hurried back in with

Margaret behind her. The younger woman looked worn but cheery. More wonderfully, she carried fresh bread, the smell of which filled the room. Beth started salivating immediately.

"The hero of Saint Louis!" Margaret said.

"Oh, please." Beth couldn't help but roll her eyes.

"You collapsed the tunnel and stopped the trolls," Margaret held out a small plate with the bread. "The Army didn't even know about it! We would've been overrun!"

"What about the boats?" Beth took a hunk and savored the warm smell before taking a bite.

"The cannons stopped the main attack," Rose said. "Some landed to the north, but Father O'Neill and the gleaners drove them back before they got into the ruins."

"Father O'Neill fought?" Beth resisted a surprised laugh.

"I don't know if he did any fighting himself," Rose said, "but he led the men and they stopped the trolls."

"How many dead?" Beth asked more quietly.

"Of ours?" Margaret answered. "It wasn't too bad. The trolls coming across the river didn't have guns."

"Hickok lost two men." Rose's voice was somber. "He says it would've been worse if the trolls that survived the tunnel weren't so busy watching you face down Chalmers. They let his men sneak up on them."

Rose bent over conspiratorially. "Hickok also said Chalmers made a huge mistake."

"Oh?"

"Mmm hmm. Chalmers signaled for the attack too early. The trolls weren't ready to go through the tunnel."

"Ah." Beth wasn't entirely surprised.

"Mmm hmm. So it took them longer than it should've."

Beth let out a long breath and then used the bread as an excuse to stop talking and just think.

"I'll get started on that soup." Margaret nodded and took her leave.

Rose sat on the edge of the chair and leaned forward. Her eyes danced with unanswered questions.

"Can I tell you about it later?" Beth asked between bites.

Rose's face fell, but she nodded. "Is there anything else you need? The Army doctor said your shoulder should be fine."

"They had an Army doctor come all the way up here?" Beth couldn't help wondering about the number of wounded down in the Barracks.

"It wasn't just for you." Rose's smile offset the implied chiding. "There are other wounded here, and over at the church." She grew more somber. "The men and boys from around here are heroes, too."

"Darn right." Hickok stood in the hall entryway. He leaned on a crutch and weariness hung on him like a blanket, but his head was unbowed.

"Bill!" Beth fought back the urge to stand and run to him. She was tired enough, and besides she was missing her trousers.

He grinned and hobbled forward. "Nice to see you awake."

"Nice to see you alive," she shot back. "Here and back at the tunnel."

"Well," he chuckled. "I'm hard to kill." He glanced at Rose, who stood.

"I'll see if Margaret needs any help with the soup." Then to Beth, "you need anything else, dearie?"

"Water, please?" Beth drained her glass and passed it

back. Then she caught the look in Bill's eye. "Maybe when the soup's ready?"

Rose nodded and took her leave. Hickok watched her retreat until the door had swung shut, then he turned back to Beth.

"That was mighty good work," he said. "I'd suspected Chalmers, but I was worried there might be more."

"Preston." She grimaced. "Chalmers said he'd killed you."

"He tried." Hickok grimly chuckled. "But your Private Johnson came through. I had my back turned when Preston drew a knife but Johnson saw him and jumped him."

"Oh? Is Matthew okay?" Her gut tightened.

"He is. Knocked the knife out of Preston's hand as he took him to the ground. Good thing, too. It was poisoned. Speaking of which…" He nodded toward her damaged hand.

She held it up and stared at it again. In the fire and lamp light, she could see the lines in her skin well enough, but not the red threads that bound her soul. They were there, though. She was sure.

"Anything we can do for that?"

"Laura said there was a way…" Beth turned to Hickok. "She helped me a lot. We need to help her." She peered toward the windows. "We'll have to go back after dark. That'll be soon."

"Maybe take Father O'Neill? That man…" Hickok snorted softly. "I've known some holy men who could fight, but he…" Hickok shook his head and pursed his lips in a small smile.

"I'm glad he told you about the tunnel," Beth admitted. "I wasn't sure he would have the chance."

"Like I said, he's an impressive man."

They fell silent while Beth chewed her bread. Hickok

sagged back in his chair and stared into space, lost in thought.

"So what's next?" she asked when she'd finished the last bite.

"I need to help tidy some things up here. Then we go home."

Beth shivered. She clung tight to her horse and leaned forward just enough to keep the night breeze off her bare neck. She couldn't do much about the cold stinging her face, but at least the trip would be quick. Hickok had loaned Father O'Neill his own horse and then insisted a "small guard" accompany them.

All ten of them. Hickok's idea of small apparently meant "enough men to ensure that any remaining trolls ran away rather than take a sniper shot at Beth." At least that's what he'd told Father O'Neill.

It was sweet. And patronizing. But this time she'd let it go.

Beth's pulse began to race as they approached the brewery. Even in the dark, the destruction of the brewery overwhelmed her. It felt like a giant had dropped stone blocks every which way. She idly wondered how she hadn't been killed. There'd been a lot more dynamite than she'd thought. How many trolls lay buried beneath?

But she let out a low breath when she spotted a dull gray glow ahead. They rode close, until she could make out the ghost's features. Laura gave her a plaintive smile. Beth pulled up on the reins a few feet away and dismounted. Her shoulder ached as she did, but soon enough she was on her feet.

"You stayed," Beth said to Laura.

She nodded. Then she gestured for her to follow.

"C'mon," Beth said to Father O'Neill, who'd dismounted right behind her. He lit a lamp and joined her.

Along with their military escort, they picked their way through what was left of the brewery until they reached the brewing room. Thankfully, one of the walls had collapsed, along with the roof.

But the kettle still stood. A ceiling beam had fallen across it and protected it from most of the rest of the debris.

Laura pointed at the kettle. Beth gestured for Father O'Neill to bring the lamp up. Its light flickered off dark ice at the bottom.

"It didn't all burn," Beth said.

"What?" Father O'Neill held the lamp further over the kettle.

"That's the poison that makes the wights," Beth explained. "I tried to burn it but the flame must've gone out. Do we have more oil?"

The soldiers started talking among themselves as Beth turned back to Laura.

"We'll take care of it," Beth said. "Right away."

Laura nodded. Then it pointed at Beth's left hand. In the low light, the red threads were once again visible. They followed the black spiderweb lines on her skin and, thankfully, stopped at the bracelets on her wrist.

"Yes. You said you know how to cure it?"

Laura nodded and pointed to Father O'Neill.

"He can cure it?"

"Me?" Father O'Neill asked.

"You." He looked surprised, but otherwise contained his reaction.

Laura nodded, and then started tracing letters in the air.

"H...O...L...Y...," Beth spelled out as Laura

continued to trace more letters. "Holy water!" Of course. What could help a soul more than something that was blessed?

One of the soldiers bustled forward. He clutched a small bottle. "More oil, Miss." He held it out to her.

"Pour it on the ice." She gestured to the other soldiers. "We need to make sure all the poison burns."

Beth stood to the side as the men got to work. Then, when everything was ready, Father O'Neil produced a match and held it out for her.

"No," she said. "You do the honors."

"Lord," Father O'Neill began, "by your power and grace, we rid this world of the Evil that sundered so many from your loving arms. Bless us, and bless all of those who strove to keep this land safe and our people free."

Laura smiled with tears.

Father O'Neill struck the match. After it flared up, he dropped it into oil in the kettle, which whooshed into flames. They crackled, and slowly the ice melted. One of the soldiers added some broken wood to stoke the fire.

Beth watched Laura. The ghost wrapped her arms around herself as she stared at the fire. When the flames began to die down, a light gray disk opened behind her. Laura looked at Beth, gave her a smile, and then disappeared, along with the disk.

"You suppose that's good enough?" one of the soldiers asked.

"Yeah," Beth said. "It's time to go home."

THIRTY-SEVEN

MARGARET AND FATHER O'NEILL threw a huge celebration the night before Beth, Hickok, and Rose planned to depart. Margaret and Rose spent the day cooking with a half dozen of the local women helping. Somehow, the gleaners came up with some beer that had been squirreled away. Apparently a small brewery still operated somewhere nearby.

Three squads of soldiers came up from the Barracks as well. They brought wagons of scrap wood that had once been troll boats. By the time dusk fell, multiple bonfires warmed the street between the Inn and church. Clusters of people laughed and drank and ate. After a bit, someone produced a fiddle and someone else a drum. When the music started, a few couples created an impromptu dance floor on the street just a dozen feet from the food tables.

Beth sat on the edge of the church steps closest to one of the fires. She closed her eyes for a moment and basked in the warmth. When she opened them, she stared at her left hand while she flexed it. Everything felt fine. Everything looked fine. Only a thin scratch still marred the skin.

"It healed nicely." Rose strolled up, her hands wrapped around a steaming mug.

"Mmm. It's still strange to think about."

"The wight poison?" Rose shuddered. "I'm glad that's gone."

"Maybe." Beth curled her hand and stretched her fingers out again. "We don't know what the trolls have, over across the river."

"True. But they've never tried anything like this before."

"They didn't have Chalmers." Beth grimaced. Or his crew. Apparently, five or six had been beguiled by the thought of ruling Saint Louis. Only two had survived, though Hickok had said he expected courts martial and hangings as soon as things calmed down.

"Such an evil man." Rose took a sip of her drink.

Beth nodded, but before she could say more, Father O'Neill came over. He nodded at them.

"Thank you, Miss Armstrong," he said. "We could not have done this without you."

"I was just one part," she demurred. "You were another, as was Rose and everyone else."

"Nevertheless, we are in your debt."

She nodded, and then an idea struck her. "Do you mean that literally?"

"Why... yes. Is there something you need?"

"I couldn't have done this—we couldn't have done this—without Laura Masterson. She stayed behind when she didn't have to."

"True."

"We need to find some way to honor her."

"Ah." Father O'Neill smiled. "I know just the thing."

"Oh?" Rose pressed.

"One of our congregants is a sculptor. I'm sure we can have a suitable statue up by the time you return."

"Return?" Beth barked involuntarily. "I... I don't know when that'll happen." She shifted her left shoulder and felt a twinge from the wound there. It still had more to heal.

"Well, when it does," Father O'Neill said, "you'll be more than welcome in our church. Even if you don't care to sing." He winked as Beth's mouth dropped and then turned and departed.

"I didn't think he noticed that," she grumbled.

"Oh, he knows quite a bit," Rose mused. "I think if he hadn't been a priest, he'd be mayor or something. Maybe governor."

Then Rose paused. A slow grin spread across her face. "Look."

The crowd had parted enough to make out Margaret waltzing with Private Johnson not far from one of the bonfires. He said something and she laughed in response. Not once did his grin fade, even as they spun in their dance.

"That's the way to win a girl," Rose sighed.

Beth chuckled. "I'll let you know when someone wins me."

"Oh, pshaw. You're already in love."

Beth raised a questioning eyebrow.

"Right there, on your hip."

Beth's hand reflexively dropped to her Colt, and Rose just laughed.

They made the long ride back to Golden City along the same Pony Express route, although at a more relaxed pace. The weather warmed slowly, and more than once they stopped for a real rest instead of simply a meal. When they reached the station where they'd fought the first wight, they found a new contingent of men living in tents and constructing a new cabin.

"Gonna burn the old one to the ground," the sergeant in charge said. "The men won't stay there. Claim there's ghosts."

"There's no ghosts." Beth had trouble keeping the amused grin off her face. It felt good to smile, though.

"She can see 'em," Hickok added.

The sergeant just shrugged. "They're still not gonna sleep there, sir."

"Fair enough," Hickok said. "Just as long as you get the station working again."

"Oh, we will, sir. All of us know how important these stations are. Just think if that order to bring the rest of the army had gotten through."

Beth waited until they were out of earshot of the sergeant before turning to Hickok.

"Order to bring the army? I didn't think Colonel Philips sent an order like that."

"Well...," Hickok chuckled. "His missing letter wasn't quite that specific. He just asked for help. But if these men think they're critical in getting the army there next time..." He shrugged and smirked.

Beth rolled her eyes and went to look for the tent Rose had secured for them.

They arrived at Julesburg to find the entire team had been replaced. The private who'd wanted to see if Beth was really a girl? Gone. As were the sergeant and the other private who'd let the station go to seed. The new crew had the entire place shiny and clean. They assembled outside and saluted Hickok before taking the horses to be cared for in the barn.

"My, these gentlemen are more polite," Rose observed as they watched the men lead the horses away. She smiled at Hickok. "Your doing?"

"I may have had something to do with it." His grin betrayed more than that.

"What happened to them?" Beth asked.

"Sergeant Meyer and Private Schwenker have been reassigned to Fort Chicago. Private Howard... was discharged. I imagine he's headed home, wherever that may be."

Beth nodded. Somehow her satisfaction felt better than she felt it ought to. Private Howard had been dumb and rude, not criminal. But the Army was still better off without him.

"Well, perhaps he can learn some manners," Rose said, "though I suppose if he didn't learn them before, he won't learn them now."

"You never know," Hickok chuckled. "But at least he's someone else's problem now."

The snow had turned into muddy slush as they approached Ma's cabin. While the air remained crisp, the late afternoon sun warmed Beth's neck and face. She smiled when she saw and smelled the smoke rising from Ma's chimney. Light glinted off one of the windows, which made Beth smile even more. She urged her horse into a trot, and Hickok and Rose followed.

When they arrived at the barn, Ma opened the cabin door. She stood with her hands on her hips and a huge smile. The shawl wrapped around her shoulders slipped part way down, but she didn't seem to mind.

"I'll get the horses," Hickok murmured as Beth dismounted.

She nodded and hurried the last few feet to throw herself into her mother's arms. The hug lasted until both women were completely out of breath.

"You're safe," Ma said when they pulled apart. She then looked Beth up and down. "Unhurt...?"

"Not entirely," Beth said, "but I'm good."

"Well come on in. I'll get some biscuits on the stove."

"Oh, that's all right, Mrs. Armstrong," Rose said as she bustled up. "Why don't you let me take care of those while you sit and talk with your daughter?"

Ma tilted her head thoughtfully and then nodded. "Let's use that honey you brought last time."

"Why that's just the thing!" Rose indicated the door. "After you?"

Inside, Ma settled into her favorite chair by the fire. It hadn't moved much, Beth noted, though there were fewer blankets draping it. Beth grabbed a chair from the table and set it nearby Ma's. Meanwhile, Rose got to work.

"So tell me about it," Ma said once she was comfortable. "All of it."

Beth began, and stopped briefly when Hickok came in. Ma gave him a faint scowl but motioned for Beth to go on. Hickok spoke quietly to Rose and then took a seat at the table, just out of Ma's immediate view. A moment later, Rose placed a mug in front of him, which he slowly slipped as he listened.

So Beth continued her story. Ma nodded and only asked a couple of questions. She wanted to know what'd happened to Margaret's mother and how Ellen Lemp's family had handled the news of her second "life" as a wight. She frowned when Beth reached the point of heading off to the breweries alone. Her frown deepened as Beth continued.

Finally, Beth broke off. "Sorry, Ma. I *had* to. There wasn't anyone else."

"I don't see why."

"I was fine." Beth bit back her exasperation.

"She was more than fine." Hickok shifted his chair to more squarely face Ma. "She was the only one who could've done it. None of the rest of us would've been able to talk with the ghost."

Ma's scowl didn't fade. "But alone?"

"I would've been there if I could've," Hickok admitted, "but I didn't find out until almost too late. As it was..." His eyes drifted to Beth.

"Yes?" Rose prompted.

"As it was, she kept me safe more than I did for her." He turned to Ma. "She saved my life more than once. Can't say I like it, but it's true. Your daughter is an impressive woman."

Ma looked at Beth, and her eyes softened.

"That's why I do it, Ma." Beth's own voice started to crack. "Not for Bill, but for Margaret, Father O'Neill, and Margaret's brother, and the gleaners, and Private Johnson. And... and even for Laura Masterson's soul."

"God bless her," Rose murmured.

Beth fell silent, and she and Ma looked at each other for a while. Slowly, Ma smiled.

"Well, you still need to stay safe, you hear?"

"I will, Ma, I will."

"That's right," Hickok added. "She will. And we'll go right back to practicing her shooting tomorrow."

"No," Beth said. "I already shoot better than you, Bill.

Tomorrow we help Ma around the farm. The day after that... we'll see."

"Well, good," Rose said, "because the biscuits will be done soon and I want to hear the rest of the story. Again, because it's so good."

Ma actually chuckled and nodded, and then gestured for Beth to go on.

Beth smiled. Later, she'd return to the Astor. But right now, it was good to be home.

AUTHOR'S NOTES

Ghosthunter follows Beth Armstrong about six months after her adventures in *Gunslinger* (available from Word-Fire Press). I wanted to capture Beth's adventures in an area of the Old West that wasn't quite ready for a female gunslinger, but wasn't quite opposed to one either. For that, I needed her to visit an area of the world that wasn't quite "civilized" but wasn't Golden City or someplace of equivalent size. I realized that the ruins of Saint Louis, which at the time of the American Civil War was the third largest city in the United States, would work well.

Barrow wights, being a stable of Norse mythology, were the ideal "monster" for the tale, though of course the true evil came from other humans. In *Gunslinger*, I established that some ghosts were "broken"—and unwilling to move on to whatever realm awaited them beyond the rift. But what if a willing soul was trapped and couldn't move on?

The next piece of the puzzle fell into place when I found the book *Lost Caves of St. Louis*, by Hubert and Charlotte Rother. Saint Louis sits on a large limestone formation that is riddled with caves. One reason the city became so populated with breweries is that those caves allowed them to keep their beer cool, thus ensuring it remained fresh longer. Many of these cave complexes have been mapped for several blocks, and it was a simple leap of logic to go from caves to tunnels.

Which brought in the trolls. Tunneling under the Mississippi River would be no small feat, but would be well within their skill, given enough time. The trolls brought the part of the "poison" through the rift from Jotunheim that would tether a soul to the body. When paired with another poison to kill the person (nightshade), we had the method to create a wight.

Then, as I slotted all the pieces into place, I realized that I'd written a mystery as much as an adventure novel. Our detective's mind is as quick as her gun.

Perhaps even faster.

ABOUT THE AUTHOR

A fourth-generation Coloradoan, Edward J. Knight only left the Denver area long enough to learn how to put a satellite into orbit. Four satellites later, he's returned to both the mountains and writing fantastical fiction. Along the way, he met the love of his life and became the father of two amazingly curious kids. He's a huge fan of tightly constructed universes and smart plots. He hopes his own Mythic West stories hold up to those standards. More of his work can be found at www.edwardjknight.com.

Want to keep on what Ed's writing, and when new releases will be out? Sign up for his newsletter at:

https://mythic-western-press.kit.com/280d39ec48

www.edwardjknight.com

ACKNOWLEDGMENTS

It takes a tribe to write a novel. First, my wife Sarah has kept me sane and been my best cheerleader and first reader. I also want to thank Griffin and Gwyneth for their patience when Daddy is off writing. I'd also like to thank Marcia Knight, Elizabeth Knight, and Steve Hartmeyer for brainstorming and proofreading, and Terry Mixon and Sam Sheddan for their on-going support. Finally, Peter Sartucci, Anne Larsen, and others from the Superstars Writing Seminars tribe encouraged me, for which I'm extremely grateful. Thank you.

ALSO BY EDWARD J. KNIGHT

Sidekick

Sharpshooter

Scout

Gunslinger

www.ingramcontent.com/pod-product-compliance
Lightning Source LLC
Chambersburg PA
CBHW072126250626
47159CB00007B/2580